INNOCENT FLOWER

Cord had been staring downward as she spoke, muscular arms folded across his large chest. She watched as he suddenly leaned over, shocked at the tremors of pleasure she felt at the sight of his shirt straining tautly against his broad back. Picking a small yellow flower, he handed it to her. "You're like this flower, Amber. Tiny, vulnerable, innocent. There for the picking, for you have no one to protect you."

He was leaning over her, so close she could see the thick lashes framing his dark brown eyes. "Until now..." he murmured huskily. "Until now, Amber..."

Powerful arms swept her against him in a crushing vise as his mouth came down on hers. His tongue parted her lips and he explored the intimate recesses of her mouth. She couldn't control the desire quivering through her body, as warm and as penetrating as the gilded sunset bathing them in glory.

Other Avon Books by
Patricia Hagan

DARK JOURNEY HOME
LOVE AND GLORY
LOVE AND WAR
PASSION'S FURY
THE RAGING HEARTS
SOULS AFLAME
WINDS OF TERROR

PATRICIA HAGAN

AVON
PUBLISHERS OF BARD, CAMELOT, DISCUS AND FLARE BOOKS

GOLDEN ROSES is an original publication of Avon Books. This work has never before appeared in book form.

AVON BOOKS
A division of
The Hearst Corporation
1790 Broadway
New York, New York 10019

Copyright © 1983 by Patricia Hagan
Cover illustration by Elaine Duillo
Published by arrangement with the author
Library of Congress Catalog Card Number: 83-91041
ISBN: 0-380-84178-9

First Avon Printing, September, 1983

AVON TRADEMARK REG. U. S. PAT. OFF. AND IN OTHER COUNTRIES, MARCA REGISTRADA, HECHO EN U. S. A.

Printed in the U. S. A.

WFH 10 9 8 7 6 5 4 3 2 1

❧ Chapter One ❧

1871

THE young woman sat alone on the worn leather seat, her gaze transfixed through the grimy train window. Lost in her thoughts, she was unaware of the admiring glances men had given her during the long journey, the envious stares of female passengers. But Amber Forrest had never dwelled on her looks. She supposed she was as attractive as any girl of nineteen. She neither grimaced nor fawned over her mirror reflection. A bit on the slender side, she was occasionally sorry not to be larger and stronger. Her diminutive size sometimes restricted her.

Across the aisle, unnoticed by Amber, a well-dressed, prosperous-looking young man stared openly, thinking she was the most beautiful woman he had ever seen. Now and then his fingers opened and closed, as though he longed to entwine them in the silky mass of silver hair trailing wistfully round her face and slender shoulders. He had never seen hair like that before.

She had glanced in his direction only once, and he gasped as she smiled absently at him, bright blue eyes sparkling beneath long, silky lashes. How could anyone have such incredibly long lashes, he wondered. And her ivory smooth skin. How he longed to touch her, to trail his fingertips down those satin cheeks. Her lips were full, almost but not quite petulant. She wore a traveling dress of lime velvet, and he could see that, despite her petite build, there was a definite swell to her bosom. Yes, she would have nice breasts. Once more his hands opened and closed and his chest rose with a quick intake of breath. *The most beautiful creature he had ever seen.*

He could contain himself no longer. He had to meet the goddess. He lifted his hand to his lips and cleared his throat. "Is this your first trip to Mexico, miss?" he asked in what he hoped was a pleasant but masterful voice.

Amber turned to stare at him curiously, blinking as though seeing him for the first time. "I beg your pardon?" It was not proper for a young lady to speak with a stranger. Grandma had always said so.

"I said, is this your first trip to Mexico?" He flashed a bright smile, leaning closer to the aisle, eager.

Amber nodded silently, then turned her gaze resolutely back to the window.

The man stiffened. He would not give up so

easily. "Where are you going?" he asked boldly. "To visit relatives?"

Amber sighed. She did not want to be rude, could not remember being rude in her whole life. And what harm, she wondered, would it do to speak to the man? He was probably feeling as lonely as she was—though she had not been feeling sorry for herself because she was so excited to be seeing her father again after all these years. Turning to look at him, she murmured shyly, "I am getting off the train at a place called Suevlo."

"Suevlo?" he echoed loudly. She moved back in her seat. Laughing softly, he gestured and said, "Don't be frightened. I was surprised, that's all. Suevlo isn't anywhere at all. It's in the middle of a wilderness. I hoped you were going all the way to Mexico City."

"No," Amber said quickly, shaking her head. "I am being met by my father...and my new family. They have a large ranch and breed bulls for fighting in Mexico City bullrings."

"Do you think you will be coming to Mexico City?" he asked, too eagerly. Amber withdrew again. Scribbling down his name and a hotel address on a scrap of paper, he held it out to her. "Here. If you do get there, be sure to look me up. I would be honored to take you to dinner."

Reluctantly, Amber took the paper, knowing she would throw it away later. "Thank you," she said coolly, then added hastily, "If you will excuse me, I would like to take a nap now."

She turned her back to him, settling down in the seat, her face to the window. For a long time she could feel his eyes on her, hear his agitated breathing. She knew he wanted the conversation to continue, and she hoped he was not hurt.

Amber allowed her mind to wander back to her childhood. She had been only twelve when her mother died. Her father left her in Louisiana in the care of her maternal grandmother and went to Mexico. He had seldom written, and Grandma hinted that he would never return, as much as saying that he had abandoned Amber. One day, there was a letter, telling of his marriage to the wealthy widow Allegra Alezparito.

Amber would not let herself believe that her father had abandoned her. After all, he had written that when her schooling was finished he would send her the money to join him in Mexico. He wrote page after page describing the happy life she would have on the bull ranch. She read that letter until it was worn to tatters, for through the next years there were only a few lines at Christmas and on her birthday.

Life with her grandmother was far from happy. The old woman insisted that they live in almost total seclusion. Amber was not allowed friends, and heaven help any young man who dared to come calling! Grandma chased people from the front porch with a corn shuck broom. Their only outings were church on Sundays and occasional shopping trips to town. Even church socials were forbidden. Grandma did not hold with square dancing or picnics or other frivolous activities.

Amber counted the years, then months, until she could escape her miserable life. But just when freedom drew near, her grandmother took to her bed and stayed there for two long years before she died. Amber nursed her night and day, pushing her dreams far into the recesses of her mind.

When the old woman died, Amber sent a wire to her father. The response was immediate. He regretted that he was unable to be there for the funeral, but he enclosed money for Amber's train ticket. No one attended the funeral except Amber, the preacher, and a few church members. A day after her grandmother was buried, Amber hastily disposed of her grandmother's small home and belongings.

What lay ahead? Her father had told her she would love life on the ranch in Mexico, and he had mentioned that his wife had a son, Valdis, in his twenties, and a daughter, Maretta. How she hoped they would all be close; a real, loving family. Amber had missed all of that.

More exhausted than she realized, she fell asleep. When someone touched her shoulder, gently shaking her awake, she sat up and stared around in bewilderment. Night had fallen, and the conductor was telling her that they were only minutes from her destination.

As the conductor left, Amber thanked her stars that she knew Spanish. It wouldn't be the first time she would do so. Since her father's decision to settle in Mexico, she had cherished a hope of someday living with him, and had fed that dream by studying Spanish, getting books however she could, making up conversations with herself, and engaging a storekeeper who knew the language fairly well in endless talks. She smiled now, thinking of his mock exasperation every time she begged him to teach her Spanish. She sent him a silent thank-you.

She quickly gathered her worn tapestry bag and purse. A large trunk containing her clothes was in the baggage compartment. She checked her reflection in the grimy window, patted her hair, then took a deep breath and closed her eyes, whispering a prayer that the future would hold everything she had longed for all those years.

The train slowed, squealing against the iron tracks. The sheltered life was behind her now. She was going to have to learn to face the world, live with other people.

The conductor took her small bag, and she gratefully took the arm he extended. He helped her down the narrow aisle to the door. She wondered if he could feel her trembling. She was so terribly, terribly excited. In a moment she would see her father again. It had been so long.

"I hope someone is meeting you, miss," the conductor said. "Suevlo isn't even a town. We don't stop here unless we have a passenger getting off. I'll bet we haven't had one in six months. I don't think we've even dropped off or picked up any mail in that long, either."

"My father will be here," she told him, leaning out the door to look up and down the track. There was no real station, only a dark, deserted little shack off to one side.

He released her arm as he stepped down to the ground, reaching behind him for a crude wooden step which he positioned for her. "Well, I don't see nobody," he said indifferently. "Maybe they'll be along in a minute."

Her trunk was unloaded, and then Amber found herself alone, backing away from the train as it began to strain forward. There was a loud burst of steam, and then it was moving. Then it was gone. She shivered, looking around the darkness. She had sent a wire telling exactly what time she would arrive. Surely, her father would not leave her standing in this godforsaken wilderness?

"Señorita Forrest?"

She jumped, whirling around to see a tall man stepping out of the shadows. There was the sudden pop of a match, and a lantern was lit. He held it above his head, and she could just make out his features. He seemed large. At first glance, he appeared to be handsome, but then she realized that his face was a bit too broad, his forehead too high. And his eyes! She actually shrank at the sight of those deep, intensely staring eyes. In the lantern's glow she detected...what? Coldness? No. It was something else, something she could not quite identify. She knew instinctively, however, that she did not like it.

He was wearing a dark brown velvet suit, jacket tapering to the waist, and a white shirt. There was a dash of scarlet in the thin cravat at his throat. He wore a flat-crowned, broad-brimmed hat, and when he tipped it she saw that he had thick black hair. His thin black mustache emphasized his Latin features, but she had known that he was Mexican.

He stepped forward and Amber saw that she was only a few inches shorter than he. His build had made him seem taller.

"Yes, I'm Amber Forrest," she told him, struggling to suppress a feeling of agitation descending over her. "Where is my father?"

"We must go now," he said quickly, reaching for her bag. "You have other luggage?"

"A trunk..." she whispered. "Please, who are you?"

He had turned to the trunk, but stopped and tipped his hat once more. "Forgive me, señorita. It is late. I am tired. My manners are asleep. I am Valdis Alezparito, your stepbrother. It is not far to the ranch. When we get there, you will meet my mother and she will explain everything. Wait here, please, while I take your trunk to the carriage."

But Amber couldn't just stand there. Something was wrong and she knew it. Trailing after him, she cried, "Please. Where is my father? Why didn't he come?"

He ignored the question. "Your trip was pleasant?" The smile he gave her was forced and his eyes were wary.

Amber once again took note of the strange eyes. She found him very disturbing. "The trip was fine, just fine. But what about my father?"

"My mother will explain to you." His eyes raked over her, lingering on her bosom, and this time his smile was genuine.

Amber realized that her stepbrother was not going to tell her anything. She did not like the nagging suspicion that was taking hold. Grandma had said that her father drank. Surely he was not intoxicated this night, of all nights?

When they were settled in the carriage, Valdis said, "It is a shame that you arrive in the middle

of the night. I would like for you to see the coun-
tryside. It is beautiful."

"I'm sure I will like it here," she said, more to
herself than to him. "It does seem strange to think
of making my home in a foreign country. I suppose
I'll get used to it."

"*Sí,* I am sure you will," he murmured. In the
darkness, Amber could not see his leering smile,
his eyes memorizing the lines of her body.

They rode along in silence for a while until Amber felt a nervous need to say something. "What
do you do on the ranch, Valdis? Are you a cowboy?"

He laughed, delighted by her innocence. "No,
señorita. I am not a vaquero. I run the business
of the ranch. You cannot see it from here by moonlight, but we are approaching my land. There are
many adobes—of brick that is colored pink—
where the vaqueros live. Some of them have families."

"You have many vaqueros?"

"*Sí.* It is a large range. You will be living in
the main house, our hacienda, and you will find
it quite beautiful. It is built on a slight rise, surrounded by gardens and tall palms."

Amber was no longer interested in the house
because she had caught him saying "my land."
According to her father, Allegra Alezparito had
run the ranch since her husband died. A famed
matador, he had been killed in a bullfight in Mexico City. Valdis gave the impression of arrogance,
as though the ranch belonged exclusively to him.

She gave herself a mental shake. Perhaps she
was too quick in forming an opinion of her stepbrother. Other than school, there had been little

opportunity to be around people, and learning how to judge character would take time. Besides, she reminded herself sternly, she was a stranger in a foreign country, and would do well to keep silent and learn. Smiling to herself, she realized this was probably the way a prisoner felt on being freed after long years in jail, wanting desperately to catch up on everything. It was going to take extreme self-discipline to restrain her impulses.

Ahead, a glow of lights broke through a ring of trees standing like sentinels around the hill of the Alezparito house. Even in the faint light Amber could tell that the house was large, even grandiose.

Valdis sat beside her in rigid silence, and after a few moments she could contain herself no longer. "Oh, do speed up the horses," she cried, giving his rein hand a brief shake. She did not see his reproachful look. "Everyone seems to be awake. My father will be waiting. Oh, I wish he had come to meet me!" She bit her lip as tears sprang to her eyes.

Valdis made no effort to move faster, and Amber felt a sudden wave of agitation but kept quiet. There was something strange, something almost formidable about him.

Valdis moved the carriage up the circular drive, coming to a stop before huge wrought iron gates that were framed by glowing lanterns. An old man stepped forward to grasp the horses' harnesses. Amber smiled at him, but he looked at her with...what? Pity? He shook his head and turned away. What was wrong with these people? First

Valdis and his imposing, intimidating manner and now this gloomy old man.

Valdis got out of the carriage, then turned to hold out his arms to Amber. She allowed him to help her down, wondering momentarily if it was really necessary for his hands to cup her exactly under her bosom and squeeze. But there was no time to dwell on what was probably nothing anyway. The reunion she had waited for all these years was at hand.

Lifting her long skirt, she brushed past Valdis and began running up the white marble steps. At the top was a wide terrace flanked by vases of beautiful gardenias, but Amber saw only the large, double oak doors.

Just as she reached the doors, they were flung open. Amber stumbled, gasping in surprise at the girl standing there regarding her distantly. She wore a blue silk gown, which dipped low to reveal very little. She had tiny breasts and almost no cleavage. A black lace shawl was draped about her shoulders, and her hair, as sleek and black as Valdis', hung loose and flowing. But her eyes were hypnotic. They changed from mellow brown to almost red as they swept over Amber, insolently studying her.

As she stood there gaping, Amber felt Valdis squeeze her arm. "This is Maretta," he said coolly as he pulled her inside the house. "Your stepsister."

"Hello," Amber said softly, nodding and smiling timidly as those angry eyes continued to blaze at her. "I'm glad to meet you, really, but...I was so anxious to see my father."

11

"So, this is little Amber. All grown up." Maretta's lips curled into the hint of a sneer. Tossing her hair, she added tartly, "Well, I am sure *you* enjoyed the ride from Suevlo, my brother."

Amber reminded herself that these were foreigners. Later, she would make every effort to understand them.

She pleaded to Valdis, "Take me to my father. Please. I don't want to wait until morning."

Maretta said coldly, "It might be wise if you waited until tomorrow, Amber, and rested tonight from your long journey."

"No! I want to see him *tonight*." She shook her head, looking up at Valdis and recoiling from his stony expression. Did he not understand her desperate need? "I know he won't mind being awakened."

Valdis and Maretta looked at each other, and Maretta murmured, "Perhaps you should tell her."

"Tell me what?" Amber turned to Valdis and clenched her hands tightly together to keep from clutching him. "Please. There is something you aren't telling me. Is he sick? Then take me to him, please."

Valdis continued to look down at her with those cold, narrowed eyes until, suddenly, Amber saw a door opening to her left. She turned to see a soft glow of candles and people seated around the room. A man stepped out and closed the door behind him, his eyes flicking curiously over Amber as he asked Valdis, "Is this the daughter?"

"*Sí*, I have just brought her from the train," Valdis responded with a punctuating sigh. He

12

made introductions. Amber did not quite get the man's long, Spanish name.

"Take her to the señora," the man suggested gently, his kind eyes on Amber. "She said earlier she would prefer to tell the young lady herself."

Valdis took Amber's arm and led her to the wide curving staircase. "Come, Amber. I am sure my mother is expecting you."

Amber hastened to keep up with him, her anxiety becoming unbearable. Why was everyone acting so strangely? Behind her, she heard Maretta saying, "*Sí*, she will be awake. The whole house is awake, and most of the valley is in the parlor."

"What is she talking about?" Amber demanded sharply. "What is going on here? Why won't anyone tell me anything? And *where* is my father? Why wasn't he here waiting for me?"

Valdis gave her an amused look. "You will soon have all your answers, señorita. My, but you are beautiful, especially when your blue eyes shine."

Amber had had enough. "Will you tell me what is going on?" she cried, jerking her arm from his grasp. "And stop holding on to me. I can walk by myself."

For an instant, she was sorry. If she had seen arrogance in his eyes before, it was nothing compared to the look of rage he gave her then.

"I endeavor to treat you like a lady, my little sister," he said tightly, "but perhaps you are one of those women who prefers rough treatment? Soon, we shall find out." There was a tight smile, and then he turned away.

Valdis continued up the stairs. At the landing,

he led her down a wide hallway lined with ornate silver lanterns. Statues lined the walls. The floor was covered by a rich beige rug into which were woven designs of birds in every color imaginable. It was truly a beautiful house.

Valdis moved quickly down the hall, eyes straight ahead, chin slightly tilted, his face set. When they stopped at a door at the end of the hall, he knocked softly. Without waiting, he turned the thick black handle and pushed open the door, gesturing impatiently for Amber to follow him.

She found herself standing in a dimly lit entrance foyer and realized that her father and stepmother's quarters took up the whole width of the massive house at that end. A lace curtain hanging in thick folds obscured whatever lay on the other side of the foyer.

Valdis swept the curtain aside and Amber followed him into the room, stunned by the lavish furnishings. The furniture was of a dark, heavy wood, ornately carved. There was a large desk against a wall, opposite the stone fireplace. In the middle of another wall, flanked by long, arched windows, was an enormous bed with a canopy of pink and red velvet fringed by gold satin.

Amber's eyes went to the tiny woman who lay there. She seemed lost in the huge bed with its puffy, lacy pillows. She raised her head to stare at Amber, wide-eyed.

Moving forward on tiptoe—for the moment seemed to command reverence—Amber whispered, "Are you my stepmother?"

"*Sí*, this is your stepmother," Valdis sighed impatiently. "We tried to persuade Amber to retire for the night, but she insisted on seeing her father. There was nothing to do but bring her to you."

"As you should have." Allegra Alezparito sat up, gathering a delicate crocheted bed jacket of soft pink over her shoulders. She beckoned to Amber. "Come here, my child. Sit down beside me. We must talk."

"I am going to bed," Valdis called over his shoulder as he left the room. "If everyone in this house and the entire valley wants to sit up all night, it is their privilege."

The slam of the door told Amber that she and her stepmother were alone. She still had not made a move toward the bed and glanced around the large room, asking nervously, "Where is my father? Does he not sleep in here? Is he somewhere else?" Her eyes filled with tears as she stared beseechingly at the woman. "Please, won't you tell me what is going on? I am so tired, and the way everyone is behaving is so frightening—"

"Come." The older woman gestured again. "Come and sit down."

Amber obeyed, dismayed to see that tears were slipping down her stepmother's cheeks.

Amber sat down on the edge of the bed, and Allegra wrapped a cool hand around hers and squeezed softly. "It is terrible to have to tell you this, my child, when you were expecting a joyful reunion. Your father had been so joyfully looking forward to seeing you. It was all he talked about for the longest time."

Amber shook her head wildly from side to side. Understanding was a cold snake wrapping itself around her heart. "You...you talk as though..."

Her voice caught and she sobbed, "Dead! My father is dead!"

When Allegra did not reply, Amber knew the anguish of truth.

"No!" she screamed, leaping to her feet. "He can't be dead. A cruel, cruel joke!" She backed away from the bed in horror, staring down at her stepmother as she continued to shake her head.

Allegra whispered, all in a rush, *"Sí,* it is true, Amber. He died two days ago. His heart, the doctor thinks. He is to be buried tomorrow. Please sit down. We must talk. We can comfort each other."

For Amber, something snapped. "He's downstairs, isn't he?" she screamed, backing away. "Down there. In that room with the candles and all those people. That's where my father is, isn't he?"

She turned and fled, oblivious to Allegra's pleas. She ran down the hall, down the stairs, stumbling, brushing by servants in the foyer, and flung herself against the parlor door. It swung open, and the man who had stepped out of the room before appeared once again. He stepped aside, stunned by her hysterical rush into the room.

The others seated around the parlor rose to their feet, gasping as Amber came to a standstill at the side of the casket. The mahogany casket sat on a bier, flanked at each end by burning white tapers. She looked through her tears at the ghastly white body inside, the head on a satin pillow. Her hands began to twitch wildly and her throat convulsed with gulping sobs. Her whole being wrenched with spasms of grief deeper than anything she had felt in her nineteen years.

She took a step forward and forced her trembling hand to touch the cold fingers clasped on his chest. She recoiled at the touch, but forced herself to reach out again.

Her father's eyes were closed, and she felt her knees buckle. She clutched the edge of the coffin for support, aware only of a determination not to give way. She had to be strong. Had to be. Now she was all alone. Perhaps, she thought wildly, perhaps she had always been alone.

She leaned forward to press her lips against his. It was as though she had kissed a marble statue.

It was her hello to her father...and her good-bye.

✖ Chapter Two ✖

AMBER lay on her side, staring into the shadows. Someone, she could not remember who, had told her this was her room. Hers? Nothing in this house was hers.

Absently, she studied the petite carved cherrywood desk and the large, ornate walnut cabinet where someone had hung her clothes. Her empty trunk sat in one corner next to a three-paneled dressing screen with a peacock embroidered on it. Thick draperies of wine velvet blocked the light at the double glass doors. She supposed there was a balcony beyond the doors. But she cared not at all. What mattered? She was suspended in a huge cobweb, and could move neither forward nor backward. She lacked the will even to try.

It had been Valdis who dragged her from her father's coffin that night, lifting her in his arms despite her sobbing protests. He had brought her here. Valdis had shown no emotion, no compassion that night or during the funeral the next day.

How long ago had that been? She had only fuzzy recollections of a young Mexican girl bringing trays of food and urging her to eat. Amber hadn't eaten, but she slept almost continually, glad for the reprieve.

But now she was awake—wide awake—and no matter how hard she tried, sleep was not going to take her away again.

She rolled onto her back and stared up at the white lace canopy. A satin comforter covered her, and she shoved it away, impatient at the sight of the gown she had been wearing for no telling how long. She could not even remember changing from the dress she had worn to the funeral.

The funeral. A lump rose in her throat as she remembered how she had stared down in horror at the raw, gaping hole in the ground—that terrible gate to eternity. Her eyes had moved to the wooden casket which contained not only her father, but the dreams of what might have been between them, and her future. All of these were lowered into the eager earth.

The sound of the door opening startled her, and she sank back on the pillows, clutching the comforter to her neck. She watched silently as a young girl crossed the room, carrying a tray, and set it down on the table beside the bed.

"Ah, you are awake! Good." The girl hurried to open the draperies, and Amber blinked at the sunshine spilling into the room.

"How do you feel? You have slept so long and eaten nothing. You must be very weak."

Amber looked up into the round, dark eyes in the pretty Mexican face. It was, she realized gratefully, a sign of caring. With a shy smile, she answered, "Yes, I do feel weak...and very hungry. But how long have I slept? And who are you?"

"My name is Dolita." The girl smiled, reaching to plump the pillows. Then she settled the tray across Amber's lap. "You have slept for almost four days and nights."

Amber gasped. "No wonder I'm starving." She looked down at the platter of eggs and the large fried steak, and her stomach rumbled eagerly. There were large, crisp brown rolls dripping butter, and a bowl of orange slices.

The girl turned away. "I am going to bring hot water for your tub. You will want to bathe and dress. Perhaps you would like a walk in the garden later, for some fresh air."

"Wait, don't go yet," Amber called so sharply that Dolita turned to stare. Forcing herself to sound calm, she said, "Tell me, please. How is Allegra? Do you think I could speak with her today?"

Dolita shrugged. "I do not know. I hear other servants talking, and they say she, too, remains in her bed and eats little. But maybe Señor Valdis has told her to stay in her room. He has been very angry lately."

"Valdis?" Amber made no effort to hide her indignation. "What right does he have to give his mother orders?"

Dolita backed away, eyes wide with fear. "Forgive me. I speak out of my place, señorita, and if the señor hears that servants are gossiping, his punishment is severe. Do not repeat what I have said, *please.*"

"No, no, I will be careful," Amber assured her, startled by the girl's panic. "Please, Dolita. I want us to be friends. No one else in this house has been so kind to me," she added. "I won't repeat anything you tell me, I promise. Just please tell me what is going *on* around here? Why does Valdis think he can order everyone around now that my father is dead?"

Dolita tiptoed back to the side of the bed, clutching her hands in front of her, and whispered, "I cannot say very much, señorita. Please understand. But I will give you some advice. You would do well never to cross Señor Valdis, for he has a violent temper. Know your place, as I know mine...as Señora Allegra knows hers. Señorita Maretta seems to be the only one who isn't afraid. Everyone else obeys him—always. You must do the same."

Amber set aside the tray, threw back the covers, and leaped to her feet. "Now that my father is dead, I have no reason to stay. So I don't care what Valdis wants."

Dolita shook her head. "I do not think the señor intends for you to leave soon. He has ordered a dressmaker from the village to come here and fit you for gowns."

Amber was aghast. "I have my own clothes!" she cried. "If there was one thing my grandmother did well, it was sew. She made me many lovely clothes."

"Señor Valdis is very particular about how the Alezparito women dress. He insists they always wear the latest fashions from Spain and Paris, and the dressmaker is constantly making new gowns. I overheard him say that your costume for the funeral was...out of date. Forgive me."

Amber sank back onto the bed, astonished. "I wore a dark blue dress and coat. They are old, but—"

"Please, I tell you only what I hear," Dolita repeated nervously. "Understand that the señor controls everything here. His word is law."

"Maybe since my father died he controls Allegra and Maretta, but he'd better not order me around."

"Oh, no, señorita." Dolita's eyes grew more fearful. "The señor has always been master here. Your father, Señor Lyman, always knew it unwise to cross him."

Amber looked away. So. Her father had been intimidated. Then her first impression of her stepbrother had been correct. He was arrogant—and probably mean, as well. The sooner she left Mexico the better off she would be. Going back to the small town in Louisiana did not appeal but she had to leave here. Perhaps she could find a new town, a new home.

She decided to finish eating, take a bath, then dress and pay a call on her stepmother. She would gather what information she could about her father, having nothing left but other people's memories. Then she would make arrangements to leave as quickly as possible.

Amber bathed quickly, then dressed in the

gingham dress that had always been a favorite. It had a high neck, with soft ruffles around her chin, and the sleeves were short and puffy. She tied the long sash in a big bow behind her, liking the way the skirt fell in gentle folds, with a wide ruffle dusting the floor. Brushing her long hair, she used a bow of matching fabric to tie it back from her face, and, with a twirl in front of the long, gold-edged mirror on the wall, decided she looked fine.

Turning to Dolita, who had been silently standing by, ready to assist, Amber asked, "Would you show me to the señora's room? This is such a big house and I don't know where I am."

Dolita shook her head firmly. "I cannot. The señor has not said you could leave your room. If I show you the way to the señora's, then he will be angry.

Amber sighed. "Really, Dolita! I can't imagine any human being provoking such fear. And he is not going to tell me when I can leave my room. Now, all you have to do is point me in the right direction. I won't say you helped me. If you don't tell me where my stepmother is, then I'm just going to have to wander around on my own, because I intend to see Allegra today!"

Dolita nodded reluctantly. "Very well. Perhaps it is best you lock horns with Señor Valdis. Then you will listen to me. When you go out this door, turn to your right and go straight down the hall. The señora's door is in the middle, at the end of the hall. Her quarters occupy one end of the upper floor."

"And where are Valdis' rooms? I don't want to

go knocking on his door by mistake."

"He has the entire third floor. A suite of six rooms."

Amber felt resentment flaring. So Valdis had a whole floor! Why did he have better quarters than his mother had? What kind of power allowed him to rule his own mother?

She left her room and hurried down the hall, anxious to speak with Allegra. Standing outside the huge arched door, Amber took a deep breath and hesitated a moment before knocking. She waited, but there was no response. She knocked again, louder, looking nervously over her shoulder. She knew the time of reckoning with Valdis would come, but she did not want it to be just then.

She turned the handle and pushed the door open. Stepping into the dimly lit foyer, she called softly, "Allegra? It's Amber. May I speak with you, please?"

There was a faint rustling beyond the foyer and Amber walked softly into the bedroom. It was very dark. She could just barely see the bed, and she called once more, "Allegra? Were you sleeping? I'm sorry to barge in like this, but I must speak with you."

The voice that answered was tired, old...and defeated. "I am awake, Amber, but you must not stay here. Valdis would not like it. Return to your room, please."

Amber bristled, making her way purposefully to the bed. "I am not going to return to my room, and I don't *care* whether Valdis likes it. I wasn't going to bring this up, because you and I don't know each other yet and I know you don't want to discuss this with me, but just why is everyone around here scared to death of your son?"

Allegra huddled even deeper into the pillows. Amber sat down on the side of the bed. "You are right," her stepmother whispered. "I do not wish to discuss this."

"All right." Amber shook her head. "I don't plan to be here very long, anyway. But I want to ask you about my father before I go. Please tell me about him."

"I do not know what you are asking me," the frightened woman said.

"I hadn't seen him in so very long. Now it's as though a stranger was buried. Tell me about him," Amber implored. "How did he live his last years? Was he happy? Did he miss me? Anything you can tell me, I will cherish. And I want to know... about his death," her voice caught on a sob. She struggled for composure, and continued, "Had he been ill?"

Some of the tension seemed to leave Allegra. Taking a deep breath, she let it out slowly, her eyes boring steadily into Amber's. Then, suddenly, she asked Amber to open the draperies. "I would like to see my beloved's daughter, see whether his light shines in her eyes...."

Delighted, Amber hurried to the window, fumbling until she found the thick-braided cord and gave it a yank. The midday sun spilled into the large room. Turning, she saw her stepmother clearly for the first time.

She found herself looking at what had once probably been the most beautiful woman in all of

Mexico. The black hair no longer gleamed, but hung limp and streaked with gray. The brown eyes were dull and sunken. But the remnants were enough to tell the story. This had been a great beauty.

Allegra Alezparito pushed back the thick quilt and moved stiffly to a sitting position. She was very thin, besides being so pale.

Allegra stared at Amber, lips parted, brows raised. "Why," the older woman cried, "you are even lovelier than Lyman said you were," she cried, tiny hands fluttering to her throat. "Your hair! The color of silver. And your eyes...oh, dear God, yes, blue, like his. And an exquisite body. Oh, to be young and as beautiful as you, Amber Forrest!" Allegra shook her head from side to side, blinking back tears. "You have the whole world before you, just as your father would have wanted."

With a sob, Amber rushed to the bed, dropping to her knees before her stepmother. "Please tell me why he died," she pleaded, assailed again by grief. "Please tell me anything about him. He must have loved you very much."

Allegra stroked the silver hair for a moment, then beckoned her to sit beside her on the bed. "I will tell you all I can," she said quietly. "The doctor said that Lyman probably never knew he had a bad heart. He died"—she hesitated briefly, then continued, her voice dropping—"in his sleep. There was no pain, no suffering. If it had to be, it was best that way."

Allegra saw Amber's hands trembling and clasped them in her own as she said, "And, yes, he did love me, Amber, just as he loved you. He was looking forward so happily to your coming here to live. I will admit that I had my doubts about your being happy here, on the ranch. It must be so different from anything you have known before. But your father wanted you here. And now you must think of this as your home."

Amber pulled her hands away to wipe at her eyes. "No," she whispered. "I can't stay here, Allegra. It isn't really my home. And, forgive me if it upsets you, but I don't feel that your son and daughter would want me here."

"Do not mind Maretta. She suffers from a love that is not returned, and it causes her to be bitter. As for Valdis..." Allegra paused to take a deep breath, as though mustering courage. "Valdis is difficult. It is best to avoid him altogether. He is proud. Too proud. But not proud enough to live up to his father's good name," she added to herself with a note of contempt.

Amber was startled. "I don't understand."

"I shouldn't have said that to you, child. I will explain, however, so that you will see why you must not rile him."

Amber listened, entranced, as Allegra admitted that Valdis was not really her son. Her first husband, Huelo Alezparito, had been married before, and that woman had died giving birth to Valdis, their only child. "Valdis was ten years old when I married Huelo, and the boy resented me. There had been only the two of them for so long, and he worshiped his father. Huelo was a great matador, known not only in Mexico but in Spain as well. Valdis basked in his father's light, and did not want to share that light, or his father's love, with me. I was only a poor peasant girl, besides being an intruder."

Amber made a face. "It sounds to me as though he just never grew up."

"There is more," Allegra said solemnly. "Valdis was a witness when his father was gored to death in the ring."

"Oh! I am sorry," Amber gasped. "I never knew how your husband died."

"Valdis was there," Allegra continued as though Amber had not spoken, "but I was not. I was here with Maretta, who was only five years old. Valdis was sixteen."

"Well, here again, I think it was a case of Valdis refusing to accept life," Amber offered. "It was a tragedy, but life has to go on." Dear me, she thought in wonder, who am I to sound so old and wise when my whole life has just been snatched away and I have no idea what's to become of me?

Allegra nodded sadly. "I know, child, but you see, Valdis would not do as his father had always wished for him to do. His father wanted Valdis to become a matador. He refuses to fight the bulls, and he knows, as I do, that others talk about this and call him a coward. This makes him bitter, and like Maretta with her hopeless love, he takes out his bitterness on everyone around him."

"Believe me," she sighed with deep resignation, "when I say it is best to stay out of his way. Valdis is what he is, and even I do not cross him. Why, I was not even allowed to take your father's name when we married!"

"Did my father ever stand up to Valdis?" Amber asked bluntly, feeling a terrible need to know.

When Allegra dropped her gaze and kept silent, Amber persisted. "Did he? Please tell me. Did they get along?"

She had to strain to hear Allegra's miserable whisper, "Like me, he knew his place."

"That is absurd!" Amber exploded, leaping to her feet. "This is *your* ranch! *You* should be in charge here."

"I think you forget your place, señorita!"

Both women jumped, startled by Valdis' cold voice. He stepped out from behind the foyer curtains, where he had obviously been eavesdropping. Allegra fell back upon the bed, shrinking before his rage. She scrambled to pull the covers up tightly to her chin.

Amber, quickly regaining her composure, stiffened and lifted her chin in defiance. "Begging your pardon, sir, but I do not have a place here at all. I shall take my leave as soon as possible."

He grinned, slowly, and the sight of his lips curled back over shining white teeth caused Amber to cringe. She determined not to show it.

"You are going nowhere, my little sister." He stood before her, boldly eyeing her from head to toe. "This is your home. It is my duty to my late stepfather to give his daughter shelter."

"That's very noble of you, I'm sure," Amber snapped, "but unnecessary." She turned to Allegra. "Thank you for visiting with me. I shall start packing my things now. Surely someone will take me to the train depot in Suevlo."

Valdis' fingers snaked out to wrap around her arm, squeezing painfully. Ignoring her cry, he pronounced, "No one will disobey me. Including you. Now go to your room and stay there until I say you may come out. You need some time for mourning—and to realize that you have no choice but to do as I say."

Amber screamed, struggling in his grasp as Allegra looked on in horror. "You aren't going to make me do *anything*, Valdis. I will find my way to Suevlo if I have to walk. Now, let go of me!"

He squeezed harder. The pain was excruciating. Despite her will to fight back, Amber was forced to stop struggling lest he break her arm. She stood limply, anguished tears streaking her face, and he continued to hold her as he spoke from between gritted teeth, "Hear me, little one, or I will make you curse the day you were born. You are going nowhere. You are staying here. In my home. For I find you extremely...desirable. You will live like a queen. But first, you must learn your place. If I have to leave my mark upon your lovely flesh, I will not hesitate to do so. Do you understand me?" He shook her. Amber could only nod.

"Good!" He released her, laughing as her knees buckled and she fell to the floor, rubbing at the angry red welts on her arm. "Besides," he taunted, "you have no money to take you anywhere. Be grateful that I am so generous as to welcome you into my home."

Amber would still not be cowed. *"Your* home?" she challenged, ignoring Allegra's whispered pleas. "This is Allegra's home. And Maretta's. And my father's, before he died. What right do you have to claim sole ownership of everything?"

His nostrils flared ominously and his fists opened and closed at his sides. "Not that it is your concern, foolish child, but Allegra deeded everything to me many years ago."

"I can't believe my father knew that," Amber murmured.

Valdis threw back his head and laughed. Allegra began to sob, and Valdis looked at her with a gloating expression and chuckled, "He found out quickly enough after he married her. I was in Spain, buying new breeding stock, when Allegra led your father to believe this was her empire. When I returned, he found out the truth." He pointed an accusing finger at Allegra, who was now sobbing wildly. "She cries because she knows he would never have married her if he had known the truth."

In a surprising show of spunk, Allegra screamed, "That is a lie, Valdis. Lyman would have married me. You know why I am crying. You know why I cry every time I lay eyes on you—"

"Shut up, damn you!" He swung at her with the back of his hand, but she ducked in time to avoid the blow, burrowing her head beneath the pillows. Turning on Amber, Valdis shrieked, "Get out of my sight! I have had enough of your insolence. Go to your room and stay there until I allow you to come out."

Turning back to Allegra, he whispered ominously, "Now I will deal with *your* insolent tongue."

Amber's eyes darted to Allegra, huddled in a tiny ball beneath the covers, shaking violently. How she wanted to help her! But what could she do? She was no match for this fiend. The only thing left for her to do was to get out while she still could. She jerked open the door and ran down the hallway to her room.

Let Valdis think her needy and dependent! She cried silently. He did not know about her money, the money she had hidden in the lining of her trunk! The money had come from sale of her grandmother's possessions, and she had planned to give it to her father. Hers now, it would take her out of this nightmare.

She reached her room and nearly knocked Dolita down in her haste to get inside.

"Señorita? What is wrong?" Dolita was right behind Amber as she ran to her trunk and fell on her knees before it. Jerking the lid open, she reached for the back.

"Valdis!" Amber spat. "He...he is evil, Dolita! I must get away from here and he doesn't want to let me go, and—" She screamed as her fingers slipped inside the lining. There was nothing there. Hooking her hand inside, she pulled with all her strength, ripping the cloth, finally yanking it free.

The money was gone.

After a long time, she looked up at Dolita. The girl was watching her with wide, frightened eyes, her hands clutched before her nervously.

"I had money in here, Dolita," Amber said tightly. "Who has been in my trunk?" She slowly got to her feet and stood before the terrified girl.

Dolita shook her head wildly. "I did not take your money, señorita. You *must* believe me. Never have I stolen anything from anyone. I did not even know you had money in there. I have not been in your trunk, and—"

"You haven't been in my trunk?" Amber echoed incredulously. "But you are my maid, aren't you? You unpacked my trunk and put my things in that chest over there, and—"

"No, no!" Dolita cried continuing to shake her head. "I put your things in the chest, but I did not take them out of the trunk. Señor Valdis took all your things and put them on the chairs. Then I put everything away."

"And what was Valdis doing in my trunk?" Amber raged.

Dolita rushed on, telling her how Valdis had brought Amber to her room the first night, after she had gone into shock at the discovery of her father's death. "By the time I was called here to your room, he had put you to bed, unpacked your trunk, found your gown...." Her voice trailed off as she saw the rush of new anger in Amber's face.

"That...that monster undressed me?" Amber gasped. "He took my clothes off and put a gown on me? Oh! Oh, I could kill him!" She whirled about. "Then he took my money! *He* has it. And now he knows I have no way of leaving! Oh, damn him! Damn him to hell!"

"Please," Dolita sobbed, holding her hands out in a pleading gesture. "Do not tell the señor I told you all of this. He will beat me. Please, you do not know the things he has done...the things he does when he is angry."

Amber bit down on her lower lip, eyes narrowed as she stared into the empty trunk. "Don't worry," she told the hysterical girl. "I won't say you told me."

Dolita asked, "But your money? How will you get it back?"

Amber sighed. "Don't worry, Dolita. I will escape that spawn of the devil, with or without money."

❧ Chapter Three ❧

FOR two long, agonizing weeks, Amber was locked in her room. Dolita was the only person she saw. The maid brought in meals three times a day. Amber begged her to explain what was going on, but the frightened girl wouldn't talk. Her gaze darted nervously around the room, as though Valdis were hiding somewhere.

On the fourteenth day, as Dolita came with breakfast, Amber cried, "I'm going crazy, sitting here not knowing anything. He can't keep me locked up forever. When is this madness going to end?"

"As I told you before," Dolita sighed, setting the tray down on the bedside table, "Señor Valdis announced that the entire household would observe a two-week mourning period. That period is over today. He may let you come out. But be careful, for he will always keep an eye on you, señorita. And do not ask the vaqueros on the ranch for help. They serve him as though he were a god. They will not help you."

"Someone must help me," Amber declared angrily. "Everyone on this damn ranch can't be a devil worshiper. *You* aren't. *You* don't care for Valdis."

"No, and I would leave if I could, but I could not find other work anywhere in the valley. You do not understand the power he has here. Please. do not try to fight him. You cannot win, señorita."

Amber gave her a probing look. "Dolita, I do not understand you. You are a beautiful girl, yet you wear dismal clothes. Is this to discourage Valdis? But surely there are young men who would love to take you away from this miserable place."

Dolita dropped her eyes and blushed, and Amber prodded further. "See? You do have a beau, don't you? Is he a vaquero here on the ranch?"

"Oh, no." Dolita shook her head quickly, firmly. "No, he is a farmer and lives with his family. He is not really my 'beau,' as you call it. Reydro is my distant cousin. I see him when I visit my aunt. He smiles at me," she added dreamily, a happy glow on her face. "I think he likes me. One day—who knows? For now..." The glow faded and her perpetual frown returned. "I work here, and I do as I am told, and I do as the señor tells me. I am lucky to have this job. I can work here because I speak Spanish *and* the languages of the Indians who work here, and also English."

"Can't you find work elsewhere?"

"This ranch is the largest in the valley, and the only one to hire workers. Others are so small they are worked by the family who owns them. I have no family, only my aunt, and with twelve children of her own, she has no room for me. I must stay here. There is no place else for me to go."

Amber sighed and began to pick at the bowl of hot corn and milk on the tray. "Maybe I could convince Allegra to leave. She can't be happy here, and surely she has relatives she could go to."

Dolita emitted a deep sigh. "She will not leave. She knows the señor would kill her if she tried. You should have seen her when he finished with her after she talked to you of private things."

Amber threw her spoon down and cried, "Did he hit her, Dolita? I don't believe it! She's a woman, and—"

"I should not have said anything." Dolita looked very frightened again and began looking around the room, afraid she had been overheard. "I only try to make you see you cannot escape him. You would do well not to try. It does not have to be so bad here, señorita. There is much luxury."

"I don't care about that," Amber snapped. "Now tell me what he did to Allegra."

Dolita took a deep breath, hesitating, then decided it was too late to keep silent. "Her servant girl, Bonita, said she had bruises on her face. She would not get out of bed for a long time, and when Bonita insisted she bathe, she saw her body and screamed. It was covered with bruises from the señor's beating."

39

Amber screamed, "That bastard! That devil! How dare he? Oh, I've got to get out of here!"

She slid from the bed. "You no doubt have a key to that door, Dolita. I'm going to see Allegra now. I want to make sure she's all right and find out if she will go away with me."

Dolita looked apologetic and murmured, "I do not have the key. There is a guard outside your door. It is he who lets me in. There is also a guard below your balcony. There is no way for you to get out of here."

Amber was shocked. This was worse than she had thought.

Casting about for something Valdis might not have thought of, she cried, "Maretta! She can't know how her stepbrother is treating her mother. You must get a message to Maretta. Tell her to come to me, to find an excuse for getting in here. I have to talk to her."

Dolita took a step backward. "No," she whispered fearfully. "I cannot take a message to her. If she told the señor, he would beat me. Do not ask this of me, please."

Amber pursed her lips, nodding. Dolita was right. She had no right to ask the girl to risk Valdis' wrath. "Then what can I do?" she asked herself out loud. "There has to be a way to get to her...."

"Do not waste your thoughts on that one."

There was an angry gleam in the girl's eyes as she said to Amber, "Señorita Maretta is just as vicious as her brother. She, too, has treated her mother cruelly. She regards her with contempt.

She knows of the beatings, believe me."

"Did Valdis beat her when my father was alive?" Amber had to know. She was vastly relieved when Dolita shook her head.

"No. There was very little fighting. The two of them stayed to themselves, rarely leaving their rooms. Señor Valdis insists on a formal dinner every Sunday evening, and it was usually only then that your father and the señora went downstairs. Valdis would sit and brag over how well he was running the ranch, and they would listen and say nothing, then hurry back to their rooms when dinner was over.

"You must understand something," Dolita rushed on. "Señorita Maretta is the only person who has any influence with Señor Valdis. She knows how to get her way with him, but she knows how far she can go. She would never help you, and she would tell him if you asked her. I am the only person you can trust. And I can do nothing for you. I am sorry."

Amber's mind was awhirl. "Maybe I won't try to leave just yet," she mused aloud. "That was a good deal of money Valdis stole from me, and I want it back. Maybe I would be wise to stay here for a while and see what I can find out. I might be able to get my money back and also find a way for Allegra to leave with me."

Dolita looked at her closely. "You are going to play a game, no?"

"I think it's the only way. I'm not going to gain anything by continuing to rebel or threatening to run away. And, you know, Dolita, that money was

41

all I had left of my family. That was my inheritance. If there's any way to prevent him, I won't let Valdis keep it."

Amber forced a smile. "If you will draw my bath, I am going to wash my hair and get dressed up. Valdis may pay me a visit, and I want to start playing my new role."

Dolita still remained skeptical. She clucked about, doing what needed doing, warning her mistress that she was playing with fire. Amber continued to fish for information. The most important thing she heard was that Valdis valued other people's opinions. He was all too aware of the gossip about his not being a matador like his famous father. Listening to Dolita, sifting through everything she said, Amber felt that Valdis had tried to counter the negative opinions by giving the appearance of being cultivated and refined. He gave lavish balls and dinner parties, bringing the best musicians in all of Mexico to the ranch. Wine and champagne were imported all the way from France, and he hired the best cooks to travel from Mexico City to prepare sumptuous feasts. He was apparently attempting to buy acceptance into Mexican society.

As it happened, Valdis did not come to Amber's room. But he sent word that Amber was expected to attend dinner that evening.

When Amber turned the doorknob at exactly 7:30 that evening, she found it unlocked. Stepping into the hall, she saw that there were also no guards. Perhaps Valdis had meant only to keep her confined for two weeks. Did he think that was enough to make her docile? He probably gave no serious consideration to her running away. After all, they were surrounded by many miles of forbidding country—all unfamiliar to Amber.

Descending the long staircase in the rose muslin gown, Amber thought it was the prettiest dress she owned. Her grandmother had crocheted tiny rows of lace around the bodice and embroidered blue rosebuds all over the billowing skirt. The gown gave her confidence.

Valdis was waiting at the bottom of the stairs, looking a little less formidable than she remembered him in an elegant red velvet waistcoat. Thick rows of white lace fluffed about the lapels, framing a yellow silk cravat. His trousers were of a shiny black material. He wore fancy embroidered boots, which Amber thought gaudy.

He stood posed with one hand on the banister, his other tucked behind his back. As she stepped down, he bowed and reached for her hand, which she stiffly gave him. He pressed warm lips against her hand, and she fought the impulse to cringe.

"Ah, you are even lovelier than I remembered, little sister." He grinned, straightening. "Your two weeks of rest have returned color to your cheeks. Come. I have been looking forward to our evening together. We shall become better acquainted. I am afraid our first encounter was marred by the sorrow that assaulted my home."

Tucking her hand in the crook of his arm, he led her to the wide double doors at the rear of the foyer, then into the large, elegant dining room beyond. Amber's gaze swept over the sparkling crystal chandeliers, lights dazzling from every prism. A large table, big enough to seat at least twenty, dominated the room. The furniture was of a heavy black wood and, like the other furnishings in the house, was ornately and delicately carved.

The walls were of brilliant mosaic tiles, and numerous potted plants gave the room a garden-like appearance. A brightly feathered bird, imprisoned in a wrought iron cage, stood, bored, in a far corner.

Valdis led her to the chair to the right of the head of the table and pulled it out for her. Then he moved to his place at the head of the impressive table. She hated sitting so close to him.

He clapped his hands sharply and a servant appeared at once with a bottle of red wine. As he poured, Amber noticed that theirs were the only two settings. "Where are Allegra and Maretta?" she asked.

"I had dinner sent to their rooms. My mother seldom comes downstairs, and Maretta is in one of her nasty moods. I thought it would be more pleasant if we were alone."

Amber wondered sadly how often her poor father had been allowed to come downstairs. Only for formal occasions?

"Tell me," Valdis said after several sips of wine, "do you find your room comfortable? If not, I would be glad to take you on a tour of my house and allow you to select something more to your liking. There are many rooms."

"No," Amber said quickly. "The room is fine, thank you.

"Besides," she added, hoping her tone was nonchalant, "I do not want to impose on your kind hospitality any longer than necessary, Valdis. I am not really a member of your family. You owe me nothing."

"Ah, quite the contrary," he smiled broadly, propping his chin on folded hands and gazing at her warmly. "I want your delicate charm, your exquisite beauty to grace my home for a long, long time. Perhaps by so doing, you can repay your father's debt to me."

Amber stared. "I don't understand. My father was in your debt?"

He waved a hand airily and reached for his glass again. "He had no skill of any value on my ranch. He was useless to me. An artist, he called himself." Valdis snorted derisively, then smiled. "But let us not talk of unpleasant things. I wish to discuss with you the lavish wardrobe I am going to have made for you. The seamstress will be coming tomorrow to take your measurements. How I envy her," he added with a bold wink.

"No! I cannot allow that. I have enough clothes." Amber shook her head firmly. Oh, she didn't want to get him riled. She wanted to gain his confidence, give her time to get the stolen money back. But how long could she allow him to speak that way of her father?

"Your wardrobe is not suitable for life here," he was saying. "I like to entertain, and since word of your beauty has already spread far and wide, I wish to have a big fiesta in your honor very, very soon. You will need a stunning gown for that, and I think red velvet will be lovely with your silver hair."

Amber forced herself to silence. Let him make his plans. She would make her own.

After a moment she asked innocently, "Would you tell me about my father? His life here?"

Valdis looked annoyed as he reached for the wine bottle. "There is nothing to tell," he said curtly. "The marriage would never have taken place had I not been in Spain at the time. He came riding through, a wanderer, and my mother fell prey to his charms. He thought this was her ranch, and he thought she was very rich. My devious mother allowed him to think these things. When I returned, they were already married. Maretta had tried to stop them, but there was nothing she could do."

Amber forgot her resolve and snapped, "My father was not a fortune hunger, Valdis. He left America after my mother died because he was so grief-stricken. He surely loved your stepmother because he would not have married for money. But there is something I don't understand about any of this. Just why is it that you control everything? Every time you mention this house, it is always *your* house. You have no respect for your stepmother, and she's treated like a...a prisoner. How do you justify this?"

His eyes were blazing, but Amber did not wither before his gaze.

"I cannot see how any of this is your business," he said tightly, "but since you are a part of this family—whether you like it or not—I will tell you that my mother was smart enough to know she was not smart enough to run the ranch when my father was killed. She did the wise thing when she deeded everything to me. Obviously, she did not tell this to your father."

He clapped his hands and several servants appeared with bowls and platters of food.

When they were once more alone, Amber said sharply, "I resent the implications you make about my father, Valdis. He would never have married Allegra for her money. And if she did not tell him she had deeded the ranch to you, that was probably because she was afraid to admit she had made a mistake."

"Mistake?" He raised a brow. "I find your unexpected spirit a pleasant surprise, little one, but do not press me too hard. I take nothing from men and very little from women, as you will learn quite soon if you do not mind your tongue."

Amber wanted to shout that she knew that included beating his stepmother, but if she did, he would know that Dolita had told her. She contented herself with, "I am not afraid of you, Valdis, so do not threaten me.

"I think I would prefer to eat in my room." She started to rise from her chair, but his hand snaked out to clutch her wrist painfully, and he applied pressure until she was forced to collapse in her chair. He released her, leaning forward to whisper harshly, "You try my patience, Amber. Sit here and eat your dinner. Later we will go for a walk in the gardens."

Choking on the angry words aching to be screamed, she forced herself to eat. Oh, how she wanted to leave! Just as soon as she had the money, she would. If she could not find what he had stolen from her, then she would steal from him, by God.

47

During the rest of the meal, Valdis talked. He talked about himself, expounding on the wonderful job he had done with the ranch. His bulls were the finest stock in all of Mexico. Amber would, he said, be very happy there. He would groom her to be the lady of the house. His mother, he declared, was senile. He hoped Maretta would marry soon and move away. He expressed his desire to entertain elaborately and was confident that Amber, with her charm and beauty, would make him the most envied man in the valley.

"It will be advantageous for both of us." He lifted his glass, while Amber sat quietly, making no move to join in the toast. "And who knows?" He leaned closer smiling broadly. "We may become good friends, much closer than merely brother and sister." Then he laughed to himself, as though harboring a deep, delightful secret.

Midway through the meal, Valdis ordered a large pitcher of sangría. Amber stared at the dark red wine and the slices of oranges and lemons and limes in the bottom of the pitcher. She thought how refreshing it looked, but she declined a glass. She would not drink with him. He was consuming enough for both of them, anyway.

When they had finished eating, Valdis stood and pulled Amber's chair back so that she could rise. She allowed him to lead her through glass-paned double doors onto a wide terrace. They were at the rear of the house.

"Beautiful, no?" Valdis said, waving his arms with a flourish.

Amber murmured in agreement, wanting not to compliment him, but thinking that it was truly lovely. A warm breeze was blowing through the dancing fronds of a nearby weeping willow, and the air was scented with jasmine. A lonely bird sang his lament of longing. Closing her eyes, Amber felt the familiar stirrings, the strange sensations that had caused her such bewilderment in recent years. Alone in her bed at night in her grandmother's house, she had felt this same encompassing loneliness mingling with a sweetly painful hunger. After a while, the dreams would begin...dreams of a handsome stranger who folded her into his arms, his lips claiming hers in a searing kiss. His hands would dance over her body, caressing her breasts, and then a strange liquid fire would fill her body, spilling forth, and she would awaken, startled and frightened. But for a while the hunger abated. Someday, that intriguing stranger would appear, and she would know him, for she had spent too many nights in his embrace not to know him well.

But the man of her dreams was not Valdis. Never Valdis. Revulsion caused her to step back.

"It is lovely, no?" Valdis placed his arm about her waist. Giving her a little shake, he laughed softly. "Relax, Amber. You say you are not afraid of me, and it is not my wish that you be. I want only for you to understand that I wish to be your friend. I want you to be happy here. This is your home now."

Amber wanted to laugh. Did he think her a complete fool? She would not be taken in by Valdis' hypocritical charm, which he would call up at will. But for the moment, she would pretend to be entranced. Let him think her a fool.

When the time was right, he would learn differently.

Valdis led her to the edge of the terrace. The mountain range was visible, stretching to the sky, and the liquid moonlight seemed to coat the peaks in snow.

"Do you see all of that?" Valdis said proudly. "It is mine. I own all that the eye can see...." Suddenly his voice became bitter, and he finished harshly, "Except on the eastern side."

Amber impishly prodded, "Why don't you own that land as well?"

He took a long, deep breath, then let it out slowly. "The pompous fool who owns that land will not sell to me. I have offered him far more than it is worth, but he is stubborn. One day he will come to me on his knees, begging me to take it off his hands."

"Why won't he sell?" Amber pushed.

"Because he is a fool!" Valdis cried. "He does not even need to use that land to raise bulls and horses, for he makes enough money as a matador."

Amber was intrigued. "A matador? How fascinating. I have never been to a bullfight. I'm sure they're cruel, so I don't really want to go—but I can't help admiring men brave enough to be matadors." As she saw him stiffen with rage, she suppressed her smile.

"You will go to the bullfights next week," he said firmly. "As a member of the house of Alezparito, it is expected of you. I myself think a man is a fool to risk his life that way. Armand Mendosa is a foolish man. But even if he does not sell his land to me, then I will probably have the use of it and the deep springs it contains when he marries Maretta."

Amber cried, "So that is the man she loves…the one who doesn't want to marry her."

"*Sí*, and I would kill him with my bare hands if it were not for the fact that their union will give me water rights. There have been no problems in the past. His family and my father's were very close. But one never knows if the cooperation will continue. Armand might build dams, or sell the property to someone who would build them, then I would have difficulty getting enough water for my stock."

"So that is why you want her to marry him."

"That and the fact that he is duty-bound to do so. I have told him he is not an honorable man if he does not live up to the agreement made by my father and his father—that he and Maretta would marry one day."

"Well, that doesn't seem fair to either of them." Amber said, and Valdis flashed her an angry look. "They were babies. What right did their parents have to promise such a thing? People have the right to fall in love, Valdis."

"It is the way. Do not interfere in something you simply don't understand."

"I'm sorry," Amber lied. Oh, it was fun to goad him!

She feigned a yawn. "Valdis, it is lovely out here, but I am very tired and I would like to go to my room now."

Without a word, Valdis turned and took her in his arms, oblivious to her indignant struggles. "I wish to kiss you good-night, little one. I want to fall asleep with the memory of your sweet lips upon my mouth."

Amber twisted her head from side to side, pressing against his chest. "Valdis, stop it!" she cried angrily. "How dare you? Stop it at once!"

Grabbing her head, holding it viselike in his hands, he kissed her, chuckling deeply over her furious struggles. When at last he released her, she staggered backward, wiping her mouth as though something poisonous had touched her.

"It will be better," he taunted, his hands on his hips, dark eyes dancing. "I can tell that you have never been kissed by a real man. I will enjoy teaching you how to please me."

With a cry of outraged horror, Amber fled back into the house, lifting her skirts so that she could run. She did not stop running until she reached the sanctity of her room and slammed the door. Sliding the tiny brass lock into place, she turned and leaned against the door, chest heaving with dry sobs.

She was startled to see Dolita standing by the bed, watching her sadly. "That lock will not hold him, señorita, not if he wants to come in," she whispered sadly.

"Oh, Dolita, what am I going to do?" Amber began to pace up and down the room. "I hate him. I really and truly hate that man."

"As well you should, for he is evil," the young maid blurted.

"I must get out of here!" Amber turned beseeching eyes to her. "But I must have the money he stole from me. I'm not worried about making my way back to Suevlo. I will walk if I have to. But

I don't have money for a train ticket, or for food, and there is no one I can borrow from. No one."

Dolita shook her head. "If I had anything, I would give it to you, señorita, but I have no money at all."

Amber asked desperately, "Is there a safe in the house? I'd never be able to break into one, but that's probably where my money is."

"There is no safe. Señor Valdis fears being robbed, so he takes his money to the bank in Cuadid, thirty miles north. Your money is probably hidden in his room."

"Then when the time is right, I will just go and search his room till I find it," Amber said.

"They say," Dolita continued in a whisper, "that Señor Valdis is in debt. He drinks too much and when he is drunk, he gambles."

Amber stepped behind the dressing screen and reached for the nightgown Dolita had left there. "Dolita, all I care about is getting out of here the first chance I get."

"Señorita, please be careful," Dolita begged nervously. "If he catches you in his room, there is no telling what he will do. And if he finds out you are planning to run away, he may post guards at your door again."

"I am leaving, Dolita," Amber said, determination hardening as she recalled the kiss. "And don't worry, I'll be careful. I know I don't dare make a mistake."

Suddenly Dolita started at the sound of the doorknob rattling. She whispered in terror, "He is trying to get in, señorita."

Amber responded calmly. "Go to the door and

ask who is there, Dolita. If he knows I am not alone, he will leave."

Trembling, Dolita did as she was told, calling out in a shaky voice. But there was no reply, only the faint sound of footsteps retreating down the hall.

Amber sighed. She was safe, but only for a while. There was, she knew, no real sanctuary for her there. There was only a relentless, lurking evil.

✥ Chapter Four ✥

AMBER stood at the edge of the palm-lined terrace. Like everyone else, she was watching the young girl on the terrace twirling about, her arms raised above her head as she clicked her castanets. Dipping and whirling to the Flamenco music of the guitars, red underskirts flipping saucily beneath black lace, the girl made a lovely picture.

But Amber's mind was on the misery her life had become, not on the party, which she had moved through like a sleepwalker.

Glancing upward, she stared at the closed draperies of Allegra's room. Amber had tried to speak with her again every day, but her door was always locked and Allegra would not respond to her knocking. Dolita had confided that servants were saying that Señor Valdis had forbidden his stepmother to speak with Amber.

Valdis. Just thinking of the man made Amber's stomach roll. How she loathed him! For the past week, he had been all politeness and solicitude. But she was not fooled by any of it. Valdis was a lecher, and a cruel man, and there was nothing she could do but endure him when he was unavoidable and dodge him whenever possible.

She moved away from the clapping, noisy crowd and loud music, grateful that Valdis was, for the moment, not hovering possessively beside her. She could see him inside, talking to three men. Business problems, she thought. He looked agitated.

Stepping down from the terrace, she entered the garden with its flowering, fragrant orange trees. A silver half-moon filtered down, casting lacy shadows on the mossy grass. A soft, warm breeze whispered through the night air. It was all so ironically beautiful, she reflected.

Suddenly, she heard Valdis' voice calling sharply, "Amber! Amber, where are you? Are you out there?"

Quickly, she ducked behind a large palm tree, pulling her long skirt tightly about her legs. As he passed nearby, she held her breath. He returned to the house after a minute, and she darted down the moonlit path, not knowing where it led, just wanting to escape Valdis for a little while.

Amber had still not found an opportunity to search his room. Dolita said she had never known him to be around the house so constantly. He had not even gone to Cuadid for his regular weekend gambling and drinking binge.

Amber plunged on into the night, lost in misery.

There had to be a way to escape...*had* to be.

The path ended at a large, wooden gate. Beyond, she could hear the soft, gurgling sound of a rushing stream. It would be nice, she decided suddenly, to kick off her tight satin slippers and wade in the cool water.

The gate opened and closed with a grating squeak, and she moved through the shadows toward the sound of the stream. Reaching the edge, she removed her shoes, then lifted her skirts waist-high, preparing to step into the water. A rumbling sound caused her to freeze.

She turned slowly, looking fearfully toward the thick, black woods beyond her. It had sounded almost like thunder. Just then she heard it again. She began to move back toward the gate, terror bubbling in her throat as the rumbling sound deepened and came closer.

Suddenly there was a crashing sound, and a huge black shadow lunged from the bushes. She screamed. Moonlight illuminated the deadly horns on the great beast's head.

The bull was staring straight at her, eyes shining like red coals. He lifted his head, and the dread sound pierced the air once more, drowning out her cry of terror.

She turned and ran, but tripped and fell to the ground. Rolling quickly onto her back, she saw that he was raising a hoof, pawing at the ground. He lowered his head and bellowed angrily again. She knew instinctively that the beast was about to charge, to send one of those spearlike horns plunging into her flesh.

Hoisting herself up on her elbows, oblivious to the skin being scraped away as she moved, she dug her heels into the ground and began to scramble backward.

There was movement behind her, and she looked frantically around to see two men crawling cautiously over the fence.

"Do not move!" One of them ordered in a deliberately calm voice. "Stay where you are."

"Watch him, Mendosa," the other man said to his partner. "He's a killer."

In the eerie moonlight she watched as the man who had first spoken removed his coat and moved forward. She did not want to look at the bull, for a fresh wave of terror ripped through her each time he bellowed. The man, however, did not take his eyes from the animal. The bull's head was lowered in readiness for attack, but the man kept moving toward him, calmly and steadily.

The stranger spoke sharply to her in a thick Spanish accent, "When he moves, get to the gate as fast as you can. Do not hesitate for a second. Move quickly."

Suddenly the bull charged, and Amber could feel the earth tremble beneath the thundering hooves.

"Toro!" the man cried, leaping in front of Amber, snapping his coat sharply. *"Toro!"* To her he yelled, "Run! Quickly!"

She scrambled to her knees and crawled a few feet before she felt strong hands grasp her around the waist and lift her high in the air. Her rescuer swung her over the fence and dropped her on the ground with a painful thud.

"She's safe," she heard him shout. "Get the hell out of there."

"Ahhh, the evening has been so boring," was the laughing reply. "I think I will make a few passes."

"Mendosa, you're crazy," the other man shouted. "He's not one to play with."

Amber got to her feet shakily, feeling a shadow of anger over being treated so roughly. Dusting off her long skirt, she moved to the gate. She could see the man called Mendosa flicking his coat, stepping quickly to one side just as the bull charged the coat.

"You're a stubborn fool!"

She looked up at the man who had lifted her over the fence as she moved to stand beside him. He felt her presence and turned to give her an angry grimace. "Will you just get out of here? You've caused enough trouble." He turned away, dismissing her.

"I only wanted to go wading," she said shakily. "I'm sorry if I caused any trouble. I didn't know there was a bull—"

"I don't give a damn," the man growled.

Stung, Amber looked away to where the other man was dancing about the charging bull. Incredulous, she could hear him laughing. "Why, I think he's enjoying this!" she gasped.

"Of course he is. He doesn't have any sense. Now, get out of here. Go back to your party."

She flamed with indignation. "Don't issue me orders. I want to thank that man, and—"

"Mendosa, if you don't get out of there, I'm going to shoot him," he warned, ignoring her completely.

"Ahhh, you would not want to kill such a magnificent beast," Mendosa said as he turned, raising his coat high above his head. The bull spun just beneath his arms. "This is Señor Valdis' prize seed bull. He would not take kindly to your destroying him."

"Then get out of there."

Amber gasped as the man pulled a gun from beneath his coat and pointed it at the bull. "Are you really going to kill him?" she cried.

"If Mendosa doesn't get out of there right now, I'm going to put a bullet through the bull's brain. Then you can explain to Valdis that your stupidity caused all this."

"If you would only let me explain," she pleaded.

"I am coming," Mendosa called. "Do not shoot him."

She watched as Mendosa lured the bull into making a pass close to the gate. As the beast rushed by, Mendosa leaped, landing beside Amber, a wide grin displaying shining, even white teeth. "Señorita Forrest, I believe," he said, bowing. "I have been looking forward to meeting you. Like everyone else in the valley, I have heard of your loveliness. But now I see that all I have heard was wrong. You are not merely lovely. You are most beautiful. Allow me to present myself—Armand Mendosa."

"I've heard of you!" she cried. "You really are a matador."

"*Sí*. I do not usually fight the bulls in their pastures, only when a lovely lady is in danger."

He flashed his smile once more, then turned to the man beside him. "This is my foreman, Señor Cord Hayden."

Cord Hayden still regarded Amber coolly, but some of the anger left him. He murmured, "Sorry if I was rough on you, but you could have been killed. That bull gored a matador in the ring last year. He should have been put to death, as is the custom, but Valdis wanted to use him for breeding."

"I'm truly sorry," Amber said desperately, "but I didn't know there was a bull here."

"Just don't go wandering around anymore," said Hayden.

Her eyes suddenly locked with his, looking up, for he was at least a head taller than she. He was, she realized, quite handsome...though there was the touch of the wolf about him. His eyes were dark brown, and framed by long, thick lashes. His lips were full, sensuous, accentuated by a thin black mustache. Black hair curled around his face, giving him almost a little-boy look—but she understood intuitively that the appearance was misleading. This was all man, a real man, and one to be reckoned with.

But there was something else about him ...something quite disturbing. It was as though she had met him before. But she told herself that she could not have.

Armand touched her arm, bringing her out of her reverie. "If you will allow me," he murmured softly, "I will see that you return to the house safely."

She wanted to tell him that the house was the

last place she wanted to be, but she kept quiet as Armand turned to his foreman and said, "I will see you back at the ranch later, all right?"

Cord Hayden nodded, tipping his hat to Amber. He turned away, but not before she saw that strange look in his eyes, as though he was having the same thoughts she was. They *had* met somewhere, sometime before. But no—that wasn't possible.

"Tell me. Why were you out here wandering the ranch alone?" Armand said as they made their way toward the distant lights and the sound of music. "I am surprised that Valdis would allow you to go off like this by yourself."

She saw no reason to lie, and blurted, "I was trying to get away from Valdis. I despise him."

To her amazement, he threw back his head and laughed. "You do not hesitate to speak what is on your mind, do you? That is good. I do not like coy women or feminine games. And I do not blame you for feeling as you do. I must admit that I share your opinion of Valdis. I must tell you also," he reached for her hand and squeezed it, "that I accepted his invitation tonight only because I wanted to meet you. Now that I have accomplished that, I am tempted to go home rather than be in the company of Valdis and his spoiled sister. I have had the best of this night, I know."

She said candidly, "I've heard that Maretta is in love with you, and that you won't marry her. Valdis is very unhappy about it."

He made a face. "Who would want to marry such a contrary woman? And she does not love me. She only wants to be Señora Mendosa. If I were a poor peasant, she would not give me a second look."

Amber said nothing, feeling that it was not her place to comment further.

"Tell me," he went on. "Why are you still here? I assumed you would return to America after your father's funeral."

She bit her lip to hold back the torrent of words. How easy it would be to pour out all her troubles to this man. He seemed so kind. But she did not know him, so she merely said, "I will leave...when the time is right."

He gave her a strange look, as though he knew there was much more to be said.

As they reached the top of the garden, they heard the lilting guitar music and the glow of dozens of lanterns spilled down on them.

Armand stopped abruptly, spinning Amber around to face him. "Before we go inside," he whispered, grinning, "I want you to know how happy I am that we met. I am glad we had some time alone together, and I am sorry it must end now. I wish..." He took a deep breath, warm, hungry eyes on her face. "I wish I did not have to take you inside."

Amber became light-headed. Here was a famous man, a fearless man, a most attractive man, and he desired her. They were standing very close, and since he was only a few inches taller than she, their lips were almost touching. "I...I thank you for saving my life...." she began, unable to think of anything else. It was an unnerving moment.

"I thank *el toro* for giving me the opportunity

to place you in my debt, señorita." He smiled. "If ever I should meet that one in the arena, I would be tempted to be merciful, for he has done me a favor."

"I should think a fierce bull like that one would be just what you matadors want," Amber said in a rush, grateful for a chance to step away from him.

He laughed, taking her hand and leading her to a nearby marble bench. They sat down together. "Let me explain," he began. "That bull will not fight again. You see, he has won."

She was genuinely confused. "I don't understand. I thought the bull always had to die." She stopped as she saw the look of pain on his face.

"When the *matador* dies, the *bull* wins," he said sadly. "You heard Cord say that the bull has killed. It was last year, a great matador named Gosa Huerto. He bled to death in moments. By custom, the bull should have been put to death afterward, but he was Alezparito stock, and Valdis stubbornly insisted he be saved for use as a seed bull. In one year, he has sired twenty-seven offspring, so Valdis' thinking was shrewd even if it went against custom."

"So why can't he be used in the ring again? There must be many matadors wanting to avenge Señor Huerto's death."

"You have much to learn," he sighed. Then, crossing left leg over right, he stared into the night as though wondering where to begin. Finally, he said, "A matador has but fifteen minutes to kill his bull. If the matador takes longer...if the bull is allowed to increase his knowledge of the matador...if he is allowed to fight again, then many matadors would die.

"You see," he went on, "bullfighting is based on a first meeting between a wild animal and a man on foot. The bull has never been in the ring before. They are not taken to the ring except to be tested for bravery, when they are exactly two years old."

"Why two years?" Amber was curious.

"At one year, they are not strong enough and at three years, they are too dangerous, too powerful. Also, they are old enough to remember the test."

"Remember?" she echoed, astonished. "What difference would that make?"

"A great difference, my beautiful one." He flashed her a smile. "To begin with, the bull is put into a corral about thirty yards across, half the size of a bullring. A picador is waiting with a kind of spear with a triangular steel point, slightly shorter than is used in a real fight. He waits on his horse with his back turned toward the gate through which the young bull has entered. No one speaks. The picador does nothing to excite the bull, for the test is to see whether or not the bull will charge without being goaded. When—and if—he does charge, his style is noted...whether he makes his charge from a distance...whether he paws the ground first...or bawls. It is noted whether the bull goes toward the horse...whether he keeps his feet back and charges with full power, pushing onward to reach the picador and horse after the pic is put into him."

Amber was horrified. "You mean the picador *stabs* him?"

"It is all a part of it. You will learn."

"I don't think I want to." She shuddered.

Armand ignored her revulsion and went on. "The bull is also watched to see whether he chops his neck around, trying to get the pic out, or if he just turns away and quits his charge because he has been hurt. If he stops fighting because he is wounded, then his owner—if he is scrupulous—will have him castrated and fattened for market."

"What do you mean, 'if he is scrupulous'?"

"No honorable breeder would sell a cowardly bull for the ring."

"What happens if the bull doesn't give up at that point?"

"Sometimes even a two-year old bull can knock over a horse and a man. If this happens, he must be taken away with the capes. But it is not good to do this, for it is not good for the bull to see the cape. It is not even good to have the bull charge more than once. It is felt that only so many pics can be accepted by a bull. If he takes two or three in his bravery test, then that is two or three less than he will take in the ring.

"Most of the time, faith is put in the lineage of the bulls. You see, a bull is not a stupid animal. This is why the bull that killed Gosa Huerto is so dangerous. He has learned that it is the matador he must fear, and not the cape. He would probably charge the man and not the cape."

"But would that not make bullfighting more of an honest sport? The bull would have a chance, then. And why do picadors stick them? Just to torture them?"

"It is going to be wonderful teaching you about bullfighting, señorita."

"Call me Amber, please," she urged, thinking how wonderful it was to have a friend here.

"And you must call me Armand," he said with a grin, then continued. "Let me explain. The picadors aim their shafts at the hump of the bull's neck in order to weaken his muscles and to lower his head for the kill. If those muscles are not weakened, and the bull has the full use of his neck, he can rear up and gore the matador quite easily. The banderilleros drive the barbs into the bull's hump to further sap his strength—though it really does little more than rile the crowd. The bull, you will learn, is regarded very highly."

He took a deep breath and grinned. "Have you learned enough to become interested? Would you like to go to the bullfight tomorrow? I will be performing."

"I...I don't think so," she stammered. She still thought it was cruel, and she wanted no part of it. She knew, too, that there was going to be a scene with Valdis when she refused to go with him.

Still, this handsome, vibrant young man had made bullfighting his profession, and there was such a warm glow between them. She did not want to do anything to end it. This attractive man had a delightful way about him.

She jumped, startled, as he touched her hand. Their eyes met and held, and she felt he was looking into the depths of her soul. He whispered, "Moonstar. That is what I shall call you. Here, in the moonlight, with your glorious hair sparkling like spun silver, it is as though you were a rare star. A moonstar."

He leaned closer, lips dangerously near. Amber could feel his warm breath on her face. "Say you will come tomorrow, my moonstar. I want to know that you are near me. I want this feeling that is growing between us to blossom in the warmth of the sun. That is what you will be for me if you are there tomorrow—my sun. We say that the best bullfighter is the sun. There is no best bullfighter if the sun is not there. You will always be my moonstar, but when I face the bull, you will be my sun. Say you will be there, Amber...for me."

She gazed into his eyes and could not move. His lips were so close she could feel them brushing hers. Oh, how she wanted him to kiss her, to take her in his arms and crush her to him, his lips devouring, possessing. Her whole body tingled fiercely. She could only stare at him, mesmerized, wanting.

The angry scream pierced their magical moment, and they sprang apart, staring at the raging woman running toward them. At first, Amber did not recognize the twisted, enraged face of Maretta.

She came at Amber with arms outstretched, fingers arched in daggerlike claws, but Armand grabbed her about the waist and stopped her, shouting to her in Spanish. Maretta struggled against him, also screaming in Spanish, but her angry eyes never left Amber.

Amber took a hesitant step forward. "What is wrong, Armand? Why is she so upset?"

"Why is she so upset?" Maretta cried. "You she-devil! You try to take my Armand from me. For this, I will kill you."

"You are not going to kill anyone, Maretta." Armand sighed. "I have told you many times that you have no right to interfere in my life."

"I have every right. We are promised. You know we are promised."

"That is a ridiculous custom and means nothing to me, as you know very well. I will marry for love and no other reason, as I have so often told you." He snorted in disgust. "A stupid custom indeed, promising babies!"

"If my father were alive and your father were alive, you would not say that. You would not dare."

"I dare many things, Maretta. Now go inside. Amber and I will be along soon." He released Maretta and gave her a gentle shove away from him.

"You will come *now!*" She hissed, moving toward Amber once more, but Armand blocked her path. Maretta cried, "It is not proper that you should be out here alone. I know she has no decency, but I should think you would know better, Armand."

"Another custom I find annoying," he chuckled, turning his back on Maretta and returning to Amber's side. "Now go inside. I am telling Amber about bullfighting."

"A pity she will not be in the ring tomorrow," Maretta spat. "I would take much delight in seeing her blood spilled in the sand."

She turned away and took a few steps, skirts flouncing, then whirled around to cry, "You must come inside now. Valdis will deal harshly with both of you." Then she turned and ran quickly up the path and into the house.

Amber said, "Perhaps we had better go in, Armand. I don't want any trouble."

He gently danced his fingertips down her cheek. "I knew I was in trouble when first I saw you, my moonstar...."

Amber was flooded by those strange feelings all over again when he pulled her tightly against him. She trembled. "I think we should go inside, Armand," she said nervously. "I can't explain now, but, you see, I already have many problems here and I must leave as soon as I can. I don't want any more trouble, and—"

"I am your friend," he interjected quickly, frowning. "I was afraid Valdis might cause you pain. You can tell me anything, Amber."

She shook her head. "I can't burden you, Armand. Goodness, you already saved my life!"

"Together we shall overcome anything," he whispered. Then his lips came down on hers without warning, gently at first, then demanding. His tongue sought hers, holding her in a kiss so deep, so scorching, that Amber trembled uncontrollably.

She struggled against him and, surprised, he released her. She stepped back quickly, staring up at him. "I...I don't think you should have done that," she murmured nervously. "We don't even know each other."

"I know enough to find you irresistible, enchanting, the most beautiful woman I have ever seen." His eyes twinkled mischievously as he added, "And I also know that you like being kissed, my moonstar."

Amber felt her cheeks flushing, and she turned toward the sound of approaching voices. Her heart beat rapidly as she saw Valdis striding purposefully toward them, looking quite angry. Maretta was hurrying after him, trying to keep up.

"Mendosa!" Valdis' voice boomed. "What is the meaning of this? How dare you lure my stepsister down here!" He came to a halt a few feet from them and stood, feet spread wide apart, hands on hips.

Armand did not back away before Valdis. He was unintimidated by Valdis' heavier build. "We do nothing wrong, Valdis," he said tightly. "And I did not 'lure' her here."

Maretta's face was twisted in anger. Shaking a fist in Amber's direction, she said to Armand, "Amber lacks the proper breeding to know it is indecent to be alone with a man, but you, Armand, you should know better."

"Now wait a minute." Amber was less nervous, and growing angry. "I resent your insulting my breeding. And I only met Armand when he saved my life!"

"Silence!" Valdis roared.

"I will not be silent!" Amber raged, furious. She was not used to being spoken to that way. "We have not been doing anything wrong, and I resent your insinuations."

Valdis' lips curled in a snarl, and he whispered raggedly, "You try my patience, Amber. I gave this fiesta for you, and you have brought shame

71

upon my house. Now go to your room and remain there. I will deal with Armand."

Amber stood her ground. "I will not be sent to my room like a naughty child, Valdis. Just who do you think you *are?*" she snapped, undaunted by his fiery gaze. "I told you. Armand saved my life. I went for a walk and accidently wandered into one of the bull pens. I might have been killed if he hadn't happened along. He distracted the bull so I could escape."

"So you just happened along, eh?" Valdis glared at Armand.

Armand's eyes twinkled as he goaded Valdis. *"Sí.* It is but a short walk on the eastern side of your property, Valdis. Remember?"

Valdis struggled with his temper, trying to ignore the reminder that he did not control that particular border. "She went into the pens? You fought one of my seed bulls? Which one?"

Armand's grin spread. "Chico. He was not so bad. I think, perhaps, he mellows with age."

"And I think you grow more insolent with age," Valdis hollered. To Amber, he snapped, "You should not have been walking about alone. There are many dangers. Now you have not only caused me embarrassment, but—" Abruptly, he stopped. Taking a deep breath, he covered his face with his hands as he struggled for control. A stiff smile on his lips, he looked at Armand and Amber in turn and said wearily, "Enough. Let us all go inside now. There are guests waiting to meet you, Amber, and my sister has been waiting to dance with you, Armand. Let us attempt to have a pleasant evening."

Maretta moved quickly, slipping her fingers around Armand's arm. With an apologetic nod to Amber, Armand turned and led Maretta toward the house.

Valdis held out his arm to Amber, but she made no move to take it. Chuckling softly, he reached out and took her hand and placed it in the crook of his arm, pressing down to hold it tightly against his side. "We will join the others, little sister," he murmured. "I wish to be the envy of every man in the valley."

"And I wish to retire for the evening," Amber snapped. "I am quite tired after my...ordeal."

Ignoring his pleas, Amber jerked her hand away, lifted her skirts, and, avoiding the terrace and the party, hurried to a side entrance. She made her way quickly upstairs. Entering the privacy of her room, she locked the door and sighed with relief. Oh, how long would it be before she could leave this place? Valdis was insufferable, and Maretta was just as bad. If only she could find her money and be on her way!

Sudden thoughts of Armand washed over her, memories of his kiss, of the feelings he had evoked. Even in the moonlight, she had known he was handsome, but when they stepped into the glow of torches along the terrace, she had realized he was truly beautiful. Here was a quandary, she told herself. Did he really find her attractive, or was he, a celebrated matador and probably sought after by many women, merely enjoying another flirtation.

What difference did it make? She shook her head. She was leaving soon. Why worry about it?

Stepping behind the dressing screen, she removed her gown and put on the satin robe Dolita had laid out for her. She then moved through the balcony doors. The night was still beautiful, with a mellow sheen of moonlight and a soft breeze.

"My moonstar! You do exist! It was not a dream!"

The softly laughing voice startled her, but she quickly gripped the wrought iron railing and leaned over to see Armand standing below, arms folded across his chest, smiling up at her.

"I found the fiesta intolerable without you," he called softly, "and since I do have to fight in the ring tomorrow, I will slip away now and get my rest. But I wanted to see you once more. I am afraid," he added mischievously, "that your stepsister will be waiting rather a long time for the sangría she thinks I went to get her."

Amber giggled. "You flirt with danger in your public and your private life, too, don't you?" she teased.

He nodded happily. "But I much prefer fighting a bull. The odds are much better."

They laughed together. Then, suddenly, their eyes met. Gazes riveted on each other, they fell silent. After a moment, Armand called softly, "You will come tomorrow. Please?"

Amber nodded. "I will, because you asked me to, Armand."

"Aha!" His wide grin broke the mood. "If you do everything I ask, then I have no problems, eh?"

Amber blushed, calling, "Yes! I mean—oh, Armand, you confuse me!"

With one last grin, he bowed, blew her a kiss,

then spun about and disappeared into the shadows.

Amber stepped inside and closed the doors, feeling warm and happy. Perhaps there was no future in this, but for however long she was in Mexico, was there really any harm in being happy?

❧ Chapter Five ❧

THE desert winds blowing lazily from the Sierra de la Madera were hot, giving no respite from the oppressive heat of the crowded arena.

Amber, in the presidential box high above the other spectators, waved her lace fan limply. Nothing, she thought, would help except for an improbable icy wind from the north.

Beside Amber, Valdis sat ramrod straight, his head held high, looking out over the multitude below him.

Amber glanced at Maretta, who sat on the other side of her brother. Maretta's eyes were shining with the happy anticipation of what was to come, and Amber wondered for the hundredth time how anyone could actually enjoy these spectacles.

Valdis suddenly leaned over and covered Amber's hand with his, but she snatched her hand away. He chuckled. "You are like a frightened little bird, lovely one. Do not be. I will explain everything that takes place."

"That won't be necessary," she said tightly. "I'm not interested, Valdis. I should not have come."

"Ah, but you should have," he said quickly, a note of reproach in his tone. "It is expected of the Alezparito family. For many years, we have accepted from time to time the invitation of the president to represent him here in his box. It is an honor bestowed on our family because of my father's glorious name."

He turned abruptly to Maretta, who seemed to be waiting for him to do so. As he nodded, she stood up and, with a single swift gesture raised her white lace handkerchief and released it to flutter gently to the ground below. The crowd screamed with delight, and Valdis said to Amber, "It is the signal to begin the parade to open the day's corrida. Allegra usually gives the signal, but I felt it best she remain at home today." His expression grew dark. "She becomes more and more senile every day. I am afraid she will embarrass us if I allow her to be seen in public."

Amber started to speak up hotly, then decided it would do Allegra no good. She kept silent. She knew very well that Valdis was deliberately keeping Allegra locked away from her.

Trumpets shrilled above the din, and Valdis leaned so close that Amber cringed. Excited, he explained, "See the two men riding out from under those arches? They are leading the procession, which heralds the entrance of the matadors."

As Valdis continued to speak, Amber scanned the procession entering the arena. The horses were prancing to stirring martial music. All around, people were screaming, arms waving as, suddenly, the three matadors of the day emerged from beneath the arch, each riding a splendid mount. Resplendent in costumes heavy with gold and silver embroidery, parade capes slung over their shoulders, they were a stirring slight.

The matadors were preceded by the banderilleros, whose costumes were similar to the matadors' but lacked the gold embroidery. The picadors wore broad-brimmed, low-crowned, beige hats, and costumes also similar to the matadors'. "See the steel armor sticking out from beneath their trousers on their right legs?" Valdis pointed to one of the picadors. "It is made of steel one-eighth of an inch thick and goes from hip to ankle. On their other leg, the armor is only knee-length. Their trousers are made of heavy chamois, and they also wear thick, protective chamois ankle boots."

As the matadors, still on horseback, approached the presidential box, the crowd roared deafeningly. The three men removed their hats and bowed. Amber felt a sudden rush as her eyes met Armand's eyes. He smiled, and she knew he was addressing himself to her alone. She could feel Maretta's angry look, but would not let herself care. Armand had been kind to her, and after all the sadness she had known, she was grateful.

Her eyes moved over him. Strong, muscular thighs strained beneath skintight knee-length trousers of richly embroidered satin. He wore a hand-drawn linen lace shirtwaist, coral pink stockings of heavy silk, and flat black slippers. His hat was made of tiny, black silk chenille balls, handsewn on heavy buckram. His sleek black hair was tied back in braids at the nape of his neck. His whole being exuded courage and strength, Amber reflected, a warm flush moving through her. She flashed a happy smile in his direction, which he returned eagerly.

A moment later, the matadors whirled their horses about and returned to the procession. As they moved away, Maretta whispered to Valdis, "He is so beautiful. I must marry him soon. Make it happen, my brother."

"It will happen," he said coldly, grimly. "Only be patient."

Amber pretended not to hear them. She gave her full concentration to the matadors, who were removing their heavy parade capes and handing them to attendants. The attendants spread the capes along the front of the wall that protected the first rows of seats. While this was being done, other men moved quickly to smooth the sand, which had been disturbed by the procession.

One of the matadors selected a heavy cape, and Valdis said it was a fighting cape. It was rose-colored on the outside, bright yellow on the inside, with a big, wide, stiff collar, and long enough to fall to a man's knees. The matador took the cape and went to stand behind a little flat wooden shelter outside the ring. It was wide enough, she noted, for two men to stand in but barely narrow enough to dodge behind.

Valdis explained as the *alguacils* rode toward

the presidential box. "They come for the key to
the red door, the *toril*, where the bull is kept."

Maretta stood, dropping the key, and to the delight of the crowd, one of the men caught it in his
plumed hat. Quickly, he turned and galloped across
the ring to hand the key to another man who stood
outside the red door. Then he raced his horse back
to the box and saluted Maretta before riding out
of the ring. Once more, men hurried forward to
sweep away the traces of the horse's hooves from
the sand.

A hush fell over the arena. All eyes were upon
the red door. The man holding the key looked at
Maretta, and when she gave the signal with her
handkerchief, he moved to unlock the door, then
ran backward. The passageway opened.

The bull appeared in a great cloud of dust and
the roll of thunder she remembered from her narrow escape. As he passed through the gate, Amber
recognized Cord Hayden astride the railing above.
He boldly attached a silken rosette to the harness
around the bull's shoulders.

Maretta swore, and Valdis hissed at her reproachfully. "I cannot help it," she cried. "I hate
that man. He is evil."

"It is his job to attach the rosette," Valdis reminded her, then whispered. "Restrain yourself,
Maretta. When we are seated in this box, everyone
watches us and hears what we say. I agree the
man is evil, but this is not the place to say so."

Amber could not resist goading them. "I think
Mr. Hayden is quite nice. He helped Armand save
me from the bull last night."

Valdis tried to quiet her with a look, but she asked, "Why did he put the flower on the bull?"

"It is a red silk rosette," Valdis said tightly. "Red is the color of our ranch. It identifies the bull as Alezparito stock."

Maretta sniffed. "She *would* defend him. They are both Americans."

"Enough," Valdis snapped, and Maretta fell silent. But she glared at Amber once more before returning her attention to the ring.

The bull moved slowly, staring belligerently around. A banderillero waved a bright red cape, and the great beast charged.

"He does this," Valdis quickly explained, "so that the matador may watch and judge whether he shows any preference in his horns, and also whether he attacks from both sides."

But Amber was not interested in the ring. Something had made her look back to Cord Hayden, still perched on the railing. He was handsome, but in a very different way from Armand. Cord was ruggedly good-looking, his hair windblown, his whole appearance a little disheveled. She thought that his appearance probably matched a reckless spirit.

He was tall, and muscular, yet lean and lithe. She wondered whether she remembered the color of his eyes correctly, and then she realized that he had seen her staring at him and was grinning. He tipped his hat, and she looked away, deeply embarrassed.

A cry went up from the crowd as the matador entered the ring, making a few passes with his cape. Valdis' explained that these passes were called 'veronicas,' meant for the matador to show his skill with the cape and demonstrate his domination over the bull.

The brassy cry of a trumpet split the air, the signal for the picadors to enter the ring. The picadors moved into position and the bull pawed at the ground. Lowering his head, he charged the nearest horse, and the mounted picador reined his steed sharply to one side while he lifted his long steel pike and planted the point between the bull's neck and shoulder blades.

Amber closed her eyes tightly, wincing every time she heard the crowd boo. They disliked this part of the fight, Valdis whispered, because of their great respect for the bull.

Another bugle blared, signaling the retirement of the picadors and the entrance of the banderilleros.

A wave of screaming filled the air and Amber's eyes flashed open. Amidst the dust clouds, the banderilleros were trying to get the bull's attention with shouts and violent gestures. The bull hesitated, then charged, and one of the men twisted his horse to safety at the same instant he planted barbed sticks, decorated at one end with colored paper, into the bull's shoulders. The crowd, Amber thought wryly, seemed to love that part as much as it had hated the driving of the pics.

The bull emitted a mighty roar as he lunged at one of the men. Then, at the last instant, he changed course and moved to the right, taking one of the other men by surprise. His horns drove into the man's horse, rupturing his belly.

Amber got to her feet. She had seen enough.

"Sit down!" Valdis ordered, reaching out to grasp her wrist, but Amber twisted away. "No!"

She moved toward the stairs, and Maretta gasped, "Oh, Valdis, do something. For a member of the Alezparito family to leave the presidential box is disgraceful! Oh! I'm afraid I may faint."

"Do whatever makes you feel comfortable," Amber said over her shoulder as she hastened away. "That is what I am doing."

Maretta went limp in her chair, and Valdis turned to minister to her—forced, for the moment, to allow Amber to leave.

She made her way down from the box, moving to the outside of the arena. Leaning against the high wooden fence, she lifted her lace fan and waved it rapidly before her face.

"Señorita Amber!"

She started to run, then realized it was not Valdis calling to her, but Armand.

As Armand reached her, he clutched her shoulders, looking at her searchingly. "Are you ill?"

"In a way," she told him bluntly. "It made me sick to see that horse being gored. I just couldn't watch anymore. I'm sorry. Please go back inside and do what you have to do. I'm going to wait out here."

"Now listen to me." He gripped her tighter, forcing her to meet his steady, unwavering gaze. "I was afraid of this. You must understand that the killing of the horses in the ring is indefensible. But it sometimes happens. I can understand your revulsion, but please, my moonstar, return to the box. I have to know that you are watching me today."

She looked at him in surprise. "Do you know what you are asking of me? I don't like any of this." She shook her head firmly.

He grinned, squeezing her shoulders. "This is my world, Amber, and now it is your world, also. You must learn to live in it. Please return to your seat. I ask you to do this for the friendship that grows between us."

She looked confused. "Armand, we just met last night, and—"

"Something is happening to us," he interrupted, cupping her chin in his hand, his eyes shining into hers. "You feel it. I feel it." He shuddered involuntarily. "God, but you are beautiful. I must go now, before I forget where we are. Please, say you will go back inside. I will hold you in my heart until we meet again."

Amber could only nod dizzily.

He released her, bowed slightly, then turned and walked purposefully back into the arena.

Amber stared after him. What was happening to her? There was a frightening emotion within whenever he touched her. What was this feeling taking hold, threatening her?

Just then, Cord Hayden stepped from behind a wooden partition, and Amber gasped, startled. He leaned back against the wall, arms folded across his chest, the play of a smile on his lips. "Well, Miss Forrest, it seems you have gotten yourself into quite a dilemma in a very short time."

How long have you been eavesdropping?" she asked coolly, accusingly.

"I wasn't eavesdropping. Just overhearing. I saw you run out, too, and I was coming to ask if anything was wrong, but Armand got to you first. Now, about your dilemma." He grinned. "You've got yourself caught between Armand Mendosa and Valdis Alezparito, the former a good man, the latter a real mean character. It's a logical choice for any decent woman, but that same choice would be dangerous."

She sighed, exasperated. "I really don't know what you are talking about, Mr. Hayden, nor why you concern yourself with my business."

"Ordinarily, I wouldn't," he answered smoothly. "Armand can usually handle himself where his women are concerned, but this time it's different. Since meeting you last night, he's talked of nothing else. I've known him a few years, and I've never seen him so taken with any woman. I can see why. You're damn beautiful," he nodded matter-of-factly, "but you're also poison because it's obvious Valdis has designs on you."

"Well, no one need have *designs* on me," she snapped indignantly. "It is my intention to leave Mexico as soon as possible. I'm not interested in Armand in the way you suggest. He's...my friend. He saved my life. As for Valdis, I hate the man." She finished, wondering why she had confided so much.

He smiled. "Well, I'm glad to hear all of this. The last thing Armand needs is to lose his head over a woman. Just make sure you let him *know* he's just a friend."

She tilted her head to stare up at him defiantly. "May I ask what is your interest in all of this?"

He shrugged. "Armand is my friend. I don't want to see him so involved with a woman that he loses his concentration in the ring. When that happens to a matador, when he doesn't have his mind totally on what he's doing, he can be killed. I've seen it happen."

He flashed her a grin that she found infuriating. "There will be some problems if he tries to court you. It's going to be hard for him to visit the Alezparito ranch, because Maretta's determined to marry him, and Valdis means to make it happen."

Amber ached to tell him to keep silent. After all, how much did she really know about this man? He might really be a friend of Valdis', and if she told him she was scheming to get her stolen money back, he might tell Valdis.

She said tightly, "Thank you for your warning, Mr. Hayden. I assure you that my first concern is also for Armand's safety, and I think you worry needlessly."

He smiled in that arrogant manner. "Men do tend to forget themselves when they fall for a pretty face," he said.

Amber snapped, "And has that ever happened to you, Mr. Hayden? Has a pretty face ever made you forget yourself?"

His dark brown eyes suddenly became stormy, flecked with red. His lips twitched, and it was apparent that she had struck a disconcerting chord.

But the moment passed just as quickly, and Cord Hayden looked at her coolly and smiled. "I would say that it has, Miss Forrest—and that is to my advantage now. While I find you quite appealing, you won't make me forget a damn thing. But you'll make me remember plenty."

Before she could reply, he tipped his hat and

walked away. She watched him go, swaggering. She saw, too, that other men instinctively got out of his way as he walked. He was not a man to be crossed.

Now there was a new feeling surging up inside her, this one more disturbing than what she had felt with Armand. It was, she reflected, as though she had felt this before...in another time, another place. But what did that mean?

"There you are!" Valdis' voice cracked, and rough hands reached out to grasp her arms painfully. He moved her along toward the arena. In an ominous whisper, he said, "I will not have you making a fool of yourself, Amber. You will come inside and sit next to me in the presidential box, and whether you enjoy what you see or not, you will act as though you do. For if you do not, when we get back to the ranch, so help me I will strip your buttocks bare and thrash you like the willful child you are."

She looked up at him and gasped, astonished, stumbling as he yanked her along roughly. "You...you wouldn't dare!" she cried.

"You listen to me." He ground out the words between clenched teeth. "I own and control everything on that ranch, and everyone—on four legs or two—obeys me. I will whip you until you beg to do my will. Do you understand me?"

Amber could restrain herself no longer. She lashed out, "I understand that you're a coward and a bully, Valdis, and I will *never* bend to your will. I would rather die! Don't you ever threaten me again!"

They had reached the outside of the presidential

box. Valdis stopped and looked at her with so much fury that it was all she could do to stop herself from trembling. "Tonight," he hissed, "you will learn what happens when you dare to defy me." He pushed her inside the box and into her seat.

Maretta glanced at her reproachfully, then saw Valdis' face and turned away.

"I am not frightened of you, Valdis," Amber snapped.

He kept silent, taking his seat without looking at her again.

Amber sat silently, looking straight out into the bullring but not seeing the scene at all. Her mind was turned inward, to the realization that she was in terrible trouble. Valdis was as intent upon having her for his own as a man could be, and everyone around Valdis was frightened of him. What, then, could she expect if she spurned him?

Keeping all expression from her face, knowing how great a mistake it would be to let Valdis know she was afraid of him, Amber willed her emotions aside and told herself to wait until she was alone: she would think this out in a safe place, away from him. For the moment, she would perform, make herself seem fearless and poised. There was, heaven knew, time enough for her jumbled emotions later on.

Amber forgot Valdis as Armand entered the ring. After a moment, her eyes went from Armand to the bull; over a thousand pounds of raw fury. He could, in a short lunge, travel faster than a galloping racehorse. He could toss both a horse and its rider into the air. He could kill a man in a few seconds.

Armand had only fifteen minutes in which to kill the bull. He had to rely on his skill with the cape and his ability to create an illusion.

She watched, heart pounding wildly, as Valdis stiffly explained that this was the third and final act of the bullfight, the most dangerous part.

A scream locked in her throat as she saw Armand, arm raised high, pass his body directly over the bull's right horn, exposing for daring seconds the femoral artery and vein to his upper thigh. The misjudgment of even an inch could mean the matador's life.

"Toro!" Armand cried, and the crowd responded unison, *"Ole!"*

Again and again Armand called out the challenge and each time he was answered by hundreds of voices making one thunderous cry of approval.

The bull, head down, shoulder muscles pierced by pics and banderillas, snorted and pawed the ground as he watched Armand's every move.

Armand stepped to his waiting attendant and accepted the heart-shaped cape of scarlet wool. Holding the cape high in the air with one hand, he used his other hand to remove his hat and began to strut in a circle, waving to the screaming crowd.

Pausing before the presidential box, Armand looked up at Amber and smiled.

"He smiles for me!" Maretta cried.

Amber said nothing. Valdis sat in stony silence.

Suddenly, Armand waved his hat in the air for a few seconds, and then, with a well-aimed pitch, landed it right in Amber's lap. With a sweeping bow, he turned to face the waiting bull.

Maretta attempted to stand, but Valdis had seen the movement coming and placed a restraining arm across her, pinning her in her seat. "No," she cried softly. "He cannot do this to me."

Amber fingered the little hat, not really understanding the significance of the gesture.

Valdis turned stiffly and said accusingly, "Armand Mendosa has dedicated the bull to you by throwing you his montera. We will discuss this tonight...when we discuss other things," he added meaningfully.

Amber sighed. None of this was her fault. Her eyes wandered to the railing, and she saw Cord Hayden watching her. He tipped his hat in an "I-told-you-so" gesture. Lifting her chin in dismissal, she looked away.

Armand was working closer to the bull, his passes death-defying before the alternate waves of sound and silence washing down from the stands.

Suddenly, he fell to his knees in the sand. The bull charged, exploding with fury into the crimson cape. Amber's hands flew to her mouth as, without so much as a glance over his shoulder, Armand lured the beast back to him in a corkscrew turn around his pivoting body.

Armand stepped back, raised on tiptoe, and, as the bull drove straight for him, head lowered, Armand drove the sword high between the animal's shoulder blades.

The bull crumpled, dying in a pool of blood.

The crowd screamed hysterically as Armand strutted proudly toward the presidential box. Every few steps he paused, taking sweeping bows to the thunderous ovation.

When he was standing just beneath the box, he looked up at Amber expectantly. She stared back, confused. What was she supposed to do at this point? While she wondered, Valdis snatched the hat from Amber's lap and angrily tossed it out of the box into the ring. She watched, astonished, as Armand reached for it and missed. The hat landed in the dirt.

Armand looked up, eyes narrowing on Valdis' glaring face. Armand turned his back and walked away, flowers raining down upon him from all around the arena.

"Good! Good!" Maretta was saying. "He missed the hat. A matador never misses the hat. You have shamed him, Valdis. He deserves it for letting the *puta* bewitch him."

Amber flared, knowing exactly what *puta* meant. Leaping to her feet, she whirled on Maretta and cried, "How dare you say such a thing, Maretta? What have I ever done to you to make you hate me so? I didn't ask Armand to throw me his hat. Now the two of you have embarrassed him in his moment of glory."

"Sit down and shut your mouth," Valdis snarled. "Do not incense me further, Amber. Already you have a merciless beating coming to you tonight."

"You won't touch me," Amber cried, moving to the stairs. "I find both of you despicable!"

Amber ran down the steps, bumping into people in her haste. She reached the main corridor out of the arena and looked over her shoulder to see that Valdis was only a short distance behind her.

Running out the main gate, she felt herself being

grabbed around the waist and she panicked. But it was not Valdis.

"Let her be, Valdis," Cord Hayden barked as Valdis skidded to a stop before him. Cord kept his grip on Amber. "I'll take her back to the ranch."

People had stopped to stare, and Valdis struggled to control himself. In a strained voice, he said, "It would not be proper. The two of you would be alone. I have no duenna to send with you."

"We have no need of a chaperon," Cord scoffed. "Besides," he added rakishly, "if I wanted to seduce Amber, it wouldn't make a damn bit of difference whether there was a duenna around or not."

Amber gasped, and Valdis stiffened. "Señor, I will ask you to hold your tongue."

"Just like you hold yours, right, Valdis?" Cord snapped, reaching out to wrap possessive fingers around Amber's arm. "Let's go."

Valdis could only watch them walk away. He did not want a scene; not with people watching. There had been too much talk in the valley already. But one day...one day, he vowed, Cord Hayden would pay for daring to defy him.

🕮 Chapter Six 🕮

"WAIT here," Cord commanded, leaving Amber near a hitching post as he went to talk to an old man standing beside a horse and wagon. Cord handed the man some money, then motioned to Amber.

"I am grateful to you," she said softly, when they were seated on the wagon's crude wooden bench, and Cord popped the reins and the tired-looking horse began lumbering forward.

"It won't be as comfortable as riding in that expensive Alezparito carriage," he told her as he stared straight ahead, "but maybe the company will be a bit more pleasant."

"I'm sure it will be," she said quickly, then felt foolish.

Cord flashed her a warm smile. "Don't be nervous with me. I don't bite. Well, not all the time.

And when I do, it's in places you'd like to be bitten."

"Sir!" Amber gasped. Then she saw the laughter in his eyes and felt easier. "Do you always say such bold things to women?"

"Only to women who blush at bold things. Now tell me why you ran out of the arena looking so upset."

She explained, and finished by saying, "I'm afraid I really didn't know what was going on at the time, only that something had happened that infuriated both Valdis and Maretta."

Cord laughed. "I'm surprised at Armand being so bold. It's a pretty big thing when a matador dedicates his kill to a señorita. When the señorita is young, pretty, and unmarried, it's usually a declaration of his intention to court her. For you to be sitting with Maretta...well, Armand is living dangerously."

Amber stammered, "I...I hardly know him." She shook her head from side to side, long hair whipping about her face in the breeze. "I never expected any of this. Sometimes I don't understand what's going on."

Cord turned to give her a probing look. "Just what *did* you expect when you came to Mexico?"

She bit her lip, determined that the pain he had suddenly evoked would not bring tears. Taking a deep breath, she let it out slowly, then said, "I don't know, exactly. I only know what I didn't expect...to find my father dead, my stepmother treated worse than a servant in her own house, and a tyrant like Valdis. He stole all the money

I had in the world in order to keep me a prisoner. All I wanted was to leave here."

Cord gently prodded, "I think you'd better tell me all of it, Amber. Start at the beginning."

She shook her head in dismay. "I have no right to burden you with my problems, and besides..." she blurted fearfully, "how do I know I can trust you?"

"Do you have any choice?" he asked plainly.

"Yes," she countered. "I can try to solve my problems myself."

"Right now you aren't doing a very good job. So why don't you just unburden on me? I am no friend of Valdis'. You can trust me."

Amber gazed at him. Again, it was as though she had known him before, somewhere. Making a sudden decision, she told him all of it. He listened quietly, staring at the road ahead as the horse plodded along.

When she had finished, he began speaking in a low voice. "I'm going to try and get you out of there, Amber, but I will have to be careful. I can't let Armand know just how desperate the situation is, and I'm going to ask you not to tell him."

She blinked. "But why?"

"Damn it, woman," he said, eyes blazing. "Don't you understand? Armand is falling in love with you. If he even thought that Valdis would lay a hand on you, he'd go charging into that house and get killed. He is a great matador, but he'd never stand a chance against a killer like Valdis."

"Killer?" Amber echoed.

"Yes, a killer," he said tightly. "I've heard some

97

ugly things, but there's no need to scare you further by repeating them. Just believe me when I say the man is dangerous, and I want you to be careful. Don't goad him, Amber. I'll work something out."

He shook his head. "Hell, I'd take you all the way to the border right now myself, but he'd have a goddamn army after us, and we'd never have a chance. We need time to plan."

Cord sensed her fear and covered her hands with one of his and squeezed. "Listen, sweetheart," he gave her a lopsided grin, "he isn't going to hurt you. He's just trying to scare you. If he wanted to hurt you, he'd have done it by now. I think he's got other plans...like marriage."

"Marriage? Valdis?"

"Gossip spreads in the valley like sand in a windstorm. I've heard that Valdis brags he's going to have the most beautiful woman in Mexico for his wife. Armand hasn't heard that, or he would have said something. Let's hope he doesn't hear the gossip. Like I said, we don't need him charging in like a white knight rescuing a damsel in distress."

They rode in silence for a while, and Cord turned the wagon from the main road and urged the horse up over a tiny knoll. Reining to a stop, he got down and wordlessly held out his arms to Amber. She allowed him to help her to the ground. He took her hand and led her around a thick hedge of sage and cactus.

She gasped in delight at the view beyond. The valley stretched in the golden sunset like giant fingers of purple mist. Dusty emerald and rose clouds wafted through the vegetation. Light bounced off the rocks, turning stone into sparkling diamonds.

"It's all so beautiful," she whispered in awe. "I have never seen anything so lovely in all my life."

Cord leaned back against a smooth, flat rock. Amber stood beside him until he lifted her and sat her on the rock. After a while, he said, "It's one of the prettiest spots I've seen in Mexico, but it can't compare with Pennsylvania."

"Is that where you are from?" she asked.

He nodded. "I'll go back there one day."

He sounded so wistful. "Can't you go back now if you miss it so? And whatever brought you all the way to Mexico in the first place? Were you running from the Rebels?" she teased.

He chuckled, but she did not miss the slight glint of anger flashing in his eyes.

"No. I didn't run from the Rebs. And, besides, what are you doing out here in the desert with a Yankee? If Armand hadn't told me you were from the South I would have known it by the butter-and-grits accent."

"I never took sides during the war," she told him somberly, quickly explaining the sheltered, removed-from-life existence she had known with her grandmother. "We were just never involved in anything. I think there could have been a battle going on right outside the window, and Grandma would have closed the shutters and gone about her business."

He had been staring downward as she spoke,

muscular arms folded across his large chest. She watched as he suddenly leaned over, shocked at the tremors of pleasure she felt at the sight of his shirt straining tautly against his broad back. Picking a small yellow cactus flower, he handed it to her. "You're like this flower, Amber. Tiny, vulnerable, innocent. There for the picking. For you have no one to protect you."

He was leaning over her, so close she could see the thick lashes framing his dark brown eyes. "Until now...." he murmured huskily. "Until now, Amber...."

Powerful arms swept her against him in a crushing vise as his mouth came down on hers. His tongue parted her lips and he explored the intimate recesses of her mouth. She couldn't control the desire quivering through her body, as warm and as penetrating as the gilded sunset bathing them in glory.

He released her and she gasped, "You...you shouldn't have done that. It was—"

"—Damn nice," he laughed, cupping her chin and brushing his lips across hers. "And you liked it."

She looked down and saw that she was still holding the fragile flower he had given her. Yes, it had been nice. She had liked it. Too much. And now she felt frightened, but within that fright was anger, and she lifted her face to look at him in a challenge. "I am not like this flower, Cord. I'm not going to let myself be weak and vulnerable. I am going to get my money back from Valdis, and I am going to leave Mexico, leave you and your kisses, and Armand and his charm, and Valdis and his power...none of these will hold me here."

He placed a hand flat against the rock on each side of her and smiled. "You are such a tiny thing to have so much spunk...like a fluffy little kitten. All playful and cute one minute, all claws and spit the next."

She wouldn't let him know how uncomfortable she was. "First I'm a flower and then a kitten. I am me, Cord Hayden, a grown woman."

"No, not grown. Not grown, little kitten. But you will be. And maybe I'll be the one to teach you."

He moved closer, towering over her. "I would like that—teaching you what a woman needs to know to please a man."

"Well, you won't get the opportunity," she snapped, furious with herself for the emotions surging within. "Now, I think we had best get back to the ranch before Valdis comes looking for me. I have enough problems with him as it is."

He was silent for a moment as he looked at her so probingly that it seemed he could see inside her soul. "Yeah, I think we better," he said finally in a husky voice. "Because if we don't leave, I'm going to give you your first lesson here and now."

He moved closer, and she braced herself for his kiss, then cursed silently at the disappointment she felt when he didn't kiss her. He merely lifted her from the rock and set her on her feet. Taking her arm, he led the way back to the wagon and helped her in.

Neither spoke again until the ranch was in sight,

then Cord tersely reminded her to be wary of Valdis. "I'm going to figure out a way to get you out of there, but I've got to contend with Armand and his infatuation. He's going to have notions of his own, I'm afraid."

"He's my friend," she reminded him stiffly. "If he knew the danger, he would want to help me."

He whirled on her. "Listen to me, damn it. Don't trifle with Armand. I told you. He needs all his concentration in that ring. Let me worry about you. Armand thinks he's in love, and when a man fancies himself in love, he gets careless. Armand can't afford to be careless."

"You wouldn't get careless, would you, Cord Hayden?" she snapped as the wagon rolled to a stop before the house. "Because you're not capable of loving anyone."

His eyes narrowed. "It's not necessary to love a woman to enjoy her," he growled. "Armand will have to learn that—the same way I did."

She wanted to ask him what he meant, but she knew, somehow, that the cruel remark came from secrets in his past, a past he kept closely guarded.

Cord got out, then placed his hands around Amber's tiny waist and set her on the ground. Releasing her immediately and stepping back, he instructed brusquely, "Go in the house. Maybe Valdis isn't back yet. Go to your room. Lock the door and stay there, and don't do anything foolish. I'll be in touch."

Amber bristled. As much as she needed his help, she resented his presumptuous attitude, and his domination. Too, she regretted the overpowering enchantment of his kisses. She was her own person once again. She would not let her vulnerable side take over. Maybe she was naive, but by God she was learning fast.

With her newborn resolutions firing her, Amber declared, "I decline your offer of help, Mr. Hayden."

He looked down at her in astonishment. With mock concern, he asked, "Have I done something to offend you, Miss Forrest?"

"It appears," she replied solemnly, "that we do not bring out the best in each other."

He threw his head back and laughed. "Give me a chance to bring out your best. I only kissed you once."

He jumped into the wagon, popped the reins, and moved into the shadows, leaving Amber standing alone, fuming.

It is my own fault, she admonished herself as she lifted her skirts and swished up the stairs. A man like Cord Hayden, she reasoned, who was handsome, charming, strong, was bound to attract women of all kinds. So he would know how to deal with each kind. He probably thought she was very stupid. He was probably snickering over the way she had melted at his touch. All right. It was too late to do anything about that now, but from that moment on she would control her emotions—and her life. She certainly did not need a man to lead her around.

Opening the front door, she was relieved to find the foyer empty and the house silent. She made her way up to her room and was about to lock herself in when she was startled by the sight of Maretta emerging from the shadows of the hallway.

"Maretta," Amber said cautiously, not missing the rage emanating from her stepsister. "You frightened me."

Maretta pushed by her and stepped into the room. "It is time we talked."

"Fine," Amber responded pleasantly, closing the door behind them. Dolita had left the lantern burning beside the bed, and in its orange glow, she saw the pinched anger on Maretta's face. Seeking to make it easier for both of them, Amber said, "I'm glad for this chance to talk and get to know each other, Maretta. To be perfectly honest with you, I've had the feeling since I came here that you hate me, and there's no reason for that. I would like us to be friends."

"Enough lies," Maretta hissed, pacing menacingly around Amber. "It is time you understood your place. I want you to stop throwing yourself at Armand Mendosa. He is a man, so he cannot be blamed for wanting what you so openly offer him."

"Now, wait!" Amber cried. "That isn't true, and it isn't fair."

"It *is* true. I know Armand. I have known him all my life. For now, he sows his wild oats, but one day he will settle down and it will be me that he marries, just as our parents wished. For the moment, I must acknowledge that there are many whores who hunger for a man as famous as he. But heed my warning," her voice rose. "I have the misfortune to have you in my family, and you will not become one of his harlots. Leave Armand alone!"

Amber gestured helplessly. "Maretta, you don't understand. Armand is my friend. He saved my life last night, as I told you."

"A matador does not dedicate the bull to a mere friend," Maretta snapped. "You have made a fool of yourself and of me, and then you rode away from the arena with Cord Hayden, who is scum."

"He knew Valdis was upset and wanted to give him time to calm down. And why do you call Cord scum?" Amber wanted to know. "Has he ever done anything to hurt you?"

Maretta colored slightly. "It is none of your concern. Just know that he is not welcome in this house. Now. I give you a warning, and if you do not heed it, then you will suffer the consequences." She leaned close, teeth bared, and whispered ominously, "It is true my brother runs this ranch and has much power and much money. But I also have power. There is a convent in the mountains where wayward young women from fine families are sent to mend their ways. I can have you sent there. I can have you *kept* there!"

Amber shook her head, feeling more pity than anger. "Maretta, I had truly hoped we could come to some understanding of each other and be friends, but I guess that is just not possible. Now *you* get something straight. I'm not scared of you or your brother or your threats. I'm not going to let you or anyone else tell me who I can or can't associate with."

"You will pay!" Maretta shook her fist, all her rage bursting forth.

Amber had reached her limit. Walking to the door, she flung it open and said, "I'm sorry we can't be friends, but if this is the way you see things about me, then I'm not listening to anything else you may have to say."

Maretta looked at her so venomously that Amber was shocked. "Very well. I have warned you," Maretta said. "Now I will give you some advice. I wish you to know that it is I who saved you from a beating tonight. Valdis was very upset with you, and I know it was his intent to give you the thrashing you deserve. But I wanted to speak with you and give you a warning, so when he had his sangría tonight, I slipped something into it so he would fall asleep. Tomorrow, when he awakens, he will have calmed down."

"Well...thank you," Amber stammered awkwardly.

"I do not want your gratitude," Maretta cried. "I want you to heed my warning and this advice. When my brother asks you to marry him, accept his proposal."

"Proposal?" Amber echoed. "You can't mean that, Maretta."

"It is his intention to marry you," Maretta said, nodding. "Accept. Become his wife and forget your foolish chasing after Armand."

Amber had lost all patience. "I have no intention of marrying your brother or anyone else. Now get out, Maretta."

Maretta flounced out of the room, and Amber closed the door wearily behind her.

Amber dropped into a chair and sat staring out the window, not really seeing the trees lining the drive, unaware, in fact, that she was where she was. Her mind was with Armand—and then, in a moment, it was with Cord. What was there about Armand that made her want to see him right at that moment? Or about Cord that made her temper flare whenever she saw him? Why should she be drawn to either of them? She had, she told herself sternly, quite enough to do in getting away from there, getting away from Valdis. She couldn't afford to think about anything except that.

Suddenly she felt smothered, and she could not, just then, bear the confines of her room. Grabbing a lace shawl, she hurried downstairs to slip quietly out the front door and into the sanctuary of the night. She moved toward the garden and soon inhaled the sweet night-blooming jasmine that clung to the orange and mango trees. Silver webs of moonlight lit orchids and bromelias. There were dahlias, cosmos, and marigolds, as well as a few succulents hugging the ground closely.

She stared beyond to the overwhelming masses of mountains, stark in the moonlight. Stepping to the edge of the garden, she saw the tilted planes and arching skies of the tableland, the rude upthrust of multicolored buttes in deserts of silver and gold, and she was deeply moved by the beauty, so secret, yet so awesome in the ghostly light.

Rubbing her arms to ward off the night chill, she moved about reverently, lost in thought. She knew that Mexico contained both baked deserts where rainfall was all but unknown and also tropical forests. There were sun-scorched, sea-level savannas, and lush grasslands dotted with trees and spiny shrubs. Tablelands were miles high, and vast dry canyons laid bare the entrails of the earth. Broad jungle rivers flowed in some places. There was the volcanic zone, running roughly across the middle of the country, of over five hundred miles.

The sound of a twig snapping brought her out of her reverie. Armand stepped into the thin stream of moonlight filtering down through the leaves, grinning broadly as he called softly, "My moon-star. Do not be afraid."

"Armand!" She laughed with relief, hurrying toward him. "What are you doing here?"

He devoured her face with his eyes. "I knew Valdis was mad, and Cord told me he brought you home so you would be away from his wrath. I had to see you, to know you are all right."

She shivered deliciously as she felt his breath, warm against her mouth. Soon his lips covered hers in a long, dizzying kiss, and his fingertips moved tantalizingly up and down her back, drawing her closer against his body. "I love you," he whispered huskily, as she tipped her head back to let him kiss her throat. "You are the woman I have waited for all my life. I must have you...for always."

Dazed, fighting to regain her will, she pushed at his chest with both hands, but he held her tightly. "Armand, no! It's all happening too soon. I'm so confused. Please. Be my friend. Don't confuse me even more."

"Ah, what is confusing about love?" he crooned, his tongue flicking at her neck. "I must have you, to awaken with you next to me in the mornings, fall asleep inside you. I want you to bear my children. I will revel to watch your beautiful belly growing large with my seed. Oh, my moonstar, say you feel this wonderful thing, too."

She struggled against him, felt her blood turning to golden, liquid fire. He was awakening those same feelings that the faceless man of her dreams had ignited. Her lace shawl fell, baring her shoulders, and he bent to cover a shoulder with his hungry mouth.

Amber lost all control as the fire swept over her body. Every nerve was taut, eager, and she felt a quivering between her thighs. He lifted her in his arms and carried her into the woods, placing her on a fragrant bed of fallen mimosa blossoms. "We mustn't, Armand. We can't—"

"I want you, my moonstar, and you know you want me," he said raggedly.

Quickly, she stood up, backing away a step. "I can't...won't...give myself to you this way. It's wrong, Armand."

She watched anxiously as he stared at her. Then, slowly, surprisingly, a smile spread across his face.

"Oh, Armand," she cried, "I've never been so far with a man. You made me want you. But it's wrong, I know it is."

He gathered her in his arms and kissed her quickly, then whispered, "Do not worry, little one. I understand that you were not teasing me. You are young and frightened, but I know you care for me. It is I who must beg your forgiveness, for I had no right to expect so much so soon."

He took a deep breath. "We will do things properly. I will court you. Valdis is your guardian now, so tomorrow I will go to him and ask for your hand in marriage." He took both her hands in his, smiling, while she stared at him in wonder.

She shook her head slowly. "It is not going to be that easy, Armand." She told him of the scene with Maretta, and the revelation that Valdis was going to propose. Then she told him about the money.

Feeling him tense with anger, she said, "You are my friend, Armand, and for now, that has to be all you can be. I have to make a life for myself. Only then can I think about falling in love."

He yanked her against him, searching her eyes in the misty moonlight as he murmured, "I am going to be more than your friend, Amber. Do not question love. When it happens this way, so suddenly, it is beautiful. Do not mar the beauty by questioning."

She shook her head. "We have to be patient."

"How can we be patient with Valdis causing trouble for you?" he cried.

Understanding the depth of his frustration, she decided to tell him more. "Armand, there is something you should know."

He looked at her sharply.

"Cord Hayden...promised to help me get away from here. He says he will work on a plan for escape. He said he couldn't just ride me away from here because Valdis would have us hunted down."

She watched his face for a sign of jealousy, and was surprised to see him smile.

"Cord is my friend, also," he said softly. "I have told him of my love for you, and he will help us. Do not worry, the two of us will get you away from here. Oh, my moonstar, when I saw you last night, I knew my life would never be complete without you. I must have you. It is love. I have waited for this all my life."

His voice faded in the tremulous mating of their lips. Both were shaken when at last he murmured, "Do not question fate, my love. Go now. Tomorrow I will pay a visit to Valdis and tell him of my intentions. If he does not agree that I may court you, then Cord and I will take you away from his house."

She cried out, "No. It can't be that way. You don't understand—" But he had quickly moved away and disappeared into the woods.

She stared into the night, reflecting on all that had happened. Armand had an entrancing effect, and maybe it *was* love. But how could she know? She had never been kissed before today, and now she had been kissed by two men, each exciting her. Why was everything happening at once?

Suddenly she heard a sound, and called out, "Armand, you are frightening me. I thought you had gone home."

There was silence. Amber felt her skin prickling. Had she heard someone, or something, in the shadowed woods surrounding her?

Lifting her skirts, she ran to the house as fast as she could. In the distance behind her was the distinct sound of footsteps in the brush, and she knew, with a terrifying flutter in her chest, that someone had been out there...watching.

❧ Chapter Seven ❧

EARLY morning sunlight flooded the room and Amber sat up, startled, then relieved as she recognized Dolita. Apprehension returned, however, when she saw the girl's face.

Dolita cried, "Señorita, you must dress quickly. Señor Alezparito demands to see you at once. He is very angry."

"He can wait until I am good and ready," Amber replied.

"That is not all." Dolita rushed to the bedside to whisper. "Señora Allegra's maid told me that the señora wishes to speak with you even though the señor has forbidden her to speak with anyone. She told her maid to say that you *must* try to get in to see her."

Amber was pleased. Flinging back the covers,

she said, "Good. I want to talk to her, too. Valdis can wait."

"Oh, no," Dolita whispered, frightened. "If you do not go downstairs now he will come up here, and if you try to see the señora first, he will find you there and both of you will be punished severely."

"Punished!" Amber scoffed. "Dolita, I refuse to cringe before that big bully. He may talk loudly and push people around, but he won't hurt me."

Dolita was aghast. "No? Señorita, it is time you knew all of it. The señor is...is a killer. It is the truth."

It was the second time Amber had heard that. "Tell me, Dolita."

The maid glanced round in that fearful way that annoyed Amber so, as though the walls had ears, and then, in a voice so low Amber could barely hear, said, "He has tortured and killed *children*...Indian children. I know, because the children all came from my cousin's village."

"Dolita, that is a very serious accusation," Amber warned.

"It is not an accusation. It is the truth. It happened about two years ago. The children had just learned to ride their ponies, and they came onto the ranch and went into one of the pens. They were chasing the bulls, teasing them, then running away. It was wrong of them, yes, but they were only children. Señor Valdis was furious. He took his men and chased them into the hills. He returned after a day. It was a week before my cousin and his people found the children—their scorched skeletons tied to charred stakes, where they had been tortured and burned alive."

Amber tried not to let herself feel what she was feeling. "I can't believe that. They would have been arrested and hanged."

"Oh, no," Dolita scoffed. "The señor is too smart for that. There was no proof, and he said he never found the children. The law would not care, not about poor Indians.

"No, señorita," she continued. "Do not underestimate him. He is not just a bully. He is evil. There have been other times when children were found in the hills dead, shot, the soles of their feet ragged and raw from running, as though they had been hunted down like wild animals."

Amber felt the bile rise in her throat as she struggled against disbelief. If what Dolita said was true, then she was in the hands of a vicious madman.

"Do not cross him, señorita," Dolita pleaded. "Even his own stepmother stays out of his way. Señorita Maretta also fears him, but from time to time she challenges him, and when she does, she suffers. I have heard her screams when he has beaten her, and I have tended her cuts and bruises myself. This isn't gossip. I know what I know," she finished raggedly, then blurted, "there is something else. Señor Valdis has given orders that you are to be under guard once again. There is someone outside the door now."

Amber took a long breath and let it out slowly. She looked at Dolita searchingly, beseeching the girl, and said, "I have to know I can trust you."

Dolita nodded. "I will do what I can, which is very little, I am sorry to say. But you can be sure I am your friend."

Amber told her about her friendship with Cord and Armand, that they were going to help her escape. Dolita smiled conspiratorially. "I have heard about Señor Mendosa's interest, for all the servants have heard Maretta's anger. But Señor Hayden," she said with a frown, "I do not know about that one...."

"What?" Amber asked. "Is there something I should know?"

"There is nothing I can tell you, except that he is so mysterious. I do know that he used to sneak in to see Maretta in the middle of the night."

Amber went cold, then hot. "Are you sure about that?" she said sharply.

"He came often, until the night she became angry and screamed and awoke the whole house. Señor Valdis was furious, but he knew only that a man had been here. Maretta would not tell him who it was. I knew, because I saw him leaving, but I never told anyone."

Amber was angry with Cord but angrier with herself for caring. Now she understood the remarks Maretta had made about Cord. She was even more glad to have Armand for a friend, for Cord Hayden was apparently immoral.

"You won't tell anyone what I have told you?" Dolita asked anxiously.

"Of course not." Amber gave her a reassuring hug and the girl smiled shyly. "We are friends,

Dolita. We have to confide in each other." She hurried to the dressing screen, calling over her shoulder, "Now I'm going to find out what Valdis wants, and then I am looking forward to finding a chance to see Allegra."

Dressed in one of the plain cotton dresses her grandmother had made, a light blue gown with a high collar, long tapering sleeves, and a slight fullness to the skirt, Amber pulled her hair back in a matronly bun at the nape of her neck. The last thing she wanted was to look appealing.

Dolita directed her to the little room at the rear of the house that Valdis used for an office, and Amber knocked softly on the heavy wood door. She heard him call to her to enter, and she stepped inside.

A large desk of heavy, carved mahogany was strewn with papers and ledgers. There was a high-backed red leather chair behind the desk with two smaller ones positioned in front. The floor was covered by a faded rug of red and gold braid. Tall bookcases lined three walls, and a large arched window afforded a splendid view of the valley behind. Despite the view, the room was stark and grim, like the man pacing angrily in front of the window.

Amber decided at once his smile was faked, for his eyes were cold. "Good morning," he said curtly, gesturing to one of the chairs. "Sit down. I wish to speak with you."

"I prefer to stand," she told him firmly, and his facade fell apart. With giant strides, he moved to her and pushed her into the chair. "I said you will

117

sit," he snarled. "And when I give an order, you will obey."

Amber tried to get up, but he gripped hard and held her in place. "Listen to me. I do not wish to harm you. I wish for us to be friends. Good friends." He emitted an exaggerated sigh. "Oh, Amber, do you not realize that you are the most beautiful woman I have ever seen, and that I want you with an agony too deep to describe?"

"That's a terrible shame," Amber retorted, eyes blazing. "I want only to leave here, and if you will give me back my money—you stole it, I know— I will be on my way."

To her surprise, he laughed, releasing her as he propped himself against the desk, arms folded across his chest. "*Sí*, I took your money, señorita, but only to keep you from doing anything foolish, like running away. Your place is here. This is now your home, and here is where you will stay."

"I'm not staying, Valdis," she told him evenly, coolly. "And you can't make me. I am leaving if I have to crawl on my hands and knees and starve while I do it."

"No, no." He shook his head from side to side, eyes twinkling. "You are going to stay here and accept my hospitality...and my good nature. You are going to learn how good I can be to you. I am going to be the king of this valley, and you, my lovely flower, are going to be my queen. You will want for nothing."

"And you are crazy!" She attempted to get up once more, but, laughing, he pushed her back down.

"Valdis," she cried, "I am warning you. You can't keep me here against my will. I am not your prisoner."

"Oh, so you warn me, eh?" he chuckled. "Warn me of whom? Do you think I am afraid of Cord Hayden? Oh, I know how he took his time bringing you home yesterday. I know everything that goes on here, just as I know you sneaked out of my house last night to wallow in the bushes with that seducer Armand Mendosa."

"You spied on me," she cried indignantly. "How dare you?"

"How dare you bring scandal to my house?" he whispered, leaning closer to cup her face in his hands and squeeze. "I seek to protect you from yourself, my innocent beauty. Armand Mendosa conquers women as he does his bulls, and he regards them the same way. Perhaps he thinks it makes him a man to be a famous matador, but if he were a real man, he would honor the pledge of our fathers and wed my sister. Pah!" he scoffed. "He hides behind a red cloak like the coward he is. And I will not have him luring you into the bushes.

"As for that gringo, Cord Hayden," Valdis went on, "he runs from something. I have not yet been able to find out what he runs from, but I will. There must be a reason he does not return to his own country. He is probably a traitor, and I will not have my future wife in his company."

"I am not your future wife," Amber cried, nostrils flaring as she fought for control of her temper. Damn him, her anger served only to amuse him.

119

"I demand that you allow me to leave here at once. If my father were alive—"

"If your father were alive," he cried, "he would be in a drunken stupor, as usual. Your father! He was a sot! A no-good drunkard who married my stepmother thinking he would get her money, and he drank himself to death like the worthless bastard he was."

"No!" Amber screamed, attempting to stand again. He restrained her. "I will not stand for your talking about him that way. You have no right!" Tears streamed down her cheeks, and she slumped in the chair.

Valdis dropped to his knees before her, wrapping his fingers around her wrists and giving her a gentle shake. "Listen to me," he commanded. "I do not wish to hurt you this way, Amber. I want only to be good to you, to love you and cherish you, and put you on the throne next to me. But you must stop fighting me, for there is no other way. You are going to be my wife. From the first time I saw you, I knew I had to have you. Never have I seen such beauty as yours. I will dress you in the finest fashions from Spain and Paris. I will give you jewels...anything you wish."

The fingers of one hand had moved slowly to caress her cheek as she stared at him stonily. Moving to the nape of her neck, he deftly undid the bun, then pulled her hair free, entwining his fingers in the long silver tresses. Pressing his lips against them, he murmured, "A goddess. That is what you are, my Amber. And you will be mine"— he raised his face and she shivered at the light in his eyes as he hissed, yanking her hair painfully—

"or I will see you dead! No man will ever have you but me!"

She cried out and he released her for a moment, then grabbed her and pulled her to her feet. He crushed her against him as his lips sought hers. "No! Don't touch me!" She struggled against him. Finally maneuvering her arm upward, she raked her nails across his face. He cried out in pain, releasing her, and she stumbled backward.

"Go!" he shrieked, clutching his wounded face. "Go to your room and remain there until I send for you. You will change your mind and marry me, or you will rot in that room!"

She fled down the narrow hallway to the foyer, where Dolita was waiting, looking frightened.

Amber clutched her and whispered in desperation, "You must help me, Dolita. I can't go to my room now. He's going to keep me locked in there, and I have to see Allegra."

Dolita hesitated a moment, but when she was confident that Valdis was not coming after them, she led Amber through the dining room to a stairway at the opposite end of the enormous house.

When they reached the second floor, Amber followed her instructions to wait in the shadows until she made sure there was no guard. Then Dolita motioned frantically for Amber to follow her to the door of Allegra's suite. "Please do not be long," she whispered. "He will come looking for you when he finds out you did not go back to your room." She turned and fled back the way they had come.

Amber did not take the time to knock, but opened the door and stepped into the shadowed foyer, calling out softly, "Allegra, it's Amber. I heard you wanted to see me, and oh, dear Lord, I need to see you."

The voice was dull, utterly devoid of emotion. "Come in, and hurry."

Amber made her way into the room and crossed to the bed, sickened by what she saw. Sitting down on the edge of the bed, she clutched the woman's cool hands and said in a rush, "You have to help me. Valdis is going to keep me a prisoner here. He says if I don't marry him, he will kill me. I have to get away. You are my only hope."

Only the dim glow of a candle burning beneath a crucifix gave any light, but Amber could see Allegra's tired, drawn face, the limp, graying hair. Allegra looked emaciated, sick, and she barely had the strength to speak.

Finally, she whispered, "I am sorry. I have no hope and I can offer none to you. I only wish I could, child."

Amber squeezed her hand gently. "You said you wanted to see me."

"Yes," she said with an apologetic nod, "but only to warn you to leave, to get away from here as quickly as possible. But if Valdis has decided you shall stay, then there is nothing you or I can do."

Amber explained quickly. "I had some money, money that came from the sale of my grandmother's house. Valdis stole it so I couldn't leave. I'm not asking for anything that was my father's ...only what was mine."

Allegra's smile was sad, and her tired eyes glimmered with tears of sympathy. "My child, if your father had had anything, I would gladly give it to you, but he had nothing. If I had anything, it would be my pleasure to give it to you. But I have nothing at all. Valdis has everything."

"There has to be a way out of here!" Amber declared. "Surely you can tell me a way out. A secret path? Anything!"

Allegra struggled to sit up, reaching out to clutch Amber's shoulder. She whispered hoarsely, "I cannot tell you how to leave here, only that you must go before it is too late. Valdis has done horrible things, unholy things. He deserves to die, and the holy mother of God, herself, would bless you if you plunged a knife into his black heart."

Amber went numb. To hear Valdis' stepmother make such a shocking declaration was overwhelming.

"Go now!" Allegra hissed, suddenly frightened. "Go before he finds you here. I have not the strength to sustain myself any longer. Go. Seek the help of anyone who is willing to help you. I hope..." She gave Amber's shoulder one last, feeble squeeze before slumping back on her pillows. She stared up and said hollowly, "I hope you kill him."

Amber sat stock-still for a moment, staring at Allegra in silence, then quietly left the room. She could not endanger her any longer. If Valdis thought she had told Amber anything at all, he would beat her, and Allegra was too weak for that.

A vaquero was standing outside the door to Amber's room, and she returned his arrogant gaze coolly. He had a scraggly beard and was dressed in disheveled clothing, gun and holster hanging just below his waist. He tried to seem fierce, but she found him slovenly, not formidable.

The Mexican grinned as he opened the door to Amber's room. "Señor Alezparito has ordered you to remain in your room."

"Fine," she snapped, brushing by him. "I'd rather be in here than out where I might run into that bastard you work for!"

She slammed the door on him and flung herself across the bed. Let him lord it over her. Armand would be there soon, and when he found out that she was being held prisoner, he would free her one way or another.

Her fingertips traced her lips as she recalled the fire of Armand's kiss. He had aroused her, made her body tremble with a hunger she knew he could feed. Yet there was that other awesome feeling, the awareness that Cord Hayden aroused more and could give more.

She shook herself furiously. Cord Hayden was not to be trusted. Just why was he here in Mexico? There were so many questions that needled. Armand, on the other hand, was a gentleman. Cord would probably want to be repaid for his help, and, she thought with a shiver, he was the kind of man who would collect his dues. Cord was not a gentleman.

The day passed with agonizing slowness. She paced back and forth on her balcony, searching for some sign of Armand's arrival.

It was almost two o'clock in the afternoon when she heard her door being unlocked and hurried back into the room to see Dolita enter with a lunch tray. The guard looked in and gave Amber a smirk, his eyes resting insolently on her bosom before he slammed the door and locked it again. Dolita set the tray down, then silently motioned for Amber to follow her out to the balcony.

"We must whisper," she ordered nervously. "Guards are all around. I know you have many questions, but I have no time. Let me tell you what I know. Señor Mendosa came a short while ago—"

"Armand was here?" Amber cried. "Is he still here?"

"No, no, he has gone." Dolita stepped back, pressing a finger to her lips. "And you must be quiet. If the guard hears anything he will go to Señor Valdis and I will be beaten. Please, señorita, if I am to help you, you must help me." Her brown eyes pleaded.

"Yes, of course." Amber nodded. "Go on, please."

"There was a big fight. Esconcia, who was cleaning in the next room, overheard and told me what happened. Señor Mendosa went into Señor Valdis' study, and they talked quietly for only a moment before Señor Valdis began to scream and shout. He yelled to Señor Mendosa that if *he* married anyone it would be his sister, and that if *you* married anyone, it would be him. He said you already told him you would be his wife. Señor Mendosa became very angry and said you would never agree to marry him. Señor Valdis ordered Señor Mendosa to get off the ranch before he killed him."

Dolita paused and Amber urged her on. "What happened then? And where is Armand now?"

"Esconcia says that Señor Valdis was holding a gun to Señor Mendosa's back as he led him out of the house. Then one of his men took him all the way to the gate. Please, señorita. I cannot stay any longer."

Stunned, Amber vaguely heard the door open and close as Dolita departed. Amber wandered back into the room and lay down across the bed, her mind whirling. There seemed no way out. There were guards at her door. She was truly a prisoner. The complete acknowledgment of her plight brought tears, and she wept until exhausted slumber carried her away.

She awoke when Dolita returned that evening to light the lanterns and bring a supper tray.

"You must eat," the girl urged. "You will become weak, like Señora Allegra."

"I don't care," Amber murmured, flinging her arm across her face to ward off the lanterns' glow.

"If you do not eat, you will be too ill to take advantage of an opportunity when it comes. Do not give up on Señor Mendosa—or Señor Hayden. Both are strong men and courageous."

The door opened, and the guard looked in and frowned at Dolita. He ordered the maid out, and then Amber found herself alone again.

She sat up and looked at the tray. There was a colorful clay pitcher filled with cool chocolate. The platter of turnovers made of stuffed corn pastry and flat little cakes made from cactus fruit made her realize how hungry she was.

Finally pushing the tray aside, she stood and walked out onto the balcony. The night was warm and still, with rolling clouds of silver and a moon casting shadows. She stared into the horizon. Damn

Valdis! She was going to escape even if she had to jump to the ground below.

Walking to the edge of the balcony, she wrapped her fingers around the ornate railing. "I will do it," she whispered. "I will make myself do it."

"I wouldn't. It's a long way down."

She jumped, whipping her head around to see a man perched on the railing at the side of the balcony. His hat shadowed his face, but she could see the arms folded across his massive chest, the shirt unbuttoned to the waist. Strong, muscular thighs strained against tight chinos.

"Cord Hayden!" she spat. "You scared me to death! What are you doing there?"

He cocked his head to one side. "I'm your guard for the night."

"You?" she sputtered. "But Valdis would never—"

"Of course not," he laughed, now standing before her. "I climbed up here, which wasn't difficult. Valdis' guards aren't very smart.

"Now then," he said, the smile disappearing. "I don't have much time and we had better discuss the trouble you're in. Armand came charging home wanting to round up men and guns and go to war with Valdis."

"Then you know about the argument they had."

"I know that Valdis told Armand you had agreed to marry him. I think it's a lie." His eyes narrowed. "I also know that you didn't listen to me. You cried on Armand's shoulder, and now he's right in the middle of this damn mess. He may get himself killed."

"You think I want that?" she countered resentfully, then hissed, "You think I'm using Armand, don't you? Well, I think it's time I set you straight on a few things, Cord Hayden, and you can pass them along to Armand when you see him. I'm going to get myself out of this mess. I don't need anyone's help, so just stay away. I'm sorry I became a...a nuisance to you."

She turned to go back inside, but Cord reached out quickly and caught her arm. She stared up at him belligerently, furious with herself for being so angry. She thought once more how overwhelmingly handsome he was, however formidable. "Take your hands away," she ordered.

"I don't take orders from anyone, particularly hysterical women," he murmured, amused. "So you just calm down and listen. It's all fine and noble that you have now decided you don't need anybody's help, but it's a little late for that. Now, I'm going to do this my way, whether you like it or not. I only came over here to tell you to stay calm. I figured you'd hear about the fight this morning and go to pieces...like a woman," he added sarcastically.

"I'm not going to pieces, sir." She jerked futilely against his grasp. "Now please leave."

"I'm going." He nodded, hands slipping to grasp her waist. "I've never met a woman yet I was willing to die for."

"And I doubt one has ever wanted to die for you, either."

He cocked his head to one side and gazed down at her as though she were merely a delightful child. "There have been times," he murmured, "when women begged to die...but not in a way *you* would understand. Not yet, that is."

She felt her cheeks flaming. "You are the most arrogant, conceited man I have ever met. I know all about you, Cord Hayden. I know how you sneaked into Maretta's room behind Armand's back—and probably ravished her."

"You don't know what the hell you're talking about," he snapped. "And I am not going to talk about that with you. Now, just don't do anything to rile Valdis."

He released her, and she stepped away, blinking back furious tears. "I don't want your help. I have news for you. I can take care of myself."

Suddenly he pulled her against him, his lips moving down on hers. Amber froze, allowing him to devour her mouth, allowing the warmth to spread through her. Then, abruptly, she gained control of herself and twisted away.

"You had no right!" She shook her head. "No right at all. What kind of an animal are you? Armand calls you his friend, and you force yourself upon a woman you know he cares about."

A frown crossed his forehead, and she knew she had, at last, hit home.

"He is my friend," he said slowly, evenly, eyes boring into her. "And, in time, he will come to realize you aren't for him. Not all men can tame that fire burning within you, Amber."

She gave her long hair a toss. "And how do you know a fire burns within me, Cord Hayden? Who are you to know so much about me?"

"I know women," he said simply, and meant it.

"But never one like me," she threw out the words

with a spirit she had never, until that moment, known she possessed.

"Perhaps." He smiled. "Who knows? I may have met a challenge for the first time in my life. But I think I'll enjoy facing it."

In a rage, she ran toward her room, then turned to whisper hoarsely, "Tell Armand not to worry about me. I will take care of myself. And if you ever dare come near me again, Cord Hayden..."

Her voice trailed off as she realized the terrace was empty. He had slipped into the night as quietly as he had come, as quietly as the nocturnal animal he was.

The dream came again that night, and the faceless man possessed her, and she felt the spasms of release deep within her belly. The mist parted, and for the first time, her lover had a face. It was Cord Hayden who held her and quenched the fire.

❁ Chapter Eight ❁

RAIN made little pattering sounds as the droplets trailed from the tile roof to cascade onto the balcony outside. The late morning sky was thick with heavy slated clouds.

Amber stared out through the double doors at the third day of rain and the fourth of confinement in her room. How much longer? She shivered.

The sound of voices lured her to the locked door, and in a minute, Dolita rushed in with a lunch tray, glancing around in fright, as always. She sat the tray down, and Amber looked down at the baked fish in a thick yellow sauce.

Dolita moved so close to Amber that she could feel the maid's breath. "I have a message from Señor Hayden."

"Cord?" Amber blinked, heart pounding. "Was he here?"

"I was at the well, drawing water, and he was in the bushes, hiding. He called to me, and when I could be sure no one was watching, I went to him. He said he will come to you tonight to take you to Señor Mendosa. You are to be ready at midnight."

Amber suppressed a cry of delight. "Tonight!" She clapped her hands together silently. "Tonight I am leaving!" But when she saw the look on Dolita's face, the sudden exhilaration disappeared.

"I am sorry," Dolita murmured, eyes downcast. "It is not what you think. Señor Mendosa insists upon seeing you, and he cannot come here, for he might not be able to control his temper if Señor Valdis discovers him. Señor Hayden says he will be able to slip in without being seen, and take you to him, but then he will bring you back."

Amber sank down on the bed and sighed. "Well, at least I will see him. And he may have some kind of plan."

"I must go now." Dolita moved toward the door. "The guard will get suspicious if I stay too long."

With too many things on her mind to think of food, Amber spent the next hour or so in her tub, excited and happy, but when Dolita returned in midafternoon, she knew something was very wrong.

"Señor Valdis," Dolita told her quickly, wringing her hands, "says you are to be brought to him at once. He has ordered sangría and wishes you to have a drink with him. He says if you refuse, the guard must bring you by force."

A few minutes later, the guard led her down

the hall and downstairs into the parlor.

Valdis was seated on a thickly embroidered sofa. Patting the place next to him, he smiled broadly and said, "I thought you might enjoy some time out of your room, *querida*. And I have some news that will delight you."

Amber sat in a chair as far away from him as possible. "Don't call me your beloved, Valdis. And yes, I would enjoy some time out of my cell, but not if it means being with you."

"Ah, is that any way for you to talk to your future husband?" he chuckled, crossing his legs, the smug expression never wavering.

Amber laughed. "I will never marry you." She leaned forward. "And how long can you continue this? How long do you think you can keep me locked in this house like a prisoner? Surely, people in the valley will start to ask questions."

"Of course." He nodded slowly. "But not for long. Which brings me to my news. We are all going on a trip to Mexico City. Your stepmother and stepsister will be going, too. It is traditional that the Alezparito family be in attendance at important events. There is to be a big fiesta in celebration of President Juarez' imminent reelection. There will be many parties, and you will go with me to all of them."

"I have no desire to go to Mexico City, Valdis," she snapped.

He went on as though she had not spoken. "Tomorrow, the seamstress will fit you for all the exquisite gowns you will need. This is the important high social season, my dear."

Amber sighed. "What does it take to get you to understand, Valdis? I have no intention of traveling to Mexico City with you."

"Oh, Amber," he chuckled softly, as though she were a headstrong child. "Surely you have learned by now that everyone does my bidding. You will go if you have to be tied down in a carriage. Do not make things unpleasant for yourself."

The study door opened and Maretta stalked in, face flushed with anger. With a quick glance of hatred at Amber, she demanded, "Tell me it is not true, what I have heard from my seamstress. You have ordered her to make gowns for this one? You intend for her to go to Mexico City with us? Tell me it is not true. I insist!"

"I tell you nothing!" Valdis leaped to his feet, his hand cracking across his half sister's face. Maretta reeled backward, sprawling into a chair.

Amber gasped. She had never before seen a man strike a woman.

"She will go with us, and I will listen to no complaints from you," he raged as Maretta looked up at him tearfully. "How dare you question what I do?"

Maretta pleaded, "Valdis, I do not want her there. Do I have to remind you what happened at the bullfight? She will bring shame upon us again."

He laughed. "What you fear is that all the men in Mexico City will have eyes for her and not you," he taunted. He returned to his seat as Maretta stared after him, rubbing the welt on her cheek.

Pouring himself a drink, he went on. "You have nothing to fear. When the announcement is made

134

at the President's Ball that Amber is to become my wife, the men will turn from her to you."

Amber cried, "You will do nothing of the kind, Valdis, because I will not marry you. And if you dare to do such a thing, I will embarrass you and your family by screaming that you are a liar."

Swirling the deep scarlet liquid in his glass, Valdis stared down into it and the colors reflected in his eyes.

Maretta turned on Amber. "You have no gratitude! My brother offers to marry you, to make you a decent woman, to give you a life other women would envy, and you dare say no! And you, Valdis"—she sneered—"you are a fool to think you will ever be accepted socially. Have you forgotten you are always excluded from all the best parties? My mother and I are invited to them all out of respect for your father, but you are considered a blemish on his honor, for you will not fight in the ring. Yet you think because you bring this silver-haired *gringa,* you will be accepted?" She shook her head vehemently as she said triumphantly, "No. You fool yourself."

Amber cringed as Valdis sent his wineglass crashing against a wall. Towering over Maretta, he railed, "You will provoke me into tearing the flesh from your worthless back! Now go! Get out of my sight before I lose control."

Maretta scurried from the room, but when she reached the doorway, and freedom, she straightened and retorted shrilly, "You will see! You will see that I am right! You will *never* be accepted. Everyone knows you for the coward you are. Only

135

a coward would beat a woman and torture children!"

He took a step toward her, and she screamed and fled. Laughing, he turned to Amber and gestured apologetically. "You must forgive Maretta. She has not been herself since she found Armand Mendosa an unwilling groom. All that will soon change, however. I had a long talk with Señor Mendosa recently, and he is learning that it would be wise to honor the arrangement his parents and ours made long ago."

Amber knew the remark was intended to rile her, so she allowed it to pass.

"Now then," he said, sitting down once more and smiling, "we shall argue no more about Mexico City."

"Perhaps you can force me to go, but you cannot force me to marry you, Valdis," Amber pointed out again. "And if you do embarrass me by announcing our engagement, then I will have no choice but to embarrass you by denying it."

She waited for his anger and was surprised when he smiled pleasantly and murmured, "That would not be wise, *querida*. You see, Maretta is quite disturbed by Armand's infatuation with your rare, exquisite beauty. I do my best to control her, but I am afraid that, despite repeated chastisement, she remains willful and headstrong. She has ...mentioned a certain convent that tames the spirits of wayward young women.

"So you see"—he waved his hands—"I am giving you a choice, not forcing you, Amber. You will either marry me or go to the convent. The nuns will make you graciously accept the wonderful life I offer you."

Amber gripped the arms of the chair and leaned forward, fighting the impulse to attack the smug, smiling face. "Did it ever occur to you to just give me back the money you stole from me and let me return to America?"

"No," he chuckled, shaking his head from side to side in maddening deprecation. "That thought has not occurred to me. I am quite sure that it won't. It is my intention to have you for my wife."

"You, sir"—she forced a tight smile as she rose— "can go to hell."

Valdis walked to the door and opened it. With a bow, he smiled. "I will give you until tomorrow morning to change your mind. If you still refuse to accompany me to Mexico City and to announce our engagement, then you leave me no choice but to notify the nuns that you are on your way."

She hurried back to her room. Dear Lord, how many hours was it till midnight? If Armand did not have a plan for getting her out immediately, then she would leave anyway, without money, taking just the clothes on her back.

✒ Chapter Nine ✒

BUT that night, after a strangely uncommuni-
cative Cord had taken Amber safely into the
forest where Armand was waiting, and had then
silently retreated to the edge of the woods, Armand reacted jubilantly to Amber's story.

"No," he said firmly. "You must not try to leave
now. There is no place for you to go, and I could
not hide you for very long. This is much better,
my moonstar. You see." He grasped her shoulders.
"I shall also go to Mexico City. The bullfight season takes me there, and I have relatives there who
will help us. My aunt. Cord and I will help you
slip away from Valdis, and you can stay with her.
It is much better this way."

Amber touched his cheek gently, hating to
dampen his sudden happiness. "And then what

happens? I can't stay hidden forever. I must find a way to return to America."

"I will take care of you," he said sharply. "You do not need to return to America. What waits for you there? You have no family, no home."

She was desperate to make him understand. "Armand, I care for you. But I'm not experienced in affairs of the heart. I have never been in love before. I must be sure. And I must take care of my*self*. I can take nothing from you."

"I understand, Amber, but you must listen. My aunt is a religious woman. Never would she keep a mistress for me, if that is what you are thinking. No, no. You will live with her, not with me. She will give you food and shelter. We can see each other whenever we want, and we can find out if this feeling between us is real."

Amber felt a tremor of hope. "But what about Valdis? He would search for me, and it won't be easy to slip away from him, anyway."

"Let Cord and me worry about Valdis. We will make all the plans, and you will be informed of all the details later. Valdis will not harm you once we get you to my aunt. You will be safe."

He cupped her face in one hand, brushing his lips across hers. She could feel him smiling. "I make the promise to you, my moonstar. Do as I ask, and if you do not fall in love with me, then there will be no bitterness. We will still be friends. But I am not worried. I will make you love me."

"Armand..." she began, but he quickly silenced her with a kiss. After a moment, she moved away. Now was not the time.

"I want to know about Cord," she began. "Why is he so devoted to you, and so protective?"

With a resigned sigh, he said, "He does not like to talk about his life, but I will confide in you, for I want no secrets between us."

Armand told of having been in Texas during the closing days of the Civil War. "My friends and I came upon a skirmish between the two armies. After the Yankees chased the Rebels away, they discovered us hiding on a ridge and thought us Rebel sympathizers and spies. We were about to be executed when Cord intervened and saved our lives. He escorted us safely to the border, and I told him he always had a home and shelter with me. A month later, just before the war ended, he came to my door.

"Something had happened to him," he continued, "though Cord never told me exactly what it was, and I did not press him. One night, when we had both had too much tequila, his tongue loosened enough that I could put a few pieces of the puzzle together and learn that his troubles had something to do with a false accusation against him, something to do with a woman. He was very bitter and he still is."

"But why does he remain here?" Amber wanted to know. "Why doesn't he return to the States and straighten it out?"

"Ah, *that* is the true mystery," he told her, eyebrows raised. "I also have learned that he is quite wealthy. Some of his men who rode with us to the border told me that he lost his whole family in the war. His parents were killed in the early months, caught in a crossfire between troops near their home. He had a younger brother who was declared missing after the battle at Gettysburg. His father, they said, was very rich, but Cord was heard to say that one day he hoped his brother would be found, alive, and he could have it all. Cord wants only to forget his past. So, a fortune awaits him, but something has hurt him terribly and he continues to brood." He looked at her thoughtfully. "No doubt, Cord has done something to arouse your curiosity about him."

She decided it best not to comment.

"Tell me," he asked pleasantly, "has Cord made amorous advances to you?" When she did not— could not—reply, he chuckled softly, "*Sí*, I can tell by your silence. But try not to be offended. You see, he thinks you are not serious about me. He thinks you are interested only because I am a well-known matador. In Mexico, young women find matadors very appealing and flirt with them. Cord has been testing you to see whether you truly care for me."

She did not know whether to be pleased or offended. If Armand was right, then Cord was to be admired for protecting his friend, while, at the same time, condemned for being so damned sneaky.

"Enough talk." Armand placed a hand on the back of her neck, drawing her face close to him. "We have not much time, my moonstar. I want to hold you." Amber shuddered with longing as his mouth claimed her hungrily.

He lowered her gently to the ground once again, his hands sliding down to pull her hard against

142

him. She could feel the thudding rhythm of his heart, and the frenzied beat matched her own.

"Let me see all of you," he whispered raggedly as his fingers slipped beneath her gown. "I want to lie beside you with only your skin between our souls."

Her voice sounded feeble, even to herself. "Armand, we mustn't. It...it isn't right. Not yet...."

"Anything is right when two people love," he said. "You are the loveliest creation God ever made. But I do not want to make you unhappy. Tell me you do not want me. I will still love you. I will wait until...until you are my wife."

"I do want you," she whispered above the rushing sound in her ears. "I want you, Armand. But it's wrong...."

Amber struggled feebly against him, dimly aware of a dull thudding sound before Armand suddenly slumped to his side, falling away from her. A hand was clamped roughly over her face, cutting off not only her scream but her breathing as well.

In horror, she stared up into Valdis' face, twisted in maniacal anger. She struggled for air.

"I should kill you, here and now," he snarled, his hand pressing harder. "I saw you sneaking out with that bastard, Hayden. I thought it was he you hungered for. But I followed you, and I watched it all. You were going to give yourself to him. You, who will be *my* wife!"

Roughly he grasped her hair. "I would not take you on the ground like a bitch in heat. But on our wedding night, I will have my fill of you. I will make you bleed from my great manhood, over and over again. Never will I tire of you...."

Amber twisted her head sharply, causing his fingers to fall directly above her teeth. She clamped down with her teeth, tasting blood at the same time he screamed in agony and ripped his flesh from her grip.

"Damn you!" he screamed, clutching his hand and falling back upon his knees. "You will be punished. I will beat the flesh from your back, and then I will make you humble yourself before me and give me pleasure until you choke—"

Amber doubled up her fist and prayed for every ounce of strength she could muster as she drove it into his face. She felt a dull, cracking pain as she made contact with his nose. He screamed again, falling backward, and she rolled away from him, tumbling over and over, finally scrambling to her feet and searching frantically for any kind of a weapon. Mercifully, her fingers closed on a large rock.

"Put it down, Amber," Valdis gasped, walking toward her with the determination of a stalking animal. "It is useless. You cannot escape. You think I am so foolish as to venture out without my men? They are all about you. And do not waste your breath searching for Hayden. No doubt he still sleeps from his encounter with a rock much larger than the one you hold in your hand. Put down the rock and come along with me, back to your room, where you must be punished. Then we will go on to Mexico City and announce our wonderful news."

Her breath came in gasps. Just ahead she could make out the shadowed outline of a large tree, and she dashed behind it. Swinging around as he stumbled by, lifting her hands high above her head, she brought the rock crashing down on the back of his neck. He went to his knees, then toppled forward in the dirt.

Tears she had been too frightened to feel trickled down and she stifled her sobs with her fists as she backed away, wanting to retreat from this devil, but seeking the courage to go to Armand's aid. And where was Cord? How badly was he hurt?

Suddenly strong hands clamped down on her shoulders, and she screamed, striking out hysterically.

"Amber! It's Cord." He held her tighter, shaking her till she went limp in his arms. Then he lowered her to the ground and knelt beside her. "Are you all right?"

She nodded, but the panic had not subsided, and she reached out with trembling hands to clutch him tightly. He held her against him as he told her how Valdis' men had taken him by surprise. "I was almost knocked out, but I had enough wit left to pretend I *was* out. Then I got the jump on them. They're out of the way for a while. What happened to Valdis?"

"I hit him with a rock." Her breathing was becoming more even, for she felt protected in his arms. Then it all came rushing back, and she cried, "Armand! You must see to Armand! He may be hurt badly."

Cord removed his arms and released her gently, standing. "Just lie quietly, Amber," he ordered. "I'll take care of him."

He turned, but froze abruptly as he found him-

145

self facing Valdis...and Valdis' gun, glinting in the shadows.

"It is tempting to shoot you and the cocky little matador, but I do not wish the scandal upon me," Valdis snarled. "It might"—he tilted his head to one side and taunted—"put a blemish upon my wedding, which I intend to be the biggest event all of Mexico has ever seen."

Cord did not flinch. "Let me take Armand— and her, too, Valdis. She's not going to marry you and she doesn't want to stay here. You're only making a lot of trouble for a lot of people."

Valdis grinned. "I will make a lot of graves if you do not obey me." Motioning with the gun, he snapped, "Do as I say. Take him and leave. Do not come back."

Cord looked at Amber uncertainly, and she sobbed, "Don't leave me, Cord. Take me with you."

"I'm afraid I'm outnumbered right now." A muscle rippled along the line of his jaw as he looked at Valdis with pure, cold hatred. How easy it would be, he thought, to choke the life from his miserable body. "Don't worry," he told her. "He's not going to hurt you. He can't afford to. Just go along with him for now. We'll get you out of this. Right now, I've got to see to Armand."

Pointing an unwavering finger at Valdis, Cord said, "If you hurt her in any way, Valdis, so help me, I'll kill you."

Valdis laughed, though he silently admitted to some degree of timorousness over the murderous gleam in his foe's eyes. "Go, *gringo,* before I change my mind and shoot you."

Cord made his way to Armand, not looking back

even when Amber began to sob. He found Armand breathing, but unconscious, and he hoisted him over his shoulder to carry him home.

Yes, by God, Cord thought to himself, a day of reckoning was coming for Valdis and it was going to come soon.

Sometime later, when Armand was awake and Cord had explained, Armand declared, "We will not go after him now. There is no need to make bloodshed. Valdis is taking her to Mexico City, and there, at one of the parties, we will take her away to my aunt's, where she will be safe."

Cord took a deep breath. Damn it, this was not the way he wanted it. Venom flowed in him. He was ready to strike. "Are you sure this is the way you want it?" he asked quietly.

Armand nodded. "It is the only way. I do not believe he will do anything so violent as to ravish her, for he wants to marry her, and Valdis is proud. He must have a virgin. And he will not beat her, because he will not want to mar her beauty. No, we can only wait until we get to Mexico City."

Cord reached for a bottle of tequila and poured them both a drink. "It's your war, amigo. I'm just a soldier in your army." He took a long swallow, and the liquid burned his throat and slid on down to sizzle in his stomach. It helped quell the fury that was becoming a part of him.

Amber struggled wildly against the ropes that bound her wrists to the posts of the bed. Her ankles were tied tightly together, the rope cutting into her flesh as it held her legs taut upon the mattress.

A gag was stuffed in her mouth, stifling her screams.

Valdis stood at the foot of the bed, a pleased expression on his face. He had changed clothes since bringing her back to the ranch, and wore a dressing gown of gold velvet, trimmed in black cording and opened to the waist to reveal a thick mat of dark hair. His arms were folded across his chest and he stood wide-legged, staring down at her naked body.

"Exquisite," he murmured huskily. "We must be married as soon as arrangements can be made for such a lavish occasion. I cannot wait much longer to possess you, my beauty."

He leaned over to dance his fingers up and down her thighs. "Like fine silk from Paris. How I will love touching you all over with my tongue...as you will love touching me."

Slowly, she realized what he was saying. He wasn't going to take her, not as long as they weren't married. But his eyes roamed over her as though she already belonged to him, and she shuddered beneath that voracious gaze just as she knew she would shudder beneath his hands. *Cord!* her mind cried. *Armand!*

She shut her mind to everything, closing her eyes to Valdis' probing gaze and the sight of her own pale, helpless body.

✥ Chapter Ten ✥

THE ride from the Alezparito ranch to Mexico City took an entire day and part of the night, and Amber, miserable, had thought it would never end. Now, despite her wretched state, she stared about at her hotel room in awe. This was the most opulent decor she had ever seen. The walls were done in a peach, white, and green paper with designs of flowers and blossoms and green vines. The deep green damask draperies hid French doors that opened onto a portico overlooking a quaint courtyard and bubbling fountain below. It was all feminine and soft. The high curving headboard of the bed was covered and tufted with a rich white satin. The bedspread of matching satin had a delicate lace coverlet.

Amber wanted only to slip between the smooth satin sheets and sleep, but a tray was brought, and she found herself devouring the tasty dish of chicken cooked in a thick wine sauce. Afterward, she opened the door to her room and found a strange man standing outside. "Señorita," he had said with a nod, lips thinly smiling beneath his bushy mustache, "I am afraid you may not go out."

She slammed the door in his smirking face. A guard! Of course, Valdis had posted a guard.

Sleep came, and Amber slipped away deeply until Dolita came in to open the draperies and flood the room with light. "What time is it? Amber cried. "I feel like I've slept for hours," Amber cried.

"*Sí*, you have," Dolita placed a tray on the little table beside her bed. "It is afternoon. Everyone else is just lying down for their siesta, and you are just waking from last night. I brought you chocolate and biscuits. After you eat, I will bring your bath. It will take a long time to do your hair, and then it is not so very long until fiesta time."

Amber stared at the food. Despite her misery, she loved the Mexican drink, made from the shavings of a bar of white chocolate and cooked in sweet milk. "Have you seen Valdis today?" she asked. "Or Maretta or Allegra?"

Dolita was kneeling before a trunk, working with the latches. "*Sí*," she said over her shoulder. "Señorita Maretta has been up since dawn, preparing for tonight. You should see her room. She has thrown all her gowns about and wants to wear none of them. A dressmaker has been called to bring her something new and very elegant."

"What is so special about tonight's party? Valdis has boasted that we had been invited to a party every night for the entire week we are here."

"The fiesta tonight is being given by General Jesu de la Prierda. He is very important, so not everyone is invited—just those who also are important."

Amber picked up a biscuit, thinking how pleased Valdis probably was. "I am worried about Allegra. She didn't look well enough to make the trip."

Dolita sighed. "I know. I worry too. She did not speak one word during all the long hours. She kept her head bowed and her eyes closed, but I know she did not sleep. Now and then I would see a tear run down her cheek. She is so unhappy. She is, no doubt, remembering a happy time when she came here...when she and your father married and spent their honeymoon in Mexico City."

Amber swallowed the lump in her throat and looked away. "Surely, there will be a special place in hell for Valdis."

Dolita nodded. Then she forced a smile. "Just keep thinking about Señor Mendosa. He will get you away. Perhaps it will be tonight."

"I don't know when it will be, Dolita." Amber pushed the tray aside. "I just pray it is soon."

Amber struggled for patience as Dolita put the finishing touches to her hair, sweeping the long silver curls up from her neck and then twisting them around to cascade to her shoulders. It had taken Dolita over an hour, and when at last she finished, Amber stood to look in the gilt-edged mirror which hung on the wall.

"Oh, *bella, bella,*" Dolita cried as she backed

away to survey Amber fully. "Señorita, never have I seen such a vision. You will make all the men swoon and fall at your feet."

Amber stared at her reflection. The dress was of purple satin, with black-trimmed ruffles cascading down the skirt. The bodice was covered with sparkling glass beads and cut low, molding her voluptuous breasts and barely covering her nipples. A long lavender lace mantilla was held atop her head with a silver comb, and the colors of her costume complemented her own silvery tresses.

"It dips too low," she moaned, staring at the hint of pale pink protruding from the tight satin. What would her grandmother say!

"No, no, it is quite proper, señorita." The girl cocked her head to one side, pursing her lips thoughtfully. "You have a good body. It is nothing to be ashamed of." She giggled mischievously, then whispered, "Señorita Maretta stuffs herself like a goose at Christmas."

Amber giggled, stopping when she heard a knock on the door. Valdis called out that Amber was to present herself in the hotel lobby at once.

"Pray for me," she whispered tersely as Dolita gave her a hug of farewell. "Pray that this is the night, because if Armand has made his plans carefully, then my nightmare is over."

Dolita blinked back tears, crossed herself, and Amber left the room.

When she reached the lobby, she was happy to see Allegra and hurried to where she stood, head bowed, and very pale. She was wearing a gray watered silk, with an edging of dark blue about the hem and ruffles cascading from her waist. Her hair was twisted in an austere bun at the back of her head, a long black lace mantilla held high at the crown by a pearl comb.

Amber thought she looked quite lovely and said as much.

Allegra lifted watery, veined eyes and whispered brokenly, "It is only a dress, my child. It is not a reflection of what is in my heart."

"Oh, Allegra," Amber cried, touching the older woman's shoulder and wanting to embrace her, but knowing she must not. "How I wish I could do something for the pain in your heart."

"My pain?" She raised an eyebrow, eyes shining for an instant. "Bless you, child, for caring about another's agony when you have so much of your own. Don't worry about me. I will welcome the day I go to join your father. It's you I'm concerned about." She stiffened as Valdis made his way down the stairs. "Speak no more. He will come to me later and demand to know what was said, and if I do not tell him, I will suffer." She stepped away and turned her back to Amber.

All the other heads were turned to Amber, however. The men were awed by her beauty and the women were plainly envious.

Maretta had waited until the last moment to make a grand entrance, standing poised on the landing at the top of the stairs in a bright red silk gown. Embroidered yellow flowers trailed about the skirt, and yards of purple gauze shirred the sleeves and bodice. The stunning outfit was capped by her shimmering black hair piled atop her head in cascades of curls held in place by a tall, thin gold comb and a long veil of red lace. But Maretta quickly realized that no one was looking. All eyes were still upon Amber, who stood stiffly beside Valdis.

Stomping down the steps, Maretta made her way to Valdis and, clutching his elbow, whispered, "It is a disgrace. She looks like a whore!"

Valdis silenced her with a look. Just then the doorman signaled that the Alezparito carriage had arrived.

Once they were in it and settled, Maretta glared at Amber, upper lip curled back as she warned, "Armand is here in the city. He may come to the fiesta tonight. I will scratch your eyes out if you so much as look at him."

Allegra shrank back against the seat. Eyes twinkling, and looking carefully at Amber, Valdis said, "I doubt Armand Mendosa will show his face here except at the bullfight."

"Yes," Maretta cried brightly. "He does perform tomorrow, and he never ventures out the night before." She threw a warning look at Amber. "But if we see him anywhere while we are in Mexico City, you keep your distance from him."

Valdis sighed. "You are behaving like a shrew. Do not worry. Everyone knows that Amber is with me, and soon they will know she is my fiancée." He could not resist taunting. "If you would spend more time enhancing your charms, perhaps you could persuade Armand to honor the pledge to marry you. I tell you this, I grow weary of waiting.

I want the water rights from his property assured, and the only way that is going to happen is for you to become a Mendosa."

Amber said coldly, "After what happened the other night, you can forget about water rights from Mendosa land."

"I will take the water by force, if need be," Valdis cried. "He knows it. He would not dare refuse me."

Amber met his fiery glare with one of her own. "We will just have to wait and see, won't we?"

"Enough!" He snapped his fingers, leaning back and breathing heavily with anger.

Maretta gave each of them a searching look. "Just what did happen?"

"You mean you didn't hear, Maretta?" Amber pretended surprise. "Valdis, you did not tell Maretta what happened in the woods?"

In a move so fast she had no time to prepare herself, Valdis' hand shot across the carriage to fasten around Amber's throat and squeeze painfully. He pulled her face close to his. "You think much of your servant girl, Dolita, no?" He grinned, speaking through tightly clamped teeth. "She is a pretty little thing. How would you like to see her tongue ripped from her mouth? I will not harm you, my future wife, but I will give Dolita what you deserve as punishment if you do not shut your mouth!" He released her, flinging her backward as she gasped for air.

Allegra spoke up. "What is she talking about? I must know."

Valdis whirled on her, and she cringed. "You

will shut up also. This is to be a pleasant evening. I am sick of your whining. One more word, and we will show Amber the only thing you are good for!"

Maretta turned away, sickened, and stared out the window.

Amber gingerly clutched her throbbing throat, wondering if there were bruises. Averting her own gaze out the window, she prayed, eyes burning with tears she dared not shed, Please, please God, let it be tonight.

The de la Prierda mansion sat atop a sweeping hill on the outskirts of Mexico City. Amber could not help but be impressed as the carriage turned into the winding road nestled between rows of jacaranda trees, heavy with fragrant blossoms. When they reached a wrought iron archway, a footman in a splendid red velvet uniform waited to help them alight. As he took Amber's arm, he seemed awed. Maretta noticed.

Another uniformed servant waited inside the massive double oak doors. Bowing, he bade them enter as Valdis told him their names. He gestured and they followed him.

Valdis told Allegra, "As soon as we are announced, find the old ladies and sit with them, out of the way. I do not want you around." Allegra nodded docilely and shuffled away.

"Valdis, you are a cruel bastard!" Amber hissed, but he merely smiled down at her.

Amber glanced quickly about the foyer, which was very large and seemed like a museum, with statues and portraits of grim-looking personages staring down from the dark-paneled walls. Three magnificent crystal chandeliers hung from the high ceiling, and the rear wall was lined with French doors, through which could be seen a flagstone terrace illuminated by torches, an impressive fountain cascading sparkling water beyond. The foyer was empty of furniture except for an occasional ornately carved chair or small table. The floor was covered in thick carpet of lush burgundy.

The butler ushered them into the large ballroom. In the center was the replica of a stone fountain, surrounded by thousands of flowers of different varieties and colors. A trough, concealed by more flowers, ran from one side of the fountain, and beautiful white swans swam about in it. Long garlands of fragrant gardenias and roses had been intertwined on ropes tied to tiny stars attached to the ceiling. The ceiling was draped in deep purple satin, giving the ballroom the appearance of a star-studded night.

The butler announced in a loud voice, "The Señora Allegra Jualisa Tofelia Alezparito. Her daughter, the Señorita Calias Maretta Alezparitô. Her stepdaughter, the Señorita Amber Forrest. Her stepson, Señor Valdis Juan Comtres Alezparito."

The room was filled with people, and everyone became politely silent when the arrival of new guests was announced. Amber looked about for Armand but did not see him, and her hopes began to sink.

A tall, stout man with narrow eyes set in a paunchy face approached. *"Buenas noches,"* he said, smiling beneath a bushy black mustache as he bent to kiss Maretta's outstretched hand. Then his gaze fell on Amber, and he cried brightly, "Ahhh, this is the lovely Señorita Forrest that has all of Mexico City talking." Amber wanted to turn and run, and Maretta glared at her once again.

"General de la Prierda," Valdis said, stepping forward with a flourish. "It is a pleasure to accept your hospitality. Unfortunately, there was an oversight last year, and I missed that party." He could not resist the barb.

The general chose not to comment. He introduced his wife to Amber, who was grateful for an excuse to withdraw her fingertips from the general's sweaty grip. "How nice of you to invite me to your home," she murmured politely.

Suddenly the general announced in a proud voice, "My son, Diego Luego Guerdo de la Prierda," and Amber found herself staring up into lackluster eyes. He was tall, thin, and...dull. It was the only word she could think of to describe him.

He bent to kiss her hand, holding on to her fingertips tightly as he stared down at her bosom and murmured, "I had heard you were beautiful, señorita, but words cannot describe such loveliness."

"Thank you, sir." She attempted to draw her hand away, but he turned sideways, tucking her fingers into the crook of his elbow.

"We shall dance," he said firmly, with a challenging glance at Valdis. "I will not allow you to stray from me this night, now that I have found you."

"Have a wonderful evening, Amber," Maretta giggled as Diego led her away.

He took her to a far corner of the ballroom, where musicians played. With Diego holding her much too tightly, they danced. "You are the most beautiful woman in the room," he said matter-of-factly, looking her over with an appraising sweep. "When my father told me that you were coming tonight, I could not believe my good fortune. You will allow me the pleasure and honor of escorting you during your stay in our city."

Amber blinked. Never had she met anyone who took himself—and her—so for granted. "Well, I don't know," she hedged, annoyed, but trying not to show it.

He raised an eyebrow and smirked, "Surely you do not prefer the company of Señor Alezparito? Everyone knows him for what he is, unscrupulous, a *bandido* in disguise. The only reason he was invited here was because he is escorting the rest of his family. And too, news of your beauty has spread throughout Mexico City."

Amber stiffened, struggling to pull away from him, but he held her tightly. "It is not by choice that I am here, señor. And I do not wish to be escorted by anyone." She looked over to where Valdis was standing, watching her resentfully. Had the threat against Dolita not been made, she would have been tempted to appeal to Diego for help. But she did not dare do that. And perhaps there was no need. She clung to the hope of Armand.

Diego continued to smile warmly. "I have heard you American señoritas enjoy trifling with men. You toy with me."

"I toy with no one, sir," she told him coolly.

"But your eyes, they glitter like the sun on water."

"My eyes are probably glittering with anger," she snapped, "because you are holding me too tightly."

His eyes widened with disbelief, the first sign of life she had seen in them. As the son of a wealthy, important man, he was not used to being rebuked.

He continued to hold her, even though she had begun to move stiffly as she stared around the room in desperation.

Then she saw him—leaning against the arched doorway which led to the terrace. His arms were folded nonchalantly across his chest. He was strikingly handsome in a dark blue velvet suit, the jacket tapering at the waist. He wore a white shirt, a splash of red in the satin cravat at his throat. His thick hair was curled slightly about his neck, giving him the look of a somewhat petulant child despite the heavily masculine aura about him. His eyes, the golden brown hue sparkling in the light of the chandeliers, smiled with amusement as he watched her struggling against Diego's embrace.

Without thinking of protocol, she jerked so abruptly from Diego that he had no time to restrain her. "Señor Hayden," she called softly, forcing herself to walk slowly toward him. "How nice to see you here."

He nodded, not moving. Glancing briefly at her bosom, he winked and murmured, "Señorita. You look lovely tonight...*all* of you."

She ignored the remark and glanced over her shoulder to see that Diego was right behind her, looking most annoyed. She wanted desperately to ask about Armand, but Diego was quickly at her side, clamping a possessive hand on her arm. He nodded to Cord and said tightly, "Señor Hayden, I believe. *Compañero* of the matador, Armand Mendosa."

Cord nodded as he continued to look at Amber, silent questions transmitting from his piercing eyes. Was she all right? Had Valdis harmed her? So many questions, but he dared not ask.

"Yes," Amber leaped at the opportunity. "Where is the famous matador tonight? I would like to wish him well in his performance tomorrow."

"The last time I saw him, he was surrounded by a dozen señoritas, Miss Forrest." Cord nodded toward the terrace. "You might find him out there in the garden, but you would have to stand in line."

Diego tugged at her arm. "We are wasting the lovely music. You shall see the matador tomorrow when I take you to the corrida. I plan to invite the entire Alezparito family to join me in my father's private box."

Cord raised an eyebrow. "Yes," he said with a grin, "I think that would be best, Miss Forrest."

Amber felt Diego tugging at her arm, but she so wanted to see Armand, to speak with him, and Cord was being no help. Then Maretta appeared, frowning. "Cord! What are you doing at this affair? You certainly do not belong here!"

"You are an authority on affairs, aren't you?" He cocked his head and grinned.

Amber did not miss the tension sparkling between the two. Maretta stood on tiptoe, looking beyond Cord, and squealed, "Armand! He waits for me!" With a swish of her skirts, she hurried out onto the terrace.

161

Amber could see a crowd of women, a blur of brightly colored gowns, and Maretta shoving her way through them.

"The music," Diego persisted, tugging at Amber's arm. "We are wasting the music."

There was nothing to do but allow Diego to lead her back onto the dance floor. One song blended into the next, and the evening wore on. Valdis and Diego tensely, but politely, vied for dances with her, and she miserably tolerated each. Cord had disappeared. She did not see Armand or Maretta.

Her eyes closed, she moved trancelike to the music, wondering if the night would ever end. Then she felt Diego suddenly stiffen and she heard a familiar voice. "You monopolize the beautiful lady, Diego. Allow your guests a chance to enjoy this delight."

Diego frowned but bowed and moved away. Amber went into Cord's arms eagerly, trembling at his nearness. "Cord, thank goodness." She breathed a sigh of relief. "I didn't think we would get a chance to talk. I was hoping to see Armand, speak with him, but—"

"He isn't going to risk arousing Valdis' suspicions," Cord interrupted tersely. "He wants him to think he's completely cowed after the other night. He's out on the terrace, forcing himself to be polite to Maretta. As long as he stays away from you, it will look like he's obeying Valdis' orders."

"Can we slip away now?" she asked anxiously, catching a glimpse of Diego's jealous stare and Valdis' scowling face as Cord whirled her about

162

the room. "I don't think I can stand another moment of this."

"Not tonight. The plan is set for tomorrow evening at the President's Ball. It will be much larger than this, and it's being held at the palace, in the city. I'll stand a better chance of getting you out, because of all the noise and all the people. Armand talked with his aunt, and she's willing. Just hold on. Things are falling into place."

"How perfect." She flashed a smile in Valdis' direction. "Make sure we slip out right after he announces our engagement. It will be quite embarrassing for him."

She relaxed in Cord's arms, allowing him to guide her to the soft rhythm. He was a good dancer, and she felt protected, and, for a little while, content.

Suddenly he held her at arm's length, eyes piercing as he asked, almost gruffly, "Amber, are you sure you know what you're doing? Is this what you want?"

"I don't understand," she replied. "You know I must get away from Valdis."

"That's not what I mean." He grimaced. "It's Armand. He's confident you're falling in love with him. I'm not. I think you're making a mistake, and he's going to get hurt. Let me get you out of all this. I can get my hands on some money, and I'll see that you're settled somewhere back in the States. Don't use Armand this way."

She went rigid in his arms. "Armand and I have no commitments. All we ask is time to see if we love each other."

163

"You don't love Armand," he stated. "You're attracted to him because he's charming and because you think you can control him. You aren't so sure you can make *me* dance to your tune."

"You're very conceited to think I want to make you do anything at all, Cord Hayden."

"I've held you." He smiled knowingly. "I've felt your body tremble with desire, Amber. You won't admit it to me, maybe not even to yourself, but you feel something for me. You aren't sophisticated enough to understand...yet."

She tried to pull away, but he held her. "Why do you persist in making me angry?" she cried.

He shrugged. "You make yourself angry, because you know I'm telling the truth."

"You think I'm trifling with Armand."

"I don't think you realize what you're doing. You're in danger and you need help and you won't let me help you. And you're confused. You're confusing desire with love. You can desire a man without loving him, but you don't realize that. I don't want you to make a mistake and hurt yourself and Armand."

Amber was trembling with rage, her voice ragged as she whispered, "You think Armand will hurt me? You think I'm like some...animal in heat, but I insist on being in love before I allow myself to be bred. Is that it? What I feel for Armand isn't really love, and what he feels for me is only lust—"

"Exactly. Armand is one of the best friends I ever had, but I tell him to his face that when it comes to women he's immature. He wants them all. Why shouldn't he? Women throw themselves at matadors."

She jerked away and hurried through the door to the terrace.

"Amber, don't—" Cord called worriedly, but made no move to follow her.

She reached the terrace and glanced around at the people. Then, glancing back over her shoulder, she saw Valdis striding toward her with Diego close behind. Frantic, she looked about wildly, then saw Armand standing to the side of the terrace, surrounded by admirers. He glanced up and saw her, but turned away. He probably didn't want Valdis to see him looking at her.

Valdis reached her then and snapped, "What do you think you are doing?"

Diego caught up with them. "It is our dance," the general's son said brusquely, reaching for her hand.

"No," Valdis told him coolly. "We are leaving now. The señorita does not feel well."

Diego looked alarmed. "I am sorry. Will she and your family be able to join me and my father in our box tomorrow?"

"Of course," Valdis responded graciously, obviously impressed by the invitation. "Please give our respects to your parents. I will escort my fiancée back to the hotel."

Diego, puzzled, silently echoed the word: fiancée? He stared after them as they moved away.

Cord, resuming his position near the French doors, watched with cold, brooding eyes.

❧ Chapter Eleven ❧

WHEN they reached the hotel, Amber was the first to alight from the carriage, anxious to escape Valdis and Maretta who had argued all the way home.

She had reached the front doors when Valdis caught up to her. He hissed, "You will go to your room and remain there until I send for you when it is time to go to the corrida tomorrow."

"Fine," she said coolly. "As long as you stay out of my room."

He looked at her in that smug way and said, "Do not worry, *querida*. I will not taste your fruit until I am entitled to the whole basket. But very soon we will be sharing not only the same room...but the same bed."

She bit back her angry retort.

Once inside her room she removed her dress and

flung it aside, then pulled a gown from her trunk, slipped it on, and crawled into bed. Outside, she heard a guard take up his nightly vigil at her door. No matter. Soon, she would be free. And with that hope, she welcomed sleep.

The sound of the door clicking open brought Amber upright and awake. As her lips parted to scream, a familiar voice called out softly, "Do not be afraid, my moonstar."

"Armand," she cried joyfully, tumbling from the bed to grope for him in the darkness. With a moan, he caught her, wrapping his arms about her to crush her against his chest. "Armand, how did you get in here?" But he silenced her with a deep kiss.

"Ah, how I wanted to do that tonight when I first saw you," he murmured, brushing her hair lovingly back from her face. "To see you and not be able to touch you is a torture I cannot endure much longer."

"But how did you get in here?" she persisted. "The guard..."

He chuckled as he struck a match. Seeing the lantern beside the bed, he crossed to light it. "Pesos do not buy loyalty," he said matter-of-factly as he sat down on the bed, patting it for her to join him. "Valdis will learn that one day. I gave the guard more pesos to let me in than Valdis pays him to keep me out. Now, he stands guard for me."

"Oh, Armand," she laughed happily, padding across the floor to sit down next to him. "I can't tell you how glad I am to see you."

His expression grew serious as he said, "To-

night, when you ran onto the terrace, you were
very upset. You had been dancing with Cord. He
has said to you the same things he has said to me,
that we should not confuse desire with love. Am
I correct?"

"Well...yes," she stammered, bewildered. Cord
had indeed taken it upon himself to mingle in
their affairs! She said as much to Armand, who
listened with maddening amusement etched upon
his handsome face.

When she had finished, he spoke as though she
were a child. "Amber, my beautiful darling, you
must understand. Cord is my friend. He does not
want me to be hurt. He is also your friend, whether
you believe that or not."

Amber was not so sure. "It doesn't matter what
he says, Armand. It's how we feel. And we really
don't know each other. That's all I'm sure of right
now."

"Very well," he began. "You will have to get to
know me. You wish to know about the real Armand? I will tell you. I am a matador. It is my
life. From the time I was a small boy, I wanted to
fight the bulls. Some men marry and later take a
mistress, but the bull is my mistress."

"But why? What makes you live with danger?
Tomorrow you could be killed," she cried.

"But I could also be killed this very night, should
Valdis walk through that door," he chuckled. He
stroked her cheek affectionately as he whispered,
"I know I could be killed, my moonstar. No matador is without fear. He lives with fear. He wakes
in the night with it. When I am actually in the

ring, in the midst of the heat of the fight, this is the only time I can completely lose fear. And when I face the time to kill or be killed, then once again my manhood is decided and won. I walk from the ring victorious...only to begin living with fear all over again."

"I think," she said, after a pause, "I understand you a little bit better now."

He laughed. "Ah, then this means you can now love me! So when do we marry?"

Amber found herself laughing at his good-natured spirit. He was so happy, so vibrant, so...so alive. Damn Cord Hayden! What she felt for Armand was the beginning of true love.

"We will marry when we are both sure it is what we want," she told him, then changed the subject. "What about Valdis? Where will he think I have gone when I disappear tomorrow night? Will he suspect you had anything to do with it?"

"No," he said bluntly. "I will be giving all my attention to Maretta tomorrow. When it is discovered that you are gone, I will continue to give all my attention to her. I will not be suspected. Perhaps you are thinking that I should be sorry for trifling with her feelings, but there are things you do not know. She deserves this treatment, believe me."

"But she loves you, Armand," Amber insisted.

He threw back his head and laughed. "I am sorry. I do not mean to make fun, but as I told you, there are things you do not know. I suppose you have a right to be told—though I have always made it a rule never to discuss the women in my

170

life. I have always thought a man who did so was a braggart, and certainly no gentleman."

He hesitated for a moment, took a deep breath, then continued. "You see, Maretta does not love me. She loves my money, my position, my family name. She tried to feel the love we were told by our parents that we should feel. When we were younger, and both quite foolish, we played together. Our bodies grew and so did the hungers within." He paused again, searching her face for understanding, then whispered apologetically, "We knew each other, Amber. Do you know what I am saying?"

He rushed on. "This went on for a few years, but as I grew older, I realized that I did not love her and told her so. She was angry and said we had to marry one day. Then, to try and make me jealous, she had an affair with a close friend. I told him I did not love her, and I gave him my blessings to pursue her if he wished.

"But," he sighed with disdain, "Maretta would not give up. She arranged for me to find them together, hoping I would become enraged. I did not. When she realized her plan had not worked, she fell in love with the other man. He was honest with her from the beginning, and he told her he was not looking for marriage. So she tried to make him jealous, as she had attempted to do with me. He was not jealous, only disgusted. He turned his back on her, and now she hates him.

"So you see"—he kissed her forehead lightly— "Maretta has tried to use two men. She deserves to have the same done to her. She is a treacherous

171

woman, a very dangerous woman. Never turn your back on her, Amber."

Amber was chewing her lower lip thoughtfully. Something was whirling inside, and suddenly it came to her. "Cord Hayden!" She sat up straight. "That's it, isn't it?" She wondered why she had not understood before. Oh, but she sometimes was naive!

"I shall not lie to you," he said quietly. "It was Cord."

"And Valdis does not know."

"No one knew but the three of us. As I say, I do not like to discuss the women in my life, and I never shall again."

He was gazing at her intently. "You speak excitedly of Cord Hayden," he said carefully. "He has held you? Kissed you? He has awakened your fire?"

Amber became wary as Armand gave her a mocking smile. "Maretta told me all about his lovemaking...that I am too gentle, too slow, and he is more than any woman can endure. She says with me, she begged only for release, but with him, she begged to die, for she could not live with such deep pleasure. Is that what you want Amber? To beg to die because you are being loved so savagely? Do you want Cord, Amber?"

"No!" she cried, astounded to hear that Maretta had said such things. "Cord has kissed me, but—"

"But you liked it!" he goaded.

He stared into her eyes, his own narrowed as he said, "Very well. Perhaps I am afraid for no reason. Perhaps I love you so much it drives me a little mad. But heed my words, Amber. If you are using me only to escape Valdis, pretending to care for me, you will regret it. Never have I cared so for a woman, and you will not play with me and then turn away."

"I have no intention of using you. Perhaps"— she took a deep breath, hating to say the words, but knowing she had to—"perhaps it would be best if I found another way to escape."

He was silent for a moment. Then he said quietly, "The decision must be yours. But do not make it now. We are both angry."

She stared at him. Why did everything have to be so difficult? And why had he become jealous of Cord? Was it Maretta's taunting?

She took another deep breath, determined to make one last effort. "Armand, I thought you understood how I feel. But you seem to feel that you own me. You don't own me, Armand. No man owns me, or ever will. When I do get married, my husband will not own my body or my soul. I will give my love...but never my freedom. Perhaps you want more from me than I can give you."

"Is this how you truly feel?" he asked quietly, calmly.

She nodded, watching his eyes mellow.

"Then I shall not worry about Cord Hayden stealing you away from me, moonstar, for he would surely demand complete obedience from a woman—in his bed and out. You would not bend to his will."

"I won't bend to yours, either."

"Ah, but you are a spitfire!"

His lips closed over hers, and once more Amber

felt the fires burning within. For precious moments they clung together, and when at last he released her, he whispered, "Forgive the jealous outburst of a man in love."

When she nodded, he kissed her once more, briefly. "I must go now. I need sleep or the bull will win tomorrow."

She gasped. "Armand, how can you joke about it?"

"Because I think sometimes that is what life is." He held her against his chest, stroking her long silken hair. "Sometimes I feel God places us here for His amusement, and that all of life is a joke for Him."

"That's blasphemy, Armand," she admonished him.

"Ah, but maybe He will think me only joking, eh?" He touched her chin with his fingertips and stepped back. "Good night, moonstar. Remember that I love you more than my life."

And he was quickly gone.

Amber put out the lantern and sat in the dark for a long time without moving. He had been upset about her feelings for Cord. Had she soothed him, or was he still disturbed?

❧ Chapter Twelve ☙

THE carriage pulled to a stop before the main entrance to the Plaza de Toros, and Amber waited for Diego to step down and turn to help her alight. Directly behind, Valdis irritably followed in another carriage with Allegra and Maretta. Amber delighted in remembering Valdis' expression when Diego arrived at the hotel with two carriages, one with room enough only for two people.

Whenever Diego gazed at her adoringly, she tried to smile, but she could not afford to trifle with Valdis.

"I do not like the way Diego fawns over you," Valdis had said bitterly, "but his family is important, so you must be nice to him. But I warn you. If you say anything to him, Dolita will suffer."

Amber remembered.

Diego brought her back to the present. "You are so beautiful, señorita," he said, beaming as he led her to the arena. "I am the envy of every man."

Though Valdis had selected it, Amber had to admit that the dress she wore was perfect for her. Deep yellow satin, it had a low, heart-shaped neckline and huge puffed sleeves that tapered to the elbows with ruffles of lace in a deeper shade of yellow. The girdle was beaded with tiny seed pearls, and these were also scattered about the skirt, beside rows of lace ruffles.

"Tell me, Amber," Diego was saying, "do you like the corrida? Even some Mexican señoritas find the sport barbarous. How do you feel?"

Amber did not hesitate. "I find it brutal and disgusting, cruel and senseless."

Diego looked at her with amusement. "Then why do you come? Just to be with me? But we could have gone for a ride in the country."

"No," she said quickly, then blushed as she realized she had spoken too clearly.

But, to her surprise, Diego laughed. "Ah, yes, we both know why you came, señorita. Gossip blows across Mexico as swiftly as the wind. Everyone has heard how Armand Mendosa dedicated a bull to you, and I saw your face last night when you saw him."

She stiffened. "You presume a great deal. Señor Mendosa saved me from a bull one night when I wandered into its field. He is a good friend."

He chuckled. "Matadors do not dedicate bulls to mere friends." He patted her hand.

176

"I don't wish to talk about Señor Mendosa," she said crisply.

"Very well." He nodded. "We shall talk about bulls, instead, and I will explain something to you. Bullfighting is indeed bloody, but it is not a sport." Diego grinned. "It is a spectacle. In a sense, it is like the plot of great literature. The plot in this novel calls for the bull to die. To deny that, to attempt to change it, would be as ridiculous as to deny the plot of *Julius Caesar* which directs that Caesar shall die.

"It is also"—he flashed her a smile—"like a ballet. Watch the performance of traditional movements. That is grace. It is a tribute to physical dexterity, but it includes the risk of severe injury.

"The main point of the bullfighting spectacle is the complete mastery of a human being over two living beings—over the bull, and over the matador, himself. For the ultimate need of the matador is to conquer his own fear. Only then can he conquer the bull."

Amber recalled Armand's admission of the night before.

"A brave man," Diego continued, "is not the one who refuses to feel fear. No, señorita, the brave man feels fear and still faces the danger that causes that fear. Matadors are afraid when they enter the ring. Even Armand Mendosa," he finished, "regardless of what he might otherwise say."

"Armand has told me of his feelings," she admitted coolly. Diego was right, but she would not reveal what Armand had confided.

Amber was now glancing around, wondering whether Armand was nearby and if he might see her. Diego was pulling her along too quickly, and she almost did not see the rut in the ground. She stumbled. Diego caught her quickly and held her up, but she could not put her weight on her foot. "I think I have twisted it," she cried. "Please, help me to sit down somewhere."

Diego glanced about anxiously, then spotted a bench just outside the arena. He helped her over and lowered her carefully onto it.

Kneeling before her, he examined her ankle. After a few moments, he straightened and said, "I see no swelling. I do not think it is badly injured, but if you would like to return to the hotel, I can send for the carriage."

"No," she said hastily, refusing to miss seeing Armand. "I will be all right. But a cool drink would be nice." She gave him what she hoped was a pained and beseeching look. "If I had something to drink and rested for a moment, I think I would be fine."

"Of course," he said with a nod. "You sit here and do not move. I will return quickly."

Diego moved away and she looked around for Armand. But the man who approached her was not the one she wanted to see.

"Very touching," he growled.

She gazed into the cold, accusing eyes of Cord Hayden.

"I've been watching your performance. Very good, Amber."

She leaped to her feet, forgetting her pretended injury, and demanded, "Why can't you leave me alone?"

He nodded at her ankle. "You acted as though you hurt yourself to get rid of Diego in hope that Armand would come running. He won't. He's inside—alone. And he's in the worst mood I've ever seen him in. What the hell did you do to him last night?"

"I...I didn't do anything," she floundered. "Now leave me alone, please. You must know how moody Armand is."

"Tell me what happened."

She felt herself bristle as memories of the conversation of the night before came flooding back. Cord Hayden had caused enough turmoil in her life, and she wouldn't say they had argued about him! Trembling, she hissed, "What goes on between us is none of your business, Cord. Now please tell me where I might find Armand. I need to speak with him." Dear Lord, she prayed, help me find the right words to make Armand realize that I do not love Cord. Make him understand.

Cord shook his head firmly. "There isn't time. Bullfights are the one thing that start on time in Mexico. Now, tell me what went on between you two last night."

She stared at him. "It is none of your business, Cord."

"He's my friend and I know him, Amber. Something is very wrong."

She glared at him but said nothing, and after a moment Cord taunted, "What happened, Amber? Did the playboy, Diego, make you a better offer than Armand?"

Her hand raised slightly, but she saw the quick flash in his eyes and knew she mustn't slap him.

"Your trouble, Cord," she said, barely controlling herself, "lies in the fact that you are obviously used to having women throw themselves at your feet. Does it really bother you so much that you can't have me the way you had Maretta?"

Surprise flashed in his eyes, but left just as quickly. "Perhaps I can," he said softly. "I have held you, Amber, kissed you, awakened the fire in you. It was much too easy. You need a stronger man than Armand. I just might be that man."

She gasped, but there was no time to answer him. Diego was approaching. He extended a cup of water to her, which she accepted gratefully.

"Diego, I'm ready to go inside now," she announced.

As he led her away, Diego studied her face in silent concern, then asked, "Is something wrong? I feel you are upset. Is it your ankle?"

"No. I am fine." She quickened her step. "I'm anxious to get inside and sit down, though."

Frowning, Diego mused, "Señor Hayden has quite a reputation with the ladies. You would do well not to be in his company. I did not like him asking you to dance last night. I will see that he keeps his distance tonight."

"That won't be necessary, Diego," she informed him. "I won't be bothered by Señor Hayden again."

They walked along a corridor and then made their way up the steps of the arena. Diego held Amber's arm tightly in case she should stumble again. She saw that they were heading toward an impressive-looking box and hesitated as she asked, "Are we sitting there?"

"*Sí,* but it is not my family's box. It is the box of President Juarez, himself," he told her proudly. "He personally invited me to sit in it. He was to be here, with his wife, but there was, I am told, pressing government business. He chose to go to his office, and his wife is preparing for tonight's fiesta."

They entered the presidential box, and Diego greeted the Alezparito family jubilantly. Maretta glared at Amber, then returned her gaze to the ring. Allegra continued to sit with head bowed, lost in her own secret world. Valdis wore a smug expression, pleased to be in the president's box.

The music grew louder, and Amber turned her attention to the ring as the procession began. When the matadors made their entrance, Maretta squealed with delight. "Valdis, look!" She pointed. "Armand stands on the right! This is his first time to do so! Oh, I am so proud!"

Valdis leaned close to her to whisper, "Do not make a spectacle, Maretta. People watch the presidential box, and we must maintain dignity at all times."

Amber quietly asked Diego, "What is Maretta so excited about?"

"Armand Mendosa is the matador of the day, with the most seniority," he explained. "He will kill the first and fourth bulls. It is an honor."

"The first and fourth bulls?" she echoed, stunned. "You mean he has to fight two bulls today? But why?"

"It is the custom on such a day of fiesta. He has done so before. The junior matador, the one standing in the center, will kill the third and sixth."

Amber looked at Armand as the matadors approached the president's box. His eyes were for her and her alone. When he smiled—so anxiously, so hopefully—her heart warmed. She would, she suddenly realized, run away with him. And whatever happened, would happen. They had to have the chance. They had to know, once and for all, if their love was real.

Suddenly Maretta leaned forward. Plucking a flower from the garland adorning the edge of the box, she flung it directly at Armand. His smile faded and his hands flew up to catch it before it hit him in the face. "He caught it!" she cried exultantly.

"I am warning you," Valdis snarled, jabbing her cruelly with his elbow.

Amber was confused. There were so many customs of the country she did not understand. Beside her, Diego sensed her bewilderment and whispered, "Poor Maretta. It is common knowledge that Armand Mendosa does not return her love and does not intend to honor the pledge of marriage made by his parents. But she does not give up." He shook his head in disgust. "She throws him the blossom to emphasize her love, and he catches it by surprise and she pretends he acknowledges her intent."

Maretta turned to smile ever so smugly, but Amber pretended not to see her.

At last, the arena was cleared, and the crowd screamed as the gate was opened and the first bull came thundering into the ring. He was huge, strong, and very frightening.

Amber felt a cold stab of fear. "Do you think this bull might be more dangerous than another?"

Diego gave her hand a reassuring pat. She wished he would stop doing that. "Armand is good matador. He is watching and will know what kind of fighter this bull will be."

Amber's eyes searched the cluster around the gate to the bull pens. She could see Armand leaning over the railing, watching. But he was not watching the bull. His head was turned in the direction of the presidential box, and he was looking straight at her. A man standing next to him said something, and he moved away from his position to reappear seconds later. As he strutted proudly into the ring, he removed his montera and waved at the crowd as they screamed in adulation.

He took his stand, holding his scarlet cape before him, his profile toward the bull.

Her hands gripped tightly in her lap, Amber turned to Diego. "Why is he out there now? I thought those other men came out first, with pics, to weaken the bull."

"They will," he assured her. "Armand is merely displaying his skill with his cape."

The bull made his first charge. A scream went up from the crowd as Armand spread his cape before the animal's snout, swinging the cape past his body as the bull followed its sweep. Armand pulled the bull closer and closer. Suddenly, as the bull made a thrusting charge, Armand gathered his cape against his body in a half veronica. The bull stopped short.

Amber watched in awe as Armand turned his back in apparent disdain of the horns, walking away in a stupendous display of mastery over the bull. The crowd roared.

Maretta squealed, "He is the bravest matador to ever live!"

"No."

Everyone seated in the box turned to stare at Allegra. For the first time, she showed an awareness that she even knew where she was. She was shaking her head, eyes dull no longer but flashing fire. "No! Your father was the bravest matador ever."

"Well...yes, of course," Maretta said slowly, stunned by her mother's surprising show of spirit. "But Armand is the bravest matador of today."

Diego leaned close to Amber. "She is probably right. Señor Alezparito was a famous matador. I saw him die. He was ripped apart, dead before they could even get to him."

Amber shuddered. "And you enjoy this?"

Valdis glared at her but Amber ignored him, turning her gaze back to the ring. A feeling of weighted despair was settling about her, lightened only by the hope that, within a few hours, she might be free.

Chapter Thirteen

AMBER forced herself to look at the ring. It would, she knew, take determination to learn to watch Armand in the ring without being terrified. But she would do it. He would expect it. Her new resolve was, she decided, smiling to herself, the one good thing about coming to Mexico. She was learning to be a woman, a strong woman.

Astride horses, the picadors made their challenges to the bull. "The junior picador will make the first delivery," Diego told her. "See how he drives the small, sharp metal point of his lance into the tossing muscle as the bull charges?"

"Ahah!" he cried suddenly. "More lancing is required. He is a strong one, this bull."

Valdis clapped his hands, and Amber looked to Diego for an explanation. "As the bull's breeder, he beams with pride," he told her matter-of-factly, "for his animal has the strength and bravery to push the picadors around. See? Señor Alezparito has reason to be proud."

Averting her gaze as a horse was grazed, Amber wondered, "But doesn't that mean the bull is unusually fierce?"

Diego did not answer her, for at that moment Armand appeared in the ring again. Diego said, "It is obvious Armand intends to be the star. Now you shall see some dexterous capework. Armand is known for his art with the cape."

Amber watched, fascinated, as Armand waved his cape at the bull. Then, as the bull made his pass, Armand turned, quickly wrapping the cloth about his body in a sweeping, poetic movement. With a dramatic sweep of scarlet satin, Armand whipped about to cut off the return charge.

The screams split the air: *"Olé! Olé!"*

Diego waved an arm toward the spirited throng. "They adore him."

Now Armand turned and strode to the waiting bearer who handed him a stick over which a small piece of red cloth had been wrapped twice. Carrying his sword and muleta in one hand, Armand removed his montera from his head and marched toward a box on the far side of the ring making a gesture. This was part of the ritual, as Armand asked permission of the plaza authority to kill the bull. Permission was granted. But instead of returning to the bull, Armand turned and strode purposefully to the box where Amber was sitting.

He stopped directly below, eyes warm and happy as he looked up at her, smiling. With precise aim,

he threw his hat, landing it once again precisely
in her lap. Hundreds of people looked to see to
whom their favorite matador had dedicated his
kill.

Valdis and Maretta, their expressions identical
rage, turned to stare at Amber. Diego shrugged,
barely managing to conceal his annoyance. "Well,
señorita. Do you accept the dedication? He awaits
a signal. You must do something. Either acknowledge his dedication or return his hat."

As she returned Armand's adoring gaze, Amber
knew she wanted to accept his gesture. Remembering the late-blooming rose she had selected
from the bouquet on her dressing table, she removed it quickly from her bodice. Standing, she
pressed the flower to her lips, then tossed it down
to Armand.

"Gracias!" he called up to her before making a
sweeping bow. He straightened, kissed the flower
while continuing to gaze up at her adoringly, then
tucked it inside his collar before turning once more
to the waiting bull, who was pawing the sand.

Valdis and Maretta sat rigidly as Amber took
her seat, trembling in wonder at what she had
done. Diego, maintaining his composure with effort, directed Amber's attention to Armand, who
now stood erect, holding the muleta with both
hands as though flagging the bull by. He explained, "Watch as he presents the muleta, held
in his right hand. It is more dangerous than if it
were held in his left hand. It is done with the cloth,
not aided by the sword."

Amber watched, paralyzed, wishing she could

just squeeze her eyes shut and not open them until it was over. Diego continued his comments, but his voice became a droning blur.

Suddenly the crowd screamed, and Amber leaped to her feet.

"I cannot believe he uses the *péndulo.*" Diego clutched her elbow to steady her. "It is an invitation for goring. Seldom does a matador do this!"

His words were drowned out by a great rolling gasp that began slowly, then rose to a scream as the bull made his charge, and Armand's brightly costumed body was hurled skyward.

Diego reached for Amber again but she backed away, shaking her head from side to side in rejection of the horror below. Clutching her throat, she fought oblivion. She would not faint. She could not do that to Armand. *Armand.*

"*Madre de Dios! Madre de Dios!*" Someone's shrill cry reached Amber. "The horns are tearing him apart!"

The bullring was filled with swirling magenta capes as toreros rushed to Armand's aid. Ring attendants rushed in from all over.

"Sit down," Diego shouted. "Armand is being helped. They have already driven the bull away. You must be calm." He turned to Allegra, who was crumpled on the floor, moaning.

Amber clutched at Diego's shirt. "I must go to him. Take me there, please."

"Where is your shame?" Maretta cried. "Never have I seen Armand perform so. His attention was on you, not on the bull."

Amber stared at Maretta. *Was* it her fault that

Armand had been gored? Was it? "Take me to him, Diego. I must see him. I must," she said woodenly.

Uniformed guards formed cordons to keep the spectators out of the ring. In a moment, a stretcher appeared. Amber knew that, in the confusion, she could escape Diego and Valdis. She did. She ran out of the box and down the steps, dashing into the crowd, and maneuvered her way toward the place she watched them carry the stretcher. Rounding a corner, she stopped at the sight of two burly guards positioned outside a heavy door. Pressing back against the wall, she watched, heart pounding wildly, as the door opened and a man in a white coat emerged. She saw the bloodstains and felt a quake of horror.

The man spoke to the guards and they shook their heads solemnly.

Amber knew it was now or never. Stepping into view, she said, "Please. I must see him. He would want to see me, I know."

The doctor's eyes narrowed as he stared at her. "Your name, señorita," he commanded brusquely.

"Amber Forrest," she told him, lifting her chin. "I want to see Armand Mendosa. We are...close. He dedicated the bull to me," she added nervously, feeling ridiculous.

The doctor nodded. "He calls your name. Come inside."

Grasping her arm, he steered her into the room. "Give what comfort you can, señorita," he said grimly. "There is nothing more to be done."

The room was small, stark; the walls of cracked, peeling plaster and the floor only dirt. A wooden

table stood to one side, covered with bloody cloths
and instruments. And in the corner, upon the single cot, Armand lay beneath a blood-soaked sheet.
A man in white was bending over him, but
straightened and gave Amber a piercing look.

"This is the woman whose name he calls," the
doctor with Amber spoke softly, and the other doctor nodded and stepped away from the cot.

Amber forced her quivering legs to take her
across the small room, which was suddenly so awesome. Reaching the cot, she gasped. Armand's
face was grayish-blue, his lips white and drawn
back in a silent grimace. His head lolled to one
side, eyes open but unseeing. She commanded her
hand to move, her fingertips to touch the red-stained fingers which poked from beneath the
sheet. Only with great effort was she able to push
the words past her heart. "Armand," she whispered tremulously. "Armand. Can you hear me?"

His glassy gaze sought to focus, and she could
feel the slightest pressure of his fingers against
hers. His voice was barely audible. "My moonstar...how I love you...."

She knelt beside him as a great sob wrenched
from the depths of her. "Oh, Armand, I love you.
Dear God, I never knew how much until this moment. Please. You must be strong. You must get
well."

"No." His voice was barely audible. He swallowed, coughed. Mustering the last of his strength,
he whispered, "No. Today, the bull wins. I am the
one to die."

"No, Armand, no!" she cried, flinging her head
from side to side, then lowering her lips to press

his bloodied fingertips to her lips, holding his hand tightly. "You won't die. I won't let you. You must live!"

"It is the final joke of God, no?" The smile he forced was a grimace of pain. "But do not worry, my moonstar. For the dying, it is not hard. I feel no pain. Only a terrible weakness. And sorrow that I did not perform well for you today."

Amber wept quietly, holding his hand against her face, for a long time.

Then she felt a hand on her shoulder and looked up into the tight-set face of Cord Hayden. She couldn't speak, but she didn't have to.

Armand moaned, and they turned to him. "Cord," he said feebly. "My friend. You will look after her. Do you promise?"

Cord nodded quickly. "You know I will, Armand."

Amber lowered her head to the cot, still cradling his hand lovingly. "No, Armand," she sobbed. "You're going to be all right. You..." She could not go on.

"My moonstar," he whispered, struggling to caress her face with his fingertips. "How I love you."

She felt his fingers stiffen suddenly, then go limp. She looked up wildly, at Cord, and then at Armand. He was quiet and still, his unseeing eyes fixed upon her.

Cord reached to take Armand's hand from her and tuck it beneath the sheet. He stared hard at his friend for just a moment, then put his arms around Amber and drew her to her feet. The doctor moved quickly to pull the sheet up over Armand's face.

Looking up at Cord in misery, she whispered, "Forget your promise to him. Let me go my own way now."

Making no reply, his lips set in a grim line, Cord silently took her from the room and they threaded their way through the mob of grieving people gathered in the corridor. When they were outside, the late afternoon sun streaming down upon them from a deep red sky, he began to walk faster, almost running, wanting to put as much distance between them and the arena as quickly as possible.

Amber stumbled, and he put his arm around her, urging her along. "Please," she sobbed, trembling. "Just let me go, Cord. Let me go."

"I'm doing what I should have done when I first found out that bastard was keeping you prisoner," he said flatly. "I'm going to see that you get away."

Making his way to his wagon, he hoisted her up onto the seat; she was too numb to protest further. He then climbed up himself, took the reins, and they headed down a narrow street leading away from the arena.

As they rode, Amber carried on a frenzied dialogue with herself. Where was Cord taking her? Was it right not to stay with Armand's body? Should she make her way, somehow, to his aunt? Underneath these thoughts was the clear knowledge that she had no choice but to let Cord rescue her from Valdis. She couldn't remain with Armand, or think of anything but escape. Beside her, Cord sat in silence. She needed those precious seconds to clear her mind and strengthen whatever was left of her will.

They hadn't gone far when Cord pulled the wagon to a halt in front of a cantina. He helped her down and they entered, and Cord greeted a plump Mexican woman, who looked up curiously from behind the bar. "I want my usual room, Rosita," he told her in a rush. "I'm leaving the señorita here. I don't know how long I'll be gone. A couple of days, maybe. I want you to make sure she stays right here."

Rosita nodded, wiping a strand of hair back from her sweaty forehead, and stepped out from behind the bar. She led the way down a dark, narrow hallway and then opened the door to a small, shadowed room at the very end of the hall. The furnishings were crude—a narrow bed with rusting iron posts, a small wooden table, and two rickety chairs. There were no windows, and only a dirt floor.

"Why are you leaving me here?" Amber cried, whirling about to face Cord.

He snapped to the Mexican woman, "Bring a bottle of tequila. See that she has food when she wants it." He watched the woman scurry away, then clutched Amber's arms, drawing her so close that she could feel his breath. "I've got to make arrangements to bury Armand, and while I'm doing all of that, I've got to make sure Valdis doesn't find you. A few more days, and you'll be out of all this."

"Let me go now," she demanded, twisting away. "I don't want your help, Cord. Can't you understand I've been through so much I can face anything?"

He whispered, "You don't have to be alone, Amber. You've suffered terribly today, and I know it hurts like hell because I've suffered the same way. But it's over. Nothing can be done about it except to grieve and...and then look to tomorrow."

She swallowed the painful lump in her throat and stared up at him with fresh tears. "Why are you doing this, Cord? Why don't you just forget about me?"

He shrugged, attempted to smile, but the effort was too much. She saw something in his eyes, something she couldn't fathom.

"Another time, another place, and you wouldn't have to ask that question, sweetheart. But right now, I can't answer it. Maybe I never will."

Brushing his lips against hers, he turned and left, locking the door behind him.

For the time being, she was alone with her memories of Armand, and her grief.

❧ Chapter Fourteen ❧

THERE was no way of knowing when night came, or morning, for in the windowless cubicle the only light came from the single lantern. She did not eat the food Rosita brought, but the tequila helped ease the pain and dim the misery.

Drunkenly, she stared up at the stains on the drooping ceiling. Cord was probably going to take her to the border and leave her there. Good. She would survive. All she wanted was to be free of Valdis and his lecherous hellishness.

Feebly, she lifted her head to take another burning swallow. The bottle was almost empty. Rosita would just have to bring another, because if she were sober she would be crying, and she didn't want to cry. Not ever again, by God.

The only real care that worked its way into her

mind was Allegra, that pitiful creature who had been so weak as to let her demonic stepson rob her of not only her material possessions but also her will. The woman was like a zombie. Whatever had he done to take away all her spirit? What could it have been? Oh, if only she could take Allegra with her to a new life!

The sound of the door being unlocked brought her to groggy awareness and she struggled to sit up, her head weighted. "Rosita?" she called, voice slurred, feeling a stabbing of remorse over having allowed herself to become so intoxicated. "Rosita, I feel sick."

But it was not Rosita's kind, anxious face that peered down at her.

"You are going to feel more than sick, bitch."

Amber shook her head wildly, the motion proving too much for her. Fangs. Maretta had fangs. And her lips were curled back, parted, as though ready to strike. She shrank back down into the thin, lumpy cot. "Go away," she whispered. "I don't want you."

"Take her!" Maretta motioned to one of two hulking men standing beside her, and they did.

"Wake up!"

Amber blinked. She felt terribly sick. Her mouth was dry, her head pounded, and her stomach was heaving precariously. Staring with bleary eyes she gasped, "Maretta! What are you doing here?" Staring quickly about, she saw that she was in an even smaller room. "This isn't the cantina."

196

Not far away, a bell clanged, and Maretta grinned. "No, you are not in the cantina. You are in the convent, where you will do penance and be exorcised of your evil spirits. The good sisters of Asmodeus are used to handling devils."

Amber reached for Maretta but felt a painful bite in each wrist. She was tightly bound by ropes, and entirely helpless. "Maretta, you can't mean to hurt me," she cried, struggling. Dear God, there had to be some way to reach this sick girl. If only she had known how disturbed Maretta really was! "You can't leave me here, Maretta."

"Oh, yes I can. You cannot be free, not now— and maybe not ever. One day, perhaps they will find you pure enough to leave, but that will be many, many years from now. You will be an old woman."

Maretta leaned closer and looked directly into Amber's face, speaking very clearly. "Never will you marry my brother and become mistress in my house. Never! Did you think to take over my home, as you took Armand? I will never let you do that, never." She finished with deadly finality, and Amber saw, too late, that Maretta had indeed been afraid of just that. She wouldn't believe that Amber only wanted to get away. No, Maretta was too desperate to see that. She believed she had no choice but to keep Amber away from Valdis, away from being mistress of the Alezparito household.

For an agonizing moment, Amber summoned all her strength and prepared to *make* Maretta understand. But just as quickly, the resolve died.

She was exhausted. And Maretta was moving away, out of the room, even as Amber opened her mouth to speak. There was no point in trying: Maretta was beyond understanding.

"Damn you!" was Maretta's parting curse. Then she was gone.

After being allowed to sleep for a few hours, the real torture began. She was taken in the dead of night to a mountain pool, where three silent nuns took turns holding her under the cold water as she struggled and thrashed. Only when drowning was imminent was she pulled to the surface, allowed to gasp for air, then pushed under again.

The purging by mountain water went on into the day, and Amber lost consciousness. There were dreams, garish nightmares of laughing black eyes, bloodied horns, blood in the sand, and Armand's death-stricken face swimming before her. She would come out of these nightmares shrieking, and the sisters of Asmodeus would murmur that the demons were leaving her.

Finally, the sisters decided she should be allowed to rest, and she was carried inside and lowered to a stone pallet, where she lost consciousness for several hours.

Amber awoke to hear herself calling Cord's name. She turned her face to the damp, musky rock wall. It was chilly, but that was the least of her pain. There were bruises all over her body, day-old rope burns on her wrists.

She heard a scurrying sound on the dirt floor but ignored it. Sleep. She wanted sleep.

Suddenly, a strange scraping sound, unlike the other noises, caused her to waken fully. Her eyes widened fearfully in the inky pit. Were they coming for her again? Oh, please, God, no, not again.

"Amber, do not be afraid."

Whose whisper? It was a woman's voice.

"It is Allegra, and Dolita. Please, whisper softly to me if you are all right."

"Yes, oh, yes!" she babbled, forcing herself up on weak, aching legs. "Yes," she hissed again.

She felt frail hands clutch her bare shoulders. Arms went about her, and she was led through the cell door, and down a dark, winding tunnel.

Once outside, she drank in the sweet night air, the air of freedom. "How did you find me?" she whispered.

"There is no time to talk." It was Dolita's voice. "We must go quickly. We have horses not too far away."

Heart pounding, Amber allowed them to help her along the rocks and through the brush, praying this was not a dream.

Allegra sensed what Amber was thinking and smiled. "It is real, my child. When Señor Hayden stormed into the ranch and accused Valdis of stealing you, I knew what had happened. I am sorry to say that several years ago, when nothing could be done with Maretta, I sent her to the convent. I thought it was a good place. But then I came to visit her, and the sisters told me I could not see her. When I told Valdis, he took some of his men

199

and we forced our way in. We found Maretta in the very cell you were in. I could only pray that was where you would be, and that we would not be caught."

Dolita grinned and lifted her skirt to reveal the knife she had strapped to her leg. "We were ready, however."

"What kind of people are those?" Amber shuddered.

"Devil-worshipers," Allegra said matter-of-factly. "I have learned that they came here from across the ocean because they were being destroyed in their own country. What law there is here leaves them alone, for they bother no one except girls whose families send them there."

"I am forever in your debt for coming after me, Allegra."

"It is time I showed some spirit. I have cowered before my stepson too long. I loved your father, and it grieves me to see how his daughter has suffered."

As they reached the tethered horses, Allegra gave brisk orders. "I will go back to the ranch and pretend I know nothing. You will go with Dolita and stay with her uncle in an Indian village. I will try to get word to Señor Hayden and let him know where you are. If I cannot, then I will find a way to get money to you, and help you get back to America."

Still astonished by the woman's courage, Amber wanted to thank her, but Allegra interrupted.

"We must separate soon, so let's hurry. Dolita will steady you while we ride, for you are very weak, child. Come! I must reach the ranch before full daylight. If I am blessed, no one will know I have been away."

With that, Allegra urged her horse forward and Dolita, grasping Amber in front of her, did the same.

❧ Chapter Fifteen ❧

INDIANS. She was going to live with Indians. Suddenly it seemed terribly important to remember all she had studied about the Mexican people and their heritage. How would they treat an American white woman? Would they even let her stay in their village? Dolita was friendly with them, of course. Maybe they would tolerate her for Dolita's sake. But she was too weary to think at all, or even to worry, so she let her mind drift while they rode.

At last, Allegra reined her horse to a stop and Amber and Dolita pulled up beside her. Beyond, through a thick grove of mahogany trees, the Alezparito ranch was visible in the early dawn. Twisting in her saddle to face them, Allegra said, "I must leave you here. Dolita, keep to the high range, out of sight."

"Allegra, it's really daylight now," Amber said worriedly. "Can you slip back inside unnoticed?"

"I will say I was out for an early morning ride. No doubt there will be suspicion"—she smiled wanly—"for I have not ventured out in so long."

"Thank you," Amber said tearfully, reaching over to clutch Allegra's hands. "Thank you. You saved my life. I just hope this is the beginning of a new life for *you*. Stand up to Valdis. Fight for your own life, as you fought for mine! Go to the law. Tell them he threatened you to make you sign over the ranch to him. Don't let him hurt you."

Suddenly a mimicking voice cracked, "Don't let him hurt you!"

Amber's heart froze. Valdis, on horseback and carrying a gun, appeared from a clump of bushes, followed by two of his men.

Allegra clutched her throat. Dolita screamed and kneed the horse, sending him crashing through the brush and out of sight. Valdis fired his gun but the two women had disappeared. "Let them go for now," he snarled, looking at Allegra. "It is you I want. Go to the house and wait for me. You have...something coming."

Peering through the bushes, Amber looked on in disbelief. Allegra lifted her chin and stared at her stepson with complete defiance. "You have beat me for the last time," she said. "You are a coward, afraid to fight the bull, but brave enough to beat a woman...*rape* a woman! Never again will you hurt me. I would rather be in my grave."

"We can arrange that," Valdis warned, pointing his gun at her.

"You cannot kill her," one of his men cautioned. "You'd be hanged. Have you gone mad?"

"Yes, he has been mad for a long, long time," Allegra said clearly. "He was mad when he came to my room and raped me, again and again, until I prayed to die!"

Amber could not believe what she was hearing, but there was no time to ponder, for Valdis shrieked, "Goddamn you! Bitch. I told you what I would do if you ever told—"

The gun exploded. Allegra fell to the ground.

Amber scrambled down off the horse and ran to kneel over Allegra's crumpled, bleeding body.

"Someone's coming," yelled one of the men. "I hear horses. Let's go!"

Valdis gave Amber a cold, dreadful smile. "I must go now to escape what my temper has caused me to do. But we *will* meet again. Run, little one. Run as far and as fast as you can, for I am going to have you one day, and when I have had my fill, I will cut your heart from your breast and eat it."

He turned and rode away, as Amber picked up her stepmother's lifeless body and cradled it, sobbing.

A few minutes later two vaqueros from the ranch thundered onto the scene, shocked and bewildered as Dolita hurriedly explained. Instructing them to report the killing to the law, she tugged at Amber's arm. "Please, señorita," she begged. "We must go. Señor Valdis could change his mind and come back for you."

Amber gently laid Allegra on the ground, then touched her eyelids to close them. Whispering a prayer for peace over the woman who had known such misery, she hurried to Allegra's horse and mounted. She and Dolita would need two horses. "What about Cord?" she asked. "How will he know where to find me?"

"We will worry about that later. Now we must go."

Amber moved her horse to follow Dolita, and when they reached the top of a rise, turned to look back. The men were lifting Allegra's body to take her home.

For Allegra, the misery was over.

❧ Chapter Sixteen ❧

THE utter desolation of the desert began without warning and went on forever. Sand and cactus spread to the mountains beyond, as far as the eye could see.

It was hot and still, and Amber felt sweat trickling from her forehead and burning into her eyes. There were deep arroyos that filled with rushing water after the infrequent rains, but were now dry, leaving only sand and gravel. And dust, endless dust.

Eventually they reached the mountains, which were covered with chaparral, pine, and firs that managed to grow in the rocky soil. Behind them lay the yucca, paloverde, and century plants of the dry washes. Willow and cottonwood trees shaded the saltbushes of the alkali sinks where once there had been water.

The higher they went, the cooler the breezes among the firs. But then, as the land dipped downward, the air was stifling again. Tall, steep cliffs ringed each side of the trail.

"And you said it was only a few hours' ride," Amber sighed.

Dolita smiled sympathetically. "You are not as good a rider as you thought, señorita, and you are weak. We are moving slowly, for I have seen how tired you are. But do not be ashamed, for those of gentle birth seldom learn to ride well."

"Then I will just have to learn," Amber retorted with an unladylike snort. Gentle birth, indeed!

"I just hope we can get word to Cord," she said after a while. "How much farther is it?"

"Just over that ridge." Dolita pointed.

After a few more minutes, they topped the ridge. Below them sprawled a dozen small clay and stone buildings. Rickety wooden fences surrounded each. Cactus spotted the wide span of sand, and a desert breeze blew balls of dancing tumbleweed down the trail before them.

They had been spotted long before they topped the ridge, and word had spread. Indian men stopped working in the fields beyond to stare curiously and small, dark-skinned children with wide, gaping eyes peered out from behind their mothers' skirts.

Amber stared back, taking everything in. This was truly another world. Thank heaven Dolita could speak their language.

Dolita spoke, reining in her horse. "You have no reason to fear these people. They are peaceful."

"The women are dressed so beautifully," Amber mused, more to herself than to her companion. "I suppose I expected buckskin and feathers."

Dolita smiled, pleased. "Both the Cora and Huichol tribes believe that a fine costume raises one's standings with the gods."

They rode on slowly down the slope to the village. Chickens scattered in front of them as they moved down the main street of the little village. Hogs rooted in the yards, and goats and cows milled about.

A soft sobbing sound caught their attention, and they looked to the right, to where a group of children were gathered in a circle. The sobbing came from the middle of that circle, rising above the taunting shouts of the other children. Amber pushed through the cluster and found a little boy about seven down on his hands and knees, face streaked with tears and mud. His filthy clothes were hardly more than rags. He looked up at Amber, first in fright, then with hostility, as his eyes became darker, angrier.

Amber held out her hand to him, but he continued to regard her warily. "Okay," she said to him gently.

She looked at the children, admonishing them with her gaze, assuming they did not understand Spanish but asking anyway, "What were you doing to him?"

Amber didn't even ask herself why she had gone toward the circle of children, or why she refused to watch the little boy being taunted. Perhaps it was the haunting presence of Armand, so recently gone, so cruelly killed. Perhaps it was Allegra's bravery before Valdis. It was probably all those feelings gathering around her; forcing her to take the child's hand in a firm grip and lead him away from the others.

By the time Amber seated herself on the ground, a few feet from her horse, the boy had lost his hostile look. But he was wary, watching her carefully, never taking his gaze from her face.

Dolita hurried over. She gasped. "Señorita. What are you doing with...with the bastard?"

"What are you talking about?" Amber asked stiffly, holding the child tightly. "Can you find his mother, Dolita?"

Dolita suddenly looked frightened. "He has no mama," she answered quickly, nervously. She died in birth. It was just as well, for she was treated much worse than this little one. She brought much disgrace upon the tribe."

Amber looked at her hard. "You mean to tell me this little boy has no mother? Who takes care of him?"

Dolita bit down on her lip, and, for an instant, Amber thought she was going to cry. Avoiding Amber's gaze, she murmured, "The padre looks after him when he can, but he is old and sick. The boy sleeps in the mission. He is given food. You must not concern yourself with him, señorita. He lives with his shame. He knows this."

The child tried to pull from Amber's grasp, but she held him tightly as she stared up at Dolita and cried, "That is the most barbaric thing I have ever heard. How can the padre allow such a thing to go on? It isn't this child's fault he was conceived out of wedlock. Who is the father? Does he even know he has a son?"

Dolita turned tear-filled eyes upon her. Amber had never seen the girl so overwrought. Gesturing wildly with her hands, she said, "His father is dead. We must go now. You must not concern yourself."

"Dolita, what is wrong?" Amber searched her face for some clue. "I've never seen you like this."

Dolita whispered, "Señorita, we must leave. Do not interfere with custom. You will only bring more trouble for the boy."

Then, so suddenly it caught Amber off-guard, Dolita screamed at the boy, waving her arms wildly. He bolted, running away, disappearing around a nearby shed.

"Oh, why did you do that, Dolita?" Amber got to her feet, trembling with fury. "What is wrong with you? I have never known you to be cruel!"

Dolita lifted her chin in defiance. "There are things you do not understand. Come, please. I want you to meet my uncle, señorita. I have tied our horses behind his hut."

Amber followed silently, vowing to ask Dolita more questions later.

Dolita's uncle was polite to Amber, respectful and distant. When he and Dolita had established that the two women could stay in his home, he bade Amber a polite welcome and the two left him. When they were out of his hearing, Dolita said, "Valdis was here some years ago... and two of the children disappeared. My uncle is afraid. The rest of the village will be afraid of us too, of our being here, for if Valdis finds us here it will go hard for them. They know this. Valdis is well known for a great distance around."

Amber sighed. Until Cord could be reached, they would have to stay here. But she hated bringing danger to these people.

"Tell your uncle I don't wish to bring trouble," Amber said quickly. "I don't want to stay here any longer than necessary. Make him see that."

She stared into the gathering dusk. No, she did not want to be here long. Cord Hayden would help. He had to.

Chapter Seventeen

DOLITA looked up at the ominous black clouds, moving like giant hands to consume the azure sky. "I do not like it," she said worriedly. "Flash floods through these deep arroyos can be deadly."

"We had to go today," Amber told her as their horses picked their way along the rocky trail. "We'd been there for almost a week. I have to know what's going on, whether Valdis has been arrested, and if I can get a message to Cord."

"I know, I know," Dolita sighed. "But I wish you had waited one more day. I do not like the looks of those clouds. Let us hurry. I will leave you on high ground while I go down to see if Señor Mendosa's housekeeper is still living in his house. If anyone would know where Señor Hayden is, it would be Jualina."

They rode for a ways in silence, and then Amber

spoke sadly, "I just can't get over the way that child is treated. Why would his own people be so cruel?"

Dolita was silent, and Amber turned to look at her. "Dolita, I have the impression you are hiding something. I've felt that way since I saw the child."

"No, no, señorita," Dolita said quickly.

There *was* something going on. Dolita was frightened, and Amber determined to find out why.

Dolita finally murmured, "The boy does not speak. The elder ones say he is cursed."

"You mean he can't talk? I thought he was just scared of me."

Dolita shook her head. "No one has ever heard him."

Amber persisted. "But surely, there is some medical reason. He might be cured, and—"

"Oh, señorita, I wish you would not concern yourself. You do not understand the ways of these people."

"Then perhaps you would like to explain 'the ways,'" Amber said, bristling.

After a long silence, Dolita nodded. "I will try to explain to you. As you probably know, Mexicans are a new race, offspring of the Conquistadores who bred with the Indian women so very long ago. The Indians were Aztecs or Mayans or Tlaxcalans. The Conquistadores just took what they wanted. The sons they sired grew up to hate them—as did their mothers! The conquerors looked on their mixed-blood offspring as worthless animals. They bragged of their own, pure Castilian blood. As the years passed, the offspring also began to brag of their Spanish blood, dismissing their dark Indian skin as the stain of the tropic sun. Those of Spanish blood, born in 'new Spain,' scorned the lowly mestizos."

"Very well, I understand about the Spanish blood." Amber was exasperated. "But what does all this have to do with that little boy being persecuted? It sounds as though there were a great many bastards in the days when the Conquistadores were raping women."

"I am coming to that," Dolita said sharply. "But we must move faster. The first drops of rain are starting. There is a cave up ahead. We may have to seek refuge there, for it is not safe to be in the arroyo if it rains hard."

They urged their horses onward, finally reaching the safety of the cave in a jagged cliff near a deep arroyo. Just as they got inside, the sky opened and rain began falling in torrents.

"It is going to be bad," Dolita said as they sat down in the cave. "I have seen these storms, and when they come so quickly, they are bad."

Amber leaned back against the cool earth wall. "There is nothing we can do about the weather, so please finish your story."

"Very well." Dolita sighed. "You see, señorita, with so much mixed blood, it has become great pride to any tribe to remain pure, free of Spanish blood. The village of Cora Indians are such a group of people. It is their law that neither man nor woman mate outside their race. Condina, the little muchacho's mama, broke the law. She was not a whore. She only loved someone not of her people.

I know this because my uncle told me the story. But her love broke the law, and it was a shame on the Coras."

"So why didn't she marry the man if she loved him?" Amber wanted to know.

"He was of another race. Mexican."

"But Mexicans are actually a race originally mixed with Indians," Amber cried incredulously. "So he was part Indian, wasn't he?"

"Not by Cora code," Dolita said. "The Coras consider themselves to be pure. The Mexican race is not pure." Amber looked exasperated, but Dolita merely shrugged. "It is the way people think, señorita. As the story was told, Condina did not tell her lover she was going to have a baby. He had never come to her, she had always slipped away to see him. He must have known—as she did—that their union could never be, and when she did not go to him anymore, he probably thought she had fallen in love with one of her own, and thought it best."

"So her people hated her?" Amber felt so tired. How she hated rigidity, customs that caused misery. "They probably *let* her die in childbirth."

"No, no," Dolita remarked quickly. "Her heart broke. That is what the shaman said."

"And what is a shaman?" Amber didn't mask her contempt, for she suddenly found herself disliking anything to do with Indian ways.

"The shaman of any tribe is very important, because he has a knowledge of sickness, sickness of body or soul. The Cora shaman was with Condina at her time, and said she died of a broken heart before her baby was born. The baby had to be cut from her body, and he almost died, too. It would have been better if he had," she said matter-of-factly.

"But where is the father? Wasn't he told? Why didn't he come and take the baby? Was he married? Or was he ashamed because he had fathered a baby by an Indian?"

Dolita was silent for a long time, and there was no sound except for the relentless pounding of the rain. Finally, she decided a hedging reply was better than none. "If he knew, then he also knew the Coras would not allow him to take his son. *If* he knew, he did the wise thing by staying away. The Coras are peaceful people, but they might have become violent had he tried to take the baby."

"Oh! They would keep the child and torment him rather than give him up? I don't think I have ever seen a group of people who needed educating more than they do!"

"I think," Dolita finally said after watching her warily for a time, "you should forget about the boy. He is used to his life. He expects nothing more."

"Well, he is going to *get* more," Amber said with more fiery determination than she had ever felt before.

Dolita was silent.

After a time, she said "The rain is slowing. There has not been enough to cause a flood, and I think we can go. We may still get wet, but it is better than spending the night here. This cave may be a shelter for wild animals." She and Amber walked back to where the horses had wandered, farther back in the cave.

They mounted and rode out and into the slow, cool drizzle.

It was nearly dark when Dolita's scream interrupted Amber's reverie, and they saw two riders thundering toward them down the arroyo.

"Bandits!" Dolita crossed herself, and Amber jerked her mount to a halt. Every instinct told her to turn and run. But the men were faster than her horse could ever be. In a moment, they were upon them and Amber found herself staring up into the mocking face of Valdis Alezparito.

He threw his right leg up and over his saddle, landing solidly on the ground. Tipping back the wide brim of his sombrero, he placed his hands on his hips, legs wide apart, and flashed a triumphant grin up at Amber. She froze.

"Tell me," he laughed above Dolita's screams, "did you know I would be coming this way? Did you plan your journey so that we could meet?"

His grin was so infuriating that Amber's fear was overwhelmed by anger. "Stay away from me, Valdis," she hissed, gripping her reins tightly. She nodded toward Dolita, who was struggling with the other man. "And tell him to leave her alone."

He continued to grin up at her. "It is amusing that while the law looks for me, I look for you. Now I have found you! I promised you something when we met again, so come down off your horse now. I wish to make good on my promise. There is a cave not too far from here, where we can be dry and cozy."

He took a step forward, and Amber yanked the reins, jerking the horse so that he reared in the air, thrashing wildly. Valdis lunged and grabbed the reins, pressing his weight on the horse's neck as he brought him down and under control. Then, as Amber beat at him with her hands, he jerked her from the saddle and flung her to the ground.

"I tell you this," he vowed, eyes wide as he towered above her, "this night I shall have you. I offered you wealth, power, as my wife, but you thought you were too good for me. Now I will take you like the slut that you are."

Amber rolled to one side, but Valdis brought one booted foot down to stomp upon her streaming silver hair. She cried with pain as she tried to pull away.

"I think I will have to hurt you to make you obey me," he said, grabbing a handful of hair and twisting it, forcing her up onto her knees. Bending her neck back, he leaned over her face and said, "You will go with me to the cave. We will build a fire, for I want to see you naked in the firelight. I have waited a long time for this. You will dance for me. You will pleasure me in a hundred ways that I will teach you. And when tomorrow comes, you will beg not to leave me. You will want to stay with me and be my whore, as you might have been my wife."

"You cowardly son of a bitch, I won't go anywhere with you," Amber bellowed in rage. "I would rather die than have you touch me."

She saw only a flash of steel before she felt the knife pressed against her throat; felt the sting as the razor-sharp edge cut into the soft flesh ever so lightly. "You may get your wish, but only after you have pleased me. I shall make you want to die!"

His breath was hot and sour. She could feel a stickiness trickling down from the cut on her throat. She could not move.

Valdis and Gerras took the women to the cave, Gerras guarding them while Valdis handled the horses. When they arrived, Gerras dragged Dolita off to help him search for firewood, for anything dry enough to burn. Valdis took a bottle from his saddlebag and tilted it to his lips. Once, he saw Amber watching and held out the bottle. "You want a drink to get you in a good mood?"

Amber sank back against the cave wall, hoping her blazing eyes transmitted her message of hate.

"Ahhh, but you shall beg for a drink before long," he chuckled, tilting the bottle again. "You will want to drink to give you strength to keep up with me, for I will show you what it is like to have a real man take you. Armand Mendosa was no real man. He gave what strength he had to the bulls, and look what happened to him!" His laughter was infuriating.

"Tell me," he taunted. "What was it like with Armand? Did he say 'please' when he wanted to touch your breasts? Did he ask your permission to spread your thighs? He was such a gentleman, was he not?"

When Amber remained silent, he went to her and, cupping her chin, whispered, "After tonight, no other man will hold any interest for you. You will want only me...love only me. If you pleasure me, then we will be together always."

He knelt before her, his tone suddenly gentle, his eyes mellowed. "I tell you this. I have yearned for you since first I saw you, but not always in the way that you think. If I had"—he jerked his head toward the outside of the cave—"I would have taken you as Gerras is taking that one. I want to give you and I wish more from you."

He trailed his fingertips gently down her cheek, but she jerked her head away and he gasped angrily. "Never turn from me again, you little fool! Do you not understand what I am trying to tell you? I am in love with you! Do you hear me?" Amber continued to stare at him, her face unreadable. A shadow crossed his eyes. "Do not make me angry. I have told you of the feelings I have for you, but do not make me lose my temper. You have seen what happens when I lose my temper."

Slowly Amber ran her fingers through her hair, shaking it about to swing freely about her face. She was stalling him, knowing she needed to catch him off his guard. She had seen what she needed— the glint of steel as the knife slipped from his boot and fell into the dirt. Gauging the distance from herself to the knife, she reached for it while pretending simply to allow Valdis to embrace her. As he kissed her, her hand touched the cold steel, fingers inching around the handle. There would be one chance and only one. If she failed, he would kill her.

Just as she brought her arm down in a swinging arc, Gerras and Dolita entered and Gerras screamed a warning. Valdis twisted to the side, and the blade missed the back of his neck, plunging instead into the flesh of his shoulder.

Amber felt the sickening thud as steel sliced into muscle, and Valdis fell away from her, falling backward, clutching his shoulder as blood streamed out of it. Amber wriggled from beneath him, screaming to Dolita, "Run!"

Valdis was swaying to and fro on his knees, blood gushing down his arm to pour from his fingers. His face was twisted in pain and shock.

"I will kill the whore!" Gerras bellowed, but by then, Amber and Dolita were almost to the mouth of the cave.

"No!" Valdis cried to Gerras. "Help me before I bleed to death."

"But she will get away!" Gerras hesitated, looking from his bleeding partner to the women disappearing into the night.

"The wound is deep," Valdis told him. "It bleeds badly. You must make a fire quickly. Take the knife and stick it into the fire, then to the wound. Make a fire from anything you can—anything."

Gerras stared at him.

"Do it, goddamnit! You want to watch me bleed to death? I will deal with her later. The cut is deep. You must do as I say. Hurry! Burn anything, even our clothing if you must.

Gerras did as he was told, and when the steel had turned white with heat, he looked at Valdis with pity.

"Do it!" Valdis gritted his teeth.

Amber pulled Dolita along in the darkness. Rain had begun again, in a steady pattering downpour. They felt their hair plastered to their faces, but

Dolita did not care. She hoped the rain would wash all the way through her skin into her soul to cleanse and purify, for she wondered if she would ever feel clean again.

Dolita sobbed, "I do not know the way in the dark. We must reach the high country and hide in the brush. It is our only hope."

Dolita was close to fainting, and Amber understood why the girl could not run as fast as she could. Several times they fell, tumbling over and over, desperate to reach the high ground. Amber kept Dolita's hand clutched in hers, dragging her sometimes until Dolita cried out, "Look! An old coyote den!"

Lightning split the sky, lighting a hollowed-out hole behind some scrub brush.

"The hills are full of dens like these," Dolita told her. "They can't know which one we hide in. Hurry. We can pull the brush in front and lie very still."

Amber started to ask what they would do if coyotes came home for the night, then kept still. She scrambled inside, Dolita right behind.

Once they were inside, Dolita began to cry. "Mother of God, when I think what he did to me I want to die."

There was nothing Amber could do but say firmly, "It's over, and we're alive, Dolita. Think only of that."

Amber leaned back against the wet earth. Closing her eyes, she suddenly saw warm brown eyes, and she cried softly, "Cord! We have to get to Armand's house and try to find Cord. It's our only hope now."

"At first light," Dolita whispered wearily, painfully, "we will go."

Amber closed her eyes once again, this time praying that she would find Cord, and praying also that the old familiar dream would come to her in her misery and comfort her.

❧ Chapter Eighteen ❧

A T last morning came, a gray mist hanging over the desert like sorrow, to bring back all of the night just past.

Amber supported Dolita as they stumbled out of the den into the clawing chill of dawn. "Just tell me the way," Amber said. "I will get us there if I have to crawl there and carry you on my back." She was fired with a greater determination than she had ever possessed.

Dolita lifted her head suddenly and pointed. "Over the next rise," she cried softly. "Armand Mendosa's house!"

Amber hurried to scramble through the brush and peer down into the valley. There was a large, sprawling house surrounded by rolling green pastures. There was no sign of anyone there.

"We are going to have to walk down there in

these rags," she told Dolita. "If you'd rather not, I'll go first and come back with clothes for you."

"I don't think anything else can shame me," Dolita responded dully. "Let us go."

They made their way down the steep slope, sliding now and then, sometimes falling. By the time they reached the whitewashed railings around the house, Jualina had spotted them from the kitchen window. She ran to them, screaming and waving her arms. The question burning in Amber's heart burst forth. "Jualina, is Cord Hayden still here?" She held her breath and waited.

"I do not know," said the woman.

Amber grabbed her and shook her, control suddenly gone. "What do you mean?" she cried. "Is he or isn't he living here?"

"I do not know," Jualina repeated, eyes wide. "I have not seen him in two, maybe three days. He says nothing to me, just comes and goes. One day, I think he will leave and not come back. Perhaps he has done so this time."

"But where does he go when he leaves?" Amber demanded, hysteria bubbling in her throat. "Surely, you know something. We have to find him, Jualina. He's our only hope."

Jualina turned to Dolita and they began conversing in their own, more familiar dialect. Amber wandered off into the main part of the house, going from room to room, absently marveling at the beautiful furnishings. All these things had belonged to Armand. Armand! She felt closer to him here...and grieved for him all over again.

Dolita came to find her, standing in the master

bedroom, lovingly fingering Armand's silk dressing robe.

"Jualina says he may come back," she said hesitantly, sorry to be intruding on her reverie. "He has not taken his clothes. But then, who knows whether he will come back. Jualina says he was always a strange one, and since Señor Mendosa died, he has been even stranger."

Amber said nothing.

"Come," Dolita touched her shoulder. "Jualina has prepared food. We are both weak."

Amber followed her into the dining room, where Jualina had laid out platters of hastily fried sausages and boiled eggs. Amber forced herself to eat, then asked Jualina if she would help her with baths for herself and Dolita. She felt, rather than saw, Dolita's grateful look.

"I will help you both," Jualina said quickly. "Dolita has told me everything, señorita. I am so sorry. I will do anything I can to help."

An hour later, wrapped in a thick towel, Amber lay down on Armand's bed and allowed sleep to take her away.

The dream came again, and she welcomed it wholly, for the man who held her was no longer a stranger. She smiled up into Cord's deep, warm eyes. He was the one she had been seeking, and found, and lost.

"Love me," she whispered in her sleep. "Please, Cord, love me."

"I do love you. I always have."

The dream was so real, she hoped never to awaken. But then her eyes were open and she saw

Cord lying beside her, his arms about her, his lips brushing hers, and she knew it was not a dream. "You're here," she whispered hoarsely. "It's real. I'm not dreaming."

"No, but I think *I* am," he laughed softly, kissing her all over her face. "Oh, Amber, how I've searched for you. I thought I'd lost you forever." He held her to him as tightly as he dared.

She told him everything, and felt him tense with fury and fear. When she had finished, and he had asked her all he needed to, he kissed her again and then, slowly and tantalizingly, began to run his hands downward, pulling away her towel to expose her nakedness completely. He rolled to one side, sliding his knee between her thighs. Gently, he began to manipulate his fingers between her legs, knowing where to touch, where to caress, and Amber felt fire coursing through her body. Her pelvis tightened, contracted, as she surrendered to the undulations sweeping through her.

It was the old dream, her secret self budding. No longer would she awaken wondering at the meaning of illusions, for illusion had become reality. In Cord's arms she had found her dream.

Still rhythmically stroking, Cord raised his head to gaze down at her and smile. "We loved each other all along, Amber, but we got sidetracked. Later, there is something I've got to tell you about me—my past, why I was so afraid to love. I'm still afraid, but right now, this is what we both need."

He spread her thighs, bending her knees, and positioned himself between. Clutching her tiny waist, he thrust himself inside her, and she gasped as the last shred of her innocence was taken.

"All of me," she whimpered, wrapping her arms about his broad back to pull him closer. "Take all of me, Cord."

"I will, honey, I will," he panted, "and I'll give you all of me."

She felt the explosion coming from deep within to spread like a hand of fire. Her cry of delight was so intense that Cord covered her mouth with his, lest the other women in the house hear. Then he took himself on to ultimate glory, filling her with the hot flow of love.

She lay beside him in wonder; gratified, fulfilled. "It is everything I thought it would be," she whispered, her fingertips touching his lips. Then painful memory shot through her, and she murmured, "It seems a sacrilege to be lying here, in Armand's bed."

"I think he would laugh about it. He laughed at a lot of things, you know. Death was one of them."

He stroked her belly. "How soon will you feel up to traveling? I'd like to head for the border as soon as possible. I'd like to settle my score with Valdis, but it's more important to get you away from here."

"But I can't leave yet," Amber told him quickly. "I have to tell you something, Cord. Dolita and I hid in the Indian village where her uncle lives. There's a little boy there. Oh, Cord, it's horrible." She went on to explain, then stopped as she saw the grim expression on his face.

"What is it, Cord?" She sat up to stare at him. "Why are you looking at me like that? I want to go back to the village and get him, take him away and love him."

"No, Amber. Leave him," he said. "Some things are better left alone and this is one of them. You can't interfere."

"But—" she started.

"His father was a Mexican. I know the story." He got up and began pulling his clothes together. "You aren't going back there. We're leaving first thing in the morning."

"Cord, don't tell me what to do! I won't be bossed around by you or anybody and—"

"The boy is Armand's son."

She stared, uncomprehending. "You...you aren't serious. Armand would never father a child and abandon him."

"Armand didn't know." He turned and looked at her. "The only reason I know is because he told me about an Indian girl he had loved. They sneaked around for about six months, and then all of a sudden, she just quit coming to see him. He didn't dare go to her village, because he knew it would mean trouble for her. He never knew she was going to have a baby, never knew she died. He just thought she dropped him because they could never marry."

"But how did *you* know there was a baby?" she asked indignantly.

"I was in a bar one night, and a drunk was mouthing off about Armand's bastard. I asked a few questions and started putting two and two together. No one ever said anything to Armand.

They didn't dare. Nobody wanted to get tangled up in that mess. Had he known, he would have gone after the kid, and it wouldn't have worked out. The Indians might even have killed him. So I never told him. I figured if it was meant for him to know, he'd find out sooner or later.

"You have to understand something about Armand," he went on, calmer now. "He was a romantic sort, and he fancied himself in love with lots of women. That's the reason I never took the courtship between you two seriously. I figured it was another one of his great romances, and that you were so desperate you were grabbing for anyone who would protect you.

"Besides," he added, grinning down at her, "I knew what was going on inside me, and I could feel the same thing happening to you. We were both fighting it, but we were falling in love."

She shook her head in wonder, then asked, "You said you were afraid to love. You were going to tell me why."

He frowned. "I don't think the time is right. One day, I'll tell you. For now, just understand when I say that I've made up my mind I'm going home and clear up a big misunderstanding. I'm no coward when it comes to defending myself and those I love and believe in, but I must admit to a fear of my own self. It's time I put fear behind me. I'm ready to go home. And you're going with me." He gave her a nod, then got up and moved to the door. "I'm going to tell Jualina to get some clothes together for you. We can buy a few things once we cross the border. And don't worry about Dolita. I'll talk to her. She can come with us or go back

231

to her uncle's village. I think she'd be safe there."

He left her, and Amber lay back to stare up at the ceiling. She could not leave the boy, especially now that she knew he was Armand's son. Why, he was all that was left of Armand. And he was helpless. She knew she would never give herself a moment's peace if she did not take that poor child from his miserable existence—Armand's son or not.

Dolita reacted happily to the news from Cord. She said to Amber, "Señor Cord is a beautiful man, and if you let your heart go, he will make you very happy."

Amber smiled at Dolita but said nothing.

All the rest of that afternoon, Amber lay in Armand's bed, her mind floating from sleep to wakefulness, her thoughts moving from Valdis to Allegra, from Armand to the child he never knew he had, and from the cruelly leering Gerras to Dolita's frightened face. At last, she allowed herself to think of Cord, to admit all she felt for him, to know how terribly she would long for him if they were parted again.

But they would be parted. This she knew. For Cord would not, perhaps could not, understand what she felt about the little bastard boy. There wasn't any point in trying to explain. She would simply have to go and take the child. Maybe she would meet up with Valdis on the way, or maybe she would be lucky for a change. But whatever the consequences, she would not ride across the border with Cord unless Armand's child was there, too. She wouldn't. She just couldn't.

Amber tossed fitfully. It meant lying to Cord and sneaking away from the ranch by herself. It meant running—again, and being alone just when she had found her love.

Maretta Alezparito clenched her teeth until her jaws ached. "You are telling the truth?" she asked of the old farmer who stood before her, head bowed as he twisted his straw hat in his gnarled, wrinkled hands.

"I tell the truth," he told her. "I heard you were offering a reward to anyone who could tell you the whereabouts of the American señorita. I saw her with a Mexican girl creeping in the brush along the ridge above Señor Mendosa's hacienda. Señor Mendosa's servant came out to wave, and they ran to her, and she took them inside."

"You have done well." Maretta let out her breath in satisfaction, then snapped her fingers and one of the vaqueros guarding her stepped forward. "Pay him," she ordered. "This is the information I have been waiting for."

The vaqueros took the old man outside, and Maretta whirled around the room in jubilation. She had known that, sooner or later, someone would spot the bitch. Now she would have her revenge. This time her simpering mother was not around to come to Amber's aid.

Her mother. Despite their mutual dislike, Maretta felt sadness at her death. And she believed Valdis was telling the truth. Someone else had killed Allegra and blamed Valdis. True, Valdis had done many ruthless things, but to shoot his stepmother in cold blood? No. It was not possible.

She would be glad when he found the real murderer and returned home to clear his name. Until then, she would do her best to keep the ranch running smoothly.

She smiled slyly. Valdis was going to be quite angry when he learned how she had dealt with the lawyers, arranging to buy the Mendosa land from Armand's estate for herself, for now she owned important property. No longer would he dictate to her! For the first time in her life, she had a position of power, and she intended to use it.

But first, she had to avenge Armand's death, and the moment was at hand. She rang for a guard and gave him a message, then retired. She wanted to be rested, to savor every moment of her new life.

🕸 Chapter Nineteen 🕸

AMBER told Cord she was resting in prepa-
ration for their long trip. Kissing her deeply,
he smiled and said he had much to do, gathering
the belongings he would take on the pack mule
that would accompany them. There would be time
for loving later. It might shock Jualina, he said,
if they slept together that night, so he went to his
own room.

Amber cried, hating to lie to him this way. She
sat in a chair before a window in Armand's room
watching the sky change from brilliant cerulean
to pale apricot, then ashen and pink, and finally
to darkest ebony. She breathed a sigh of relief as
the moon rose, casting a pearly glow all over the
night. She would need that light.

At last, it was late enough. Cord would be in
bed. The house was still. She dressed and made

her way stealthily to the room where Dolita was sleeping. Awakening her, she warned her not to make a sound, then told her, "Hurry and get dressed. We are leaving."

"I do not understand," Dolita protested.

"I'll explain later. Please, Dolita. Hurry. We've got to make our way in the dark. I'll go and get two horses ready. Meet me in the stable."

Within moments, Dolita was hurrying into the stable to where Amber waited with the bridled horses. There had not been time for saddles.

"Now tell me why you have gone mad," Dolita demanded harshly. "Why are you running away from Señor Cord when you love him? When he loves you?"

Amber looked at her accusingly, for surely Dolita had known the truth all along. "I know who's the father of that little boy."

"How...how did you find out?" she gasped, crossing herself. "Mother of God, who would tell you such a thing? Señor Hayden? But how did he know?"

"He knew. He never told Armand, so Armand didn't know. But I know, and now I'm going back there and get that child."

"No, no." She shook her head wildly. "They would never let you take him. Even though he is despised, he is part of their tribe, and they would never allow him to leave."

Amber mounted her horse. "They aren't going to know about it till it's too late. I'll take my time, pretend to be hiding there. They will let me stay. When the time is right, I'll do it. I must, for Armand...and for the child's sake."

"But Señor Cord is going to be furious," Dolita protested, waving her arms. "You cannot do this."

"I'm doing it. Now, please, tell me if you're coming with me."

After a moment's hesitation Dolita mounted. "Very well. If this is what you insist upon, then I have no choice but to obey you. You did not desert me last night. You may have saved my life. I will help you—but I still think you are mad."

They moved cautiously, waiting until they were a safe distance from the house before prodding their horses into a trot. The ground beneath was rough and covered with small rocks, making sharp chipping sounds as the hooves rhythmically touched down. Turning her face against the cool night wind to look at Dolita, she saw that the girl looked frightened. "Please," Amber whispered, stretching to give her arm a reassuring pat. "It's going to be all right. Really."

Dolita said nothing, but her expression was grim. It would take time to get to the village, and it was very dark despite the moonlight. Many things could happen.

They entered a narrow arroyo. Cactus and scrub brush growing above on the mountainside blotted out the moonlight in patches now and then, causing them to fall into total darkness.

Suddenly, a shrill cry split the silence, and Dolita gasped and reined her horse to a sudden stop.

"Dolita, it's a coyote," Amber called softly. "Or some other wild animal. And it was a long way off."

"Not a wild animal. Not a long way off." Dolita

peered into the shadows, trembling. "It was a human—and not human."

"Human and not human?" Amber laughed nervously. "Really, Dolita, there's nothing to be afraid of."

Realizing that Amber was not slowing down, Dolita kneed her horse on.

They rounded a bend...and froze. Ahead, illuminated by the ghostly crimson glow of a torch, was the bloody dripping head of a cockerel, nailed to a crude wooden cross. The silent breeze gently ruffled its feathers. Dolita crossed herself, but Amber could only stare, transfixed.

Concentrating solely on the cross, the women did not see the two faces watching them from the ridge above, faces painted blood red, wide white circles drawn about the eyes and downward to circle noses and mouths.

✾ Chapter Twenty ✾

MARETTA closed her eyes and lifted the glass to her lips, draining the contents in one long swallow.

She was only mildly startled to hear the soft clink as the fresh carafe of sangría touched the rim of the bathtub, and she didn't bother to look around. This maid was so much more obedient and attentive than that stupid Dolita, she thought with satisfaction. Here she sat in her wonderful tub, the girl hovering nearby to make sure her glass was kept full.

"You are a good servant," Maretta sighed, taking another long sip. "You fulfill my every desire."

"Every desire, sweetheart?" a masculine voice growled. "There are a few things servant girls can't do for you."

Maretta sat up, water sloshing over the sides

of the tub. "Cord!" she cried, staring wide-eyed at the handsome, smiling face above her. "What are you doing here? How did you get in the house? I have guards—"

"Your guards aren't very efficient," he drawled. "They drink tequila and fall asleep. I had no difficulty crawling up to your balcony once it got dark."

Maretta smiled. "Will you share my drink...and my bath?"

"Both invitations are too good to turn down," Cord said with a grin. He unbuttoned his shirt and jerked it off, and Maretta shivered at the sight of his broad, muscular chest.

He unbuckled his belt, unfastened his trousers, then stepped out of them and kicked them out of the way. He wore nothing beneath.

He stepped over the rim of the tub and lowered himself in, spreading his legs and bending his knees so that Maretta was encircled within his legs. Drawing his feet closer, her own legs became entwined about him, and she could feel his stiffening shaft against her thighs. The warm, encompassing water lent a dreamlike quality to the encounter.

She leaned forward, eyes half-closed, and wrapped her arms around his neck as she pressed her oil-slick breasts against his chest. "Cord, *mi amante*," she whispered huskily, her tongue flicking out to trace his lips. "How I have missed you! So many nights I have lain awake remembering how you held me, touched me, set me on fire. I was afraid you would not come to me ever again."

He reached to cup her face with one strong hand, bringing his lips down to claim her mouth. His voice was husky. "Did you think I could ever turn my back on what we had?"

"Oh, Cord! Cord!" She began covering his face with kisses, her fingers grasping his hair and holding him closer. "How I adore you! Never have I wanted a man as I want you!"

His hands moved to slide down her back, to cup her buttocks and press her firmly against him. His swollen member slipped between her thighs, and he rode her against him without penetration. She began whimpering as the delightful sensations rippled through her. "I was here a couple of nights ago," he whispered as he continued to drive her toward frenzy, "but you weren't here."

"Oh, Cord," she begged frantically, her fingernails digging into the firm flesh of his back. "Take me, please take me now."

He grinned. "We've got lots of time, sweetheart. You'll be begging me to stop before this night ends. Now, I want to know where you went that night. Who's the new man in your life, eh? Who's trying to steal you from me?" He began to thrust his hips upward, driving himself even more tantalizingly between her thighs. "I know I haven't been around much lately, but I've had things to do. I promised Armand I'd look after Amber, but she took off before I could send her back to the States. I've just been so busy. So tell me who's moved in to try and take my place."

"Oh, no one, no one...." she moaned, barely able to speak over the trembling waves of heat in her body. "No one, I swear it. You are the only one for me, forever and always. Oh, how I love you...want you—need you."

"Tell me who he is, Maretta," he whispered as he undulated his hips. "You don't get what you want till I get what I want. That's the way this game is played."

She raised her face to look at him with eyes that mirrored anguish...as well as deep lust. "I was not with a man that night, Cord. You must believe me. Oh, please, please believe me."

Cord clamped his hands on her thighs, holding them still, preventing her from moving. "You're going to tell me where you went that night," he whispered. "Or it's over. Start talking."

"It was not what you think, Cord. Believe me. I did not sleep with a man. It was...business, about the ranch. Please."

"Business!" He spat in disgust. "You expect me to believe that?" He gave her a rough shake that sent more water splashing over the tub rim. "Tell me, Maretta. Did your business have anything to do with Amber and Dolita's disappearance?"

"Oh, why do you care about that slut?" she cried. "Cord. Forget her."

"Not until you tell me where you took them."

Desperate, she told him everything. While she talked, Cord realized she was telling the truth. He asked slowly, cautiously, his mouth moving slowly over hers. "Who helped?"

"Puetas," she gasped, trembling. "I know him only as Puetas."

Cord swore. He knew he should get up, dry himself, dress, and leave. But he couldn't quite make himself do it. He felt the desire still within him, and with one swift movement, he pulled her legs upward and entered her. In just a few moments, he took them both to sweet release.

Cord reached the squat structure where he remembered Puetas bunked and peered inside. It was dark. He stood perfectly still as moments ticked by, wanting to make sure there was no movement within. When he was sure the Mexican cowboy was asleep, he moved to the door.

It opened with a squeak, and Cord knew Puetas was instantly awake and fumbling for his gun. Cord lunged across the room for the bed and grabbed the man's throat, pressing him down on his back. Slowly, Cord began to squeeze the life's breath from his body.

"It's me—Hayden," Cord said in a deadly voice. "In a few more seconds, you're going straight to hell unless you tell me what I want to know."

Beneath him, Puetas made gurgling noises and struggled frantically to nod.

Cord released the pressure ever so slightly. "Do you know where Valdis Alezparito is hiding out?"

"*Sí.*" The sound was barely audible. "*Sí.*"

Cord moved away quickly to stand beside the narrow cot. His eyes had become adjusted to the darkness, and he could make out Puetas' trembling form.

"I will tell you," Puetas gasped, clutching at his painfully constricting throat. "I am not willing to die for that one."

Cord smiled. "No," he drawled. "You aren't going to tell me, you son of a bitch. You're going to take me there. Get your worthless ass up and get dressed. And remember," he added slowly, "I can find him myself eventually. You're just making things a little easier, so it won't bother me a bit to kill you. Remember that, and don't get any ideas."

"No, no. I will make no trouble." Puetas moved cautiously as he got out of bed and reached for his trousers. "I will take you there, but please, do not tell him it was I who betrayed him."

"Move," was all Cord would reply.

Puetas obeyed.

✺ Chapter Twenty-one ✺

CORD rode directly behind Puetas, ever alert should the vaquero get any notions. He thought miserably of Amber, at the mercy of that bastard. Mercy! Valdis Alezparito was the worst kind of rogue because he was, in fact, a coward. And cowards went to extremes to try to make up for their lack of courage by exercising every brutality they could, whenever they could.

His hands gripped the reins tightly, wanting the pain of the leather cutting into his flesh to take his mind off his anger. How he wanted to choke the life from Alezparito! But now was not the time for heroics or vengeance. All that mattered was getting Amber out of there. And once he did, by God, he was going to *make* her leave Mexico with him. There was no way she could take Armand's boy from the village, though he could well understand her wanting to do so. The Indians would kill the child before they would let him go.

Cord had finally come to understand his feelings for Amber, and they had nothing to do with the promise made to Armand on his deathbed. Amber was unlike any woman Cord had ever known. She was beautiful, but spirited and intelligent as well. Oh, he had fought against his feelings, struggling to keep his vow never to love another woman, regarding them all as treacherous. He had struggled hard.

Cord bitterly recalled those first days after Amber's disappearance. He drank heavily, but could not wash away the memory of sparkling eyes and hair like liquid silver.

Just as he had vowed to move heaven and earth to find her, the letter had come from Major John Wesley Powell, Cord's commanding officer during the Civil War.

Thinking of that letter provoked other memories, painful memories, the bloody days of the war, fighting for something he believed in...and trying like hell to stay alive so he could return to Christina.

Christina.

Cord smiled bitterly, there in the darkness as they rode.

Tall, slender, her eyes the color of spring grass, her hair a mass of ginger curls, Christina's beauty seemed sculpted. She had an air of confidence and dignity about her that was almost a coldness. Both her family and his were rich, prominent, and everyone approved of their planned union.

Cord frowned as he felt the agony return. Yes, he had loved her, planned to marry her, and all the time she was a two-timing slut with no more scruples than a worn-out old whore. To the cream of Society she presented a picture all grace and charm. A real lady. And while she was writing him long letters of love and devotion, for him and for the Northern cause, she was bedding a brawling dock worker.

When he came home on leave and heard her tearful tale about the bastard raping her, he'd gone completely crazy and stormed down to the waterfront to give the man a sound beating and scare him to death. But it hadn't worked out like that. The guy had a knife. And Cord had a gun. He used it.

He had thought it a clear case of self-defense and gone back to war. A week later, Major Powell informed him that the man he had killed was the son of a prominent New York banker who had rebelled against his family's strict upbringing and left home for a different kind of life. The family was screaming murder and wanted justice, and Christina was brokenhearted and telling everyone that Cord had gone after the poor soul in a rage of jealousy. Cord had met Armand by then, and when Major Powell told him the thing for him to do was disappear for a while, Cord took his advice and had come to Mexico. The war was technically over, anyway, so he didn't feel he was a deserter.

Cord found peace in Mexico, and he knew it was better to stay there than go back and face a hangman's noose. But as time passed, and all feelings for Christina dissipated, he wanted to go back and clear his name. To hell with her reputation. Let the world know what a slut she was.

Now had come Powell's letter telling him that Christina had suffered a breakdown, brought on, possibly, by the remorse she'd been carrying. She had admitted inciting Cord with a lie. She had had a fight with her lover, and he had threatened to tell Cord of their affair, so she lied to Cord to save herself. If Cord would return, the Major wrote, there would be a hearing. Cord would be cleared. He would be able to pick up the pieces of his life in America.

Powell had also written of plans for an expedition to explore the upper Colorado River and the region called the Grand Canyon. A skilled organizer and promoter, Powell had raised funds to finance their private expedition. The major was a dedicated teacher and scientist, and the loss of his arm during the war was compensated for by his knowledge, his dreams, and his experience. He was set to go, and the expedition was to begin in late May.

Cord wanted to go. He wanted to go bad. The thrill of exploration fired him, and he wanted to be a part of discovering the navigation possibilities of the Colorado River.

Cord shook away his reverie. Right now the important thing was freeing Amber.

"We are almost there," Puetas called softly, urgently. "He hides in the mountain just beyond the next rise, in a big cave, about an hour's ride."

"Have you been in the cave?" Cord quickly asked.

"Yes. It is big, and there are many small alcoves. I know which one Valdis sleeps in, and that's probably where he is keeping the señorita. Set me free, and I will show you the way inside."

"Don't bargain with me," Cord said brusquely. "I'll blow you in half if you don't show me the way."

"So?" Puetas forced a gruesome laugh. "What difference does it make to me who pulls the trigger? When Valdis finds out I betrayed him, he is going to kill me."

Cord thought a moment, realizing Puetas was right.

"At least give me a chance," the Mexican pleaded. "I swear before the Holy Mother that I will not lie to you. I will show you the way, then I will just keep on riding away from here. I do not wish to die."

"All right," Cord said finally. "Lead the way in, and I'll let you go by yourself from there."

"You will not be sorry," Puetas assured him. "I promise."

✎ Chapter Twenty-two ✎

A MBER lay on her back, stunned with exhaustion and terror, as she had been for days. Beneath her, the crude straw mattress prickled and stung her naked flesh. Above her, flames from a torch danced eerie patterns on the cave's ceiling.

It was damp, and she was hungry. How long had it been? Two days? She was too dazed to know. She made no sound. For the moment, mercifully, she was alone. She had not dared look for Dolita, pretending she was still in a stupor, but she prayed that Dolita was all right. Dolita. With a wrenching of her heart, she imagined Dolita being ravished again by Gerras, and she despaired.

Amber dozed, and when she awoke she heard the sound of soft weeping. Dolita! She was not far away! "Don't cry," Amber whispered. "We've got to get out of here."

"No," Dolita moaned. "We are doomed. There is no way out."

"Listen to me!" Amber lifted herself from the mat and whispered fiercely. "We can't give up. There has to be a way out of here, and I'm going to find it."

Dolita said woodenly, "And what if you are found missing? What if Valdis comes for you? There is only one thing we can do. We must pray."

"We'll hide and we'll look for some weapon to defend ourselves." Amber shook her head. "Oh, I don't *know* what we'll do, Dolita. I just know we've got to try. If we go down, we go down fighting."

They rose unsteadily and moved to the opening in the rocks that led to the main part of the cave. In the last glow of the torch, Amber saw Dolita crossing herself.

Amber was not Catholic, maybe not really anything, but she took a deep breath and did the same thing.

🎕 Chapter Twenty-three 🎕

THERE was no moon. Thick black clouds had rolled across the mountains to cover the sky. The wind, steadily rising, was the only sound as it whistled up and around the trees, causing limbs to clatter like giant bones.

Cord could barely make out Puetas, riding just ahead.

Suddenly Puetas reined in so sharply that Cord jerked to one side to keep from running into him. Puetas whispered nervously, "We should go on foot from here. We are going inside from the secret way," Puetas decided.

"How do you know about this secret way?" Cord asked suspiciously.

Puetas said, "I was with Valdis when he found this cave, years ago. We explored the passageways, and we thought we were lost until we found a tunnel leading upward. We crawled out to find we were behind a big growth of cactus and brush. I know where that is. Nowhere else is there such a dense growth."

Slowly they made their way up a rocky incline, pausing when they reached a spot directly over the main entrance to the cave. Below, a large campfire burned, flames leaping to illuminate the men gathered there. One man was playing a guitar, another a mandolin, while two women danced, skirts whirling as the onlookers whistled and shouted at the sight of the prancing bare legs.

Cord leaned close to Puetas and whispered, "Do you know how many men Valdis has got?"

Puetas was silent, thoughtful, as he contemplated the figures below. "I think fourteen. Counting Valdis, fifteen."

Cord quickly counted the men gathered around the fire, saw bottles being passed back and forth and figured they were probably as drunk as they seemed. Good. That much was in his favor. But not in his favor was the fact that Valdis was missing, which meant he was inside, and maybe with Amber. He clenched his jaw tightly.

"Let's get on with it," he said harshly.

"You must follow me closely," Puetas whispered as they continued up yet another incline. "There are many rocks. Do not slip and roll into their campfire," he added, lightness in his voice for the first time.

"And what are we supposed to do once we get to the opening?"

"Try to get through without having our flesh torn to the bone. It will not be easy. As I said, it was many years ago that we were here. The cactuses are probably bigger, the brush thicker. Once we get through, we will drop through the hole. It is not too long a drop. From there, we move through the main tunnel."

Cord hoped Valdis would be asleep, and not with Amber and Dolita.

"You do remember for sure where Valdis sleeps?"

"Yes. I was here not long ago. On our right, after we get into the big tunnel, there will be three alcoves. His is the middle one. We must be careful, though, for coming in from the secret way, there is a crack in the earth, perhaps as wide as we are tall. We have to jump across it."

Cord frowned. He still did not totally trust the man.

"Here," Puetas called softly. "It is here. Ayah! The thorns are sharp. We cannot make our way through."

"Hell yes, we can." Cord groped in the dark and pushed Puetas aside. Feeling about gingerly, he winced as the sharp briars pricked his fingers. "Pull your shirtsleeves down around your hands," he ordered. "We'll just have to push our way in."

They unbuttoned their cuffs and doubled their hands up beneath the fabric. Ducking their heads, after pulling their hat brims low, the two men began to push into the tangled cluster of cactuses.

Both felt the sharp needles rip at their clothing, then at their flesh.

At last, Puetas stumbled forward into the vertical opening and was almost pitched down into the cave. "We are here," he gasped. "Now we have to bend to our knees and drop down."

"Wait!" Cord pushed on through. "If I go first, it might be a trap. I could be falling to my death. If you go first, you might just keep on going and sound the alarm."

"I think it is time you trusted me," Puetas said solemnly.

"Uhn-uh." Cord took his gun from his holster. "We're going to drop down at the same time, and if I hear one sound besides your feet hitting the ground, the next sound will be this gun going off. Understand?"

Puetas nodded wearily.

Cord crouched, toes hanging over the edge of the hole. Quickly, he holstered his gun. "Go!" he commanded. They dropped together, landing a second later on their feet. Straightening, they listened for noise. But there was only silence and damp darkness.

Puetas tugged gently at Cord's arm, motioning for him to follow. They moved several feet, then Puetas leaned close. "We must crawl forward on our knees very slowly. The crack is nearby. We will jump across it."

Cord fell to his knees, side-by-side with Puetas, crawling. Soon his heart quickened. "This is it," he whispered.

They stood, backed up to get a running start, and charged across. Fear was a rock in Cord's throat as he felt himself leaping into nothingness. How wide was the crevice? How deep?

They landed suddenly, pitching forward onto their hands.

"Not much farther," Puetas hissed breathlessly as they got to their feet. "Come."

They moved forward, inching their way. Suddenly, with instinct honed during his years in the war, Cord froze to absolute stillness. Someone was near. He could hear breathing, could sense a rapid heartbeat.

Cord hesitated, but only for a second. Whoever was near had most likely heard them. His impulse was to shoot, but he knew that would bring all of Valdis' men, so he held himself in check. Taking a deep breath, he let it out slowly, calling softly, "I've got a gun on you. Don't move."

There was a sob, then the anguished whisper. "Cord. Dear Cord, is that your voice?"

"Amber!"

He was nearly knocked off-balance as she threw herself into his arms. He gathered her closely with one arm, holding his gun tightly with the other. "Let's go," he whispered to Puetas, "before someone sounds an alarm."

"Wait." Amber trembled against him. "Dolita. Over there. She's fainted."

"I will get her," Puetas murmured, moving blindly forward.

Cord continued to grasp Amber against him until Puetas whispered, "I have her. She is unconscious. How are we going to get her across the crevice?"

There was no way they could leave her behind, and they could not risk trying to wake her up because she might start screaming.

"There's a big crevice back there, maybe six feet

wide," Cord told Amber. "It's the only way to get out of here without going out the front way. Do you think you can jump across?"

Amber took a deep breath. Jumping six feet in the darkness seemed like a leap straight into hell. "I don't see that I have a choice," she replied. "But what about Dolita? Cord, I won't leave her."

"Neither will I," he said gruffly. Turning to Puetas, he ordered, "Give her to me. I'll make the jump with her. Then I'll come back for Amber and hold onto her as she jumps. You go on ahead."

Puetas made no move. "Did you hear me, man?" Cord said harshly. "Give her to me and you go on and jump."

"No," came the stubborn reply. "If you cannot trust me by now, then go ahead and kill me. You take Dolita and go across. I will hold Amber's hand when she jumps."

It was, Cord told himself, one of those times when a man has to trust another man. "All right," he said finally, taking a deep breath as he holstered his gun, then reached out to take Dolita in his arms. "We'll do it your way, Puetas."

"Puetas?" Amber echoed softly as she felt Cord drop her hand and unfamiliar fingers clutch at the hand. "But didn't you used to guard me? Cord! He...he's one of Valdis' men!"

"Amber, I don't have time to explain," Cord snapped, hoisting Dolita's limp body over his shoulder. "Just jump. And don't worry."

Amber looked about wildly in the darkness. There was no time to argue. Allowing Puetas to lead her forward, she prayed Cord knew what he was doing.

Puetas explained brusquely, "We will take several steps backward. When I squeeze your hand, begin running. When I give your hand a yank, jump as hard as you can. I will pull you as much as I can. Can you do it?" he asked.

Amber was barely able to choke out her reply. Fear was spreading, making her believe she was smothering.

Cord, with Dolita, made the jump safely. Then, clutching Puetas' hand tightly, Amber took the steps back, and then, feeling the hard pressure of his fingers, ran forward. When she felt him tug and leap, she called on every bit of strength within her.

They threw themselves into the darkness, feeling suspended in midair. Time stopped. And then, with a painful thud, she pitched forward, crying out painfully as her chest hit the side of the chasm, smashing the air from her lungs.

Puetas' hand was torn from Amber's as she fell. He landed safely on the far side of the chasm, knowing even as he landed that Amber hadn't made it. He heard the awful thud as her body smacked into the earth.

Amber made no sound. There was a slicing pain in her lungs as she fought to suck in precious air. Her hands, clutching rocks, were torn and bleeding, and the blood made her hold slippery. She could not hang on much longer, and she knew it.

Cord shoved Dolita into Puetas' arms and crawled down the side of the chasm, grasping Amber's arms. He hauled her up over the side and, with only a pause for one deep breath, held her to him and began running with her in his arms.

They made their way to a jutting path leading up, Puetas carrying Dolita. Suddenly, light appeared behind them. Cord did not stop to turn and see what it was. His single thought was to get Amber out of the way. He set her down, dropped into a crouch, and whirled toward the light, gun drawn.

Beyond the crevice they had just crossed was Valdis, moving steadily forward, a rifle at the ready. Another man was beside him, carrying a torch and a gun.

Valdis screamed, "Goddamn you! For this you will die!" He fired, and Cord leaped behind a jutting rock, the bullet hitting stone with a whining echo.

"Leap across the crack, Gerras!" Valdis commanded.

Cord fired at the two men. He heard an agonizing scream and knew he had hit one of them. Then, knowing the gunfire would bring all of Valdis' men running, he scrambled quickly up the path. Puetas and Dolita were far ahead, and he dragged Amber with him, both gasping.

Puetas pushed Amber behind him, and moved to help Cord. "Ayah! What has happened?" Puetas' words were lost in the echoes of other gunshots. Cord gave a short gasp of pain and began to lose his handhold on the earth. He slid backward, and Puetas barely caught hold of his wrists before another shot was fired. Without hesitation, Puetas jerked Cord up and out of the hole.

"You are hurt," Puetas protested to Cord as he and Amber reached Puetas. "I must see to your wound!"

"Later," Cord snapped, gritting his teeth against the pain. "You're going to have to carry Dolita through the brush to the horses. Amber can hang onto your belt and follow. I'll try to keep up, but if I fall back, *keep going*. Get the women out of here as fast as you can."

They pushed their way forward, struggling through the tearing thorns and the brush. The skies opened and rain came down in torrents. Amber's long hair became tangled in cactus, and Cord told her to grit her teeth as he yanked it free.

Stumbling their way in the drenching rain, they finally reached the horses. Cord knew his foot was bleeding badly, for he could feel the stickiness inside his boot. He struggled up into the saddle, pulling Amber up behind him, leaving Dolita to Puetas.

"Follow me," Puetas cried.

They rode through the stormy night, hair plastered to their faces, clothes drenched. Puetas led the way, Dolita lying across his lap. Cord winced with pain, and Amber clung to his waist, her head pressed against his back. Behind them, they heard, very faintly, the shouts of Valdis' men. But as they continued deeper into the mountains the sounds grew fainter, and they knew that they were going in opposite directions.

After they'd plodded through the mud and brambles and brush for an hour, the rain let up and the clouds parted to give a little light.

"Up ahead," Puetas cried. "Another cave. Perhaps a wolves' den. We must be careful, but at least we are far away from Valdis, and soon it will be light. We can rest." He turned in his saddle to look at Cord. "Are you badly hurt? Where did the bullet hit?"

"My foot," Cord told him dully, seeing that the way was wide enough for them to ride two abreast, and urging his horse to fall in beside Puetas. "I think the bullet went all the way through. It's bleeding bad, but I'll be all right. It could have been a hell of a lot worse. Where are we, anyway? It seems like we've been climbing steadily."

"We have. We are in the mountains of Sierra Madre Occidental, just south of the Yaquí River. Nogales is about a two days' ride. Valdis and his men will not look for us here."

Puetas went inside the cave first to make sure there were no animals there. Cord lowered himself gingerly from the saddle and turned to help Amber, who said, "No. I can take care of myself. Let me help you inside. I want to look at that wound, and then we need to see about Dolita."

Puetas hurried to gather twigs and scraps of dry brush lying just inside the mouth of the cave. Everything outside was soaked. He built a fire and then, placing Dolita nearby so she would be warm, he went to Cord, slumped against a wall. Slipping a knife from its hiding place inside his pants, he sliced through the leather of Cord's left boot.

"I should have searched you," Cord said tartly when he saw the weapon.

Puetas grinned. "I could have killed you any time I chose. It was my pleasure to know this."

Cord raised an eyebrow. "Why didn't you?"

Puetas shrugged as he tugged gently at the boot. "I felt sorry for the women, and I thought I could

help, then go back to my life. Now I am running
with you."

"I'm not running, and neither are you. I'll take
care of Valdis in my own good time. All I wanted
to do was get Amber out of there." Cord winced
with pain as the boot was removed from his injured foot.

Amber knelt beside him, using the hem of his
shirt against the wound. She had been wearing it
and now she was naked again. Puetas averted his
gaze. "I think the bullet did go all the way
through," she said, lifting worried eyes to meet
his in the glow from the fire, "but you're still bleeding. We need a tight bandage to stop it."

"I will get my saddle blanket and tear it into
strips." Puetas hurried to the horses, tethered just
inside the cave.

Cord reached out to cup Amber's face in his
hands. He gazed at her, pushing his pain from
his mind. "Are you all right?" he asked, eyes
searching hers. "Did the bastards hurt you, my
Amber?"

"No," she murmured, stirred. "I'm not sure what
happened, but I think Valdis was too drunk to
bother me. I'm afraid Dolita wasn't as fortu-
nate..." She saw the way he was looking at her
and fell silent, then reached for what was left of
the shirt and put it on.

They heard Dolita moaning and turned to look
in her direction. Cord urged, "Go see to her."

Both Amber and Puetas moved to the girl's side,
and she stared up at them with wide, frightened
eyes. Amber clutched her hand and told her they
were safe, but Dolita looked from Amber to the

man beside her, then shrank back and cried, "It is you! Puetas!"

"No, no! He helped us," Amber explained quickly. "He carried you on his shoulder through the brush and thorns and rain. He's our friend now, Dolita. You don't have to be afraid anymore."

"It is true." He nodded, eyes twinkling. "It is my shirt you are wearing." He tugged at the sleeve, baggy on her thin arm. "I will look after you, while Amber looks after Señor Hayden. He was wounded. I must bandage him now." He did so, quickly.

"I'll tell you everything in the morning." Amber gave Dolita what she hoped was a reassuring smile and turned back to Cord.

It didn't take him long to fall asleep. She brushed a dark tendril back from his forehead and kissed him, then lay down close beside him, in case he should need her.

✒ Chapter Twenty-four ✒

IT was late in the day when Amber awoke, groggy and sore throughout her body. Lifting her head from Cord's shoulder, she looked around, disoriented. Slowly, it all came back. The capture... Valdis. Thank God for Cord. She smiled down at him, saw that he was sleeping peacefully. Checking the bandage on his foot, she was satisfied that it had stopped bleeding at last. She stood and stretched, uncomfortably damp in the rainsoaked remnants of Cord's shirt. The fire Puetas had built was out, so she began gathering more twigs and scraps of wood to light it again. Then, since everyone still slept soundly, she removed the ragged shirt and propped it on a stick near the fire to dry.

Checking on Dolita, she smiled to see that she was asleep with Puetas' arms protectively about her. Moving away, she tiptoed to the cave entrance. It was, she guessed, midafternoon, for the sun was beginning to make its descent behind the surrounding mountains. The landscape that greeted her was painted in a golden haze, fringed by fertile green grasses of the valley below. Hills and gullies and rock formations spread as far as she could see, and great whitecaps of clouds floated by in the cerulean blue sky as though directed by an unseen pulley. Amber felt as peaceful as she had in a long time.

Stepping outside, she found a flat rock, warmed by the sun, and sat down, pulling her knees up to hold her chin as she wrapped her arms around her legs. The sun felt wonderful. She thought about returning to retrieve her shirt, then decided not to risk waking the others. Besides, she wanted the time alone for reverie. She sat there, still for a long time, going over all that had befallen her since she'd left the States. By the time Cord spoke, she was so lost in her daydreaming that she jumped, startled. "A true sun goddess," he said.

"Oh! I didn't hear you!" she gasped, covering her bare breasts with her arms and pulling her legs up against her even tighter. She stammered, "I...I left your shirt to dry. It was still wet."

He limped over and sat down beside her. His face was shadowed by beard stubble, but he seemed without pain despite his wound. "Naked you came into my arms, and naked you shall leave," he murmured, reaching out for her.

She pulled away and cried, "No, Cord. We mustn't. And your foot—you shouldn't even be walking on it. You're going to start it bleeding again."

"It's fine," he said evenly. Suddenly he gripped her arms. "Why did you run away?" he demanded fiercely, eyes devouring hers. "You did run, didn't you? Don't you know I'm trying like hell to love you? I want us to make a future together. I thought you cared for me—until I woke up to find you gone."

"It's the boy." She began to cry, looking up, beseeching his understanding. "My heart went out to him before I even knew he was Armand's. I can't abandon him to the kind of miserable life I know he's living."

Without replying to her statement, he informed her, "I'm taking you back to the States with me and leaving you somewhere safe. One day, I'll come back and find you. If you've met another man, I'll have to accept it. But by God, I'm going to get you out of Mexico."

"You can force me to go with you, but you can't make me stay. I'll find a way to get back."

He leaned forward, eyes blazing. "Woman, why do you have to be so stubborn? I told you. Those Indians won't *let* the boy go." He shook his head slowly. "You beautiful, stubborn little fool."

Ignoring her protests and the pain of his wound, he lifted her in his arms and carried her to a grassy knoll conveniently hidden by thick shrubs. He lowered her to the ground, and they gazed into each other's eyes, the magic beginning. With a deep moan, he pulled her over him, taking turns fastening his lips to each nipple. Amber sighed

267

deliciously, thrusting her bosom in offering.

He devoured each nipple to rosy hardness, then slipped his hand between her legs, moving gently. She was ready for him, he knew, but instead of taking her, he teased, teased until she was writhing, begging for fulfillment.

"I will love you forever," he whispered. "Say you love me, Amber. Say it!" he commanded.

"Cord, I do love you," she whimpered, clinging to him. "But—"

He kissed her, long, hard, as he turned her over and lay on top of her. He gave a hard thrust, and she cried out, but the cry quickly turned to sighs and moans as he cupped her buttocks and rocked her to and fro.

He waited until she had reached her pinnacle of ecstacy, then took himself to his own crest. He felt tears falling from Amber's eyes, and knew they were tears of rapture.

They held each other close, gazing into each other's eyes with adoration. Finally Cord whispered, "Can you say you don't want to go with me, Amber?"

She started to speak, to attempt to convince him about the boy, but he held his fingertips to her lips and said, "Let me talk. There's something you need to know, something that might make you understand me."

And he told her of Christina, and then about Major Powell's expedition.

She listened to every word, and she did understand him better. But that did not change how she felt about the boy, and she tried to tell him that. He frowned and stood up and walked away. When he returned, having found a long stick to use for a cane and having fetched her shirt, he tossed the shirt at her. "It's still a bit damp. Stay out here in the sun, and it will dry."

He walked back to the cave, shoulders stooped, head down. She called to him, but he kept right on going. Quickly putting on the shirt, she hurried after him. He *had* to understand about the boy.

Before she could talk to him, she found Dolita and they hugged. "He wants me to go home with him, but I can't leave the boy," Amber cried. "Even if I hadn't found out he's Armand's, I still couldn't have deserted the child. If Cord won't help me, then I'll just find a way to do it alone."

Dolita looked downcast. "I hope you are not angry with me for not telling you the truth about the boy. I felt I shouldn't."

"No, I understand. I just hope you understand the way I feel about him."

"No, I don't," Dolita said bluntly, looking directly at Amber. "I think you are making a mistake. But I will not refuse to help you. I will take you back to the village, but I do not plan to stay there for long. I have another uncle in Soinota, and I want to go there and make a new life—far from here and that fiend Valdis."

"Neither of us will be staying long. Just help me get the boy's trust, and then we'll be on our way."

Amber gave her a hug, tears of gratitude stinging her eyes. She could not have come so far without Dolita's help, and the poor girl had suffered so much because of Amber.

Cord approached, eyeing them suspiciously, and

asked in a tight voice, "Are you discussing plans to go back to the village?"

"Yes." Amber would not lie to him. If he was too stubborn to understand, then he didn't really love her. "I am going. If you won't come with me, then I will go alone. My mind is made up."

"Fine." Cord picked up a bottle of tequila and sat down, taking a drink. He had already had several.

Nervous, Dolita got up and went outside, leaving them alone together.

Cord stared at Amber with stormy eyes. "Both of you do whatever you want. I'm sick of worrying about you. I've kept my promise to Armand. I've offered to take you to the States, maybe make a life together one day, but you have to be so goddamned stubborn. You won't listen to reason. Fine, get yourself killed by the Indians or Valdis. I'm not going to ride herd on you till you come to your senses."

"No one is asking you to ride herd on me!" Amber stood up.

"I'll get on with my life," she said furiously, "and you can get on with yours." For long moments, silence crackled between them.

"I guess we're not going to agree, are we?" she finally asked hoarsely, and when he did not answer, she walked away.

Cord watched her go as he reached once more for the bottle. The most beautiful woman he had ever known, and also the most impossible. Maybe she was right. Maybe they just weren't going to agree.

* * *

As night crept upon them, Cord took his bedroll and went outside the cave, while Amber bedded down near the fire. She pretended not to notice when Puetas drew Dolita into the shadows; tried to block out the sound of their whispered giggles.

Outside, Cord sat very still, listening to the lonely whisper of the wind as it rustled through the trees. At last, quietly, he gathered his things. He mounted his horse, anger keeping him from telling Amber goodbye. Maybe, he thought bitterly, he should have kept the vow he'd made never to give a damn about another woman.

Cord rode into the night. He did not look back.

❦ Chapter Twenty-five ❦

AMBER sat on the hard ground, the Indian children gathered about her. Spring had arrived, and they were gathered beneath the newly leafed branches of a cottonwood tree. Round-eyed, brown-skinned faces watched her with curious interest. They understood no Spanish, and, of course, no English. The days passed quickly, and as Amber devoted her every waking hour to little Armand, as she called him, the other children and the adults had began treating her like an exotic pet.

Puetas had offered to go after Cord, to talk to him, but Amber had dully told him not to bother. He had looked at her strangely but said nothing more, and he, Dolita, and Amber then had made their way to the Indian village.

The Indians were wary when they saw Amber

and Dolita again, accompanied by yet another stranger, but Cuelo decreed that they be tolerated as long as they did their share of work in the village. That meant helping in the fields. Cuelo warned the strangers and his niece not to interfere with local customs.

Amber did not object to the work. It gave her time to be with the little boy. She learned that the name he answered to, when anyone bothered to speak to him at all, was "Malo," meaning "bad." Amber bristled and declared, "Not anymore! Since he has no name of his own, I'll christen him 'Armand.'"

Dolita shook her head and wandered away. Amber was going to face a big disappointment, for the boy was hopelessly hostile.

Amber smoothed the front of her dowdy buckskin dress and, shading her eyes against the glare of the bright spring sunshine, scanned the rough landscape beyond where the crops were being planted. Spotting Puetas and Dolita toiling side by side in the field, she made her way over to join them. As she approached, Dolita exchanged a worried glance with Puetas, then said to Amber, "There may not be time to make friends with little Armand. Yesterday, one of the men out hunting saw a stranger, a man who looked like a bandit and was watching the village. When he saw the hunter, the stranger rode away. Puetas and I have talked, and we think it was one of Valdis' men. It may not be safe for us here any longer."

Amber's twinge of fear was overshadowed by her agitation. "We can't go to pieces every time a stranger is seen in the mountains, Dolita. You two can leave any time you wish, but I'm not leaving without that boy."

Puetas eyed her warily. "The Indians here do not interfere in what does not concern them. They will not defend us if Valdis comes. They will stand back and let us be taken. I will be killed for betraying Valdis, and you and Dolita would be better off dead. Should Valdis and Gerras take you again, this time, they will make you beg for a quick death."

Amber shuddered, but refused to let Puetas see how upset she was. "I'm not running. Besides, Valdis has probably succeeded in buying off the law by now and gone home. He probably thinks the four of us crossed the border weeks ago."

"He wants you," Puetas said simply. "He told me he had never desired a woman more fiercely. He vows to have you or die. And you must remember, Valdis fears nothing."

Amber nodded grimly. "I know." And she did.

An hour later, Amber and the still-wary child were sitting together near the fire. Amber looked down at the boy and felt a warm rush to see a rare bright smile on his face. Impulsively, he squeezed her hand tightly, and in that moment she knew that it was going to be all right between them.

Amber pointed to a distant hill. "Armand, there are beautiful cactus flowers up there. Would you show me the way up? I would like to find a cool place to sit and be quiet, and I want you with me."

He understood enough, and they began to climb, and several times Amber almost slipped. "I'm not a mountain goat," she said with a laugh. The boy laughed with her.

Finally they reached a large flat rock overlooking the valley below. He sat beside her, and she slipped her arm about him. They sat in silence, and Amber looked down into the valley. She could see the Indians working in the fields, and the thought came to her that it was a bleak existence. Had she been born into it, perhaps she would be content, for she would know no other life. Grinning to herself, she wondered what her grandmother would think, to see her in buckskins!

The peaceful glow was darkened by thoughts of Cord. If only he were here! The three of them could leave together and make a new life. But Cord was gone...and this knowledge hurt badly. There was only herself and little Armand. Well, together, they would make that new life.

Suddenly she turned to look at the boy and asked, "Would you like to go away with me, Armand? Leave Mexico and go to America? I could find a place for us to live, some kind of work to do. I would take care of you. You will never hurt again." She hugged him. "I know you don't completely trust me yet, but you will."

The boy picked up a stick. Handing it to her, he pointed to the dirt.

"You want me to draw you a picture?" Amber asked, pleasantly surprised. He made no reply, and she slid from the rock and fell to her knees before him on the ground. Drawing a crude outline of what she hoped the United States and Mexico looked like, she pointed to Mexico, then to him, and said, "You are here. And here is where we will go."

To her delight, he nodded.

Amber leaped to grab him in her arms. "You understand, Armand! You understand that I want to take you with me. And you want to go, don't you?"

He could only smile, but that was enough. He understood, and he wanted to go with her. That was all that mattered.

They sat on horseback on a rise above and to the north of Amber and the boy. They had been watching the Indian village since dawn, hidden within a thick clump of sage and brush.

Valdis Alezparito's chest swelled with rage, and Gerras turned to look at him and ask, "It is the American, no?"

Valdis nodded grimly. "My scout was right. It is Amber. But why is she here? I thought she would be with Hayden, but no one has seen him anywhere at all, and I have had many men looking." He pointed to the village. "Something else. I am sure the traitor-dog, Puetas, is there also. And, no doubt, the *puta* you want, Gerras."

Gerras grinned, and in response, Valdis' lips twisted into the cold grimace that, for Valdis, passed for a smile. "I carry the scar of the silver-haired beauty, and you carry the scar of the American. We both hunger for vengeance. We shall have it."

"You want to ride in there now?" asked Gerras.

"We will wait until they are sleeping, and take them by surprise. The only shot I want fired is one that wounds Puetas. But don't shoot to kill. I prefer to slit his throat and let him feel his life's blood draining slowly away." Valdis nodded toward Amber and the boy. "You know the boy?" He grinned. "It's Mendosa's bastard."

Gerras' eyes widened. "The half-breed? But why is he with her?"

"Perhaps she knows he is the son of Armand Mendosa. If so, this could be good, for she will be obedient if she thinks we might hurt the boy."

Gerras matched his grin. "I believe our luck is changing."

Unseen and unheard, Puetas slipped from his hiding place in the rocks above them; trembling, cold sweat dotting his forehead. He had heard everything the two men had said.

🦋 Chapter Twenty-six 🦋

CUELO, looking agitated and gesturing impatiently, was waiting when Amber and the boy returned from their walk. He held up a dead rabbit and shook it, speaking in his tongue, which she did not have to understand to know why he was angry. He wanted the rabbit cooked for his supper, and expected her or Dolita to prepare it.

Just as she was about to apologize for her lack of knowledge in cleaning wild animals, Armand reached to take the rabbit from Cuelo. The boy hurried away. That seemed to satisfy the old Indian, and Amber knew that the boy was skinning the animal.

A little later, Armand brought back the rabbit, smiling proudly. He built a fire, fashioned a skewer from a stick, and in no time, was turning the rabbit over the flames. Amber was amazed. When it was done, Cuelo came and ate, much more than his share, and Amber wished there were more for Armand. When he reached for a piece of the meat, Cuelo slapped his hand away and doled out only a small bite for the child.

"It won't be like this much longer," she said to the boy, giving him what was left on her own clay plate—which was almost all she had been served. "Soon, there will be plenty for you to eat, Armand. I promise."

He looked at her and grinned, as though he understood.

Dusk turned to a cool night of purple skies and dancing silver stars. The village people settled down early for sleep, for planting time was upon them, and they were weary from their long day in the fields.

Amber stretched out on a pallet. It was not too uncomfortable, and the clean, pungent aroma of the sagebrush and pine stuffing was pleasing. The night was chilly, so she made sure there was enough wood on the fire at the entrance to her lean-to. She snuggled beneath one of the thin woven blankets and tucked the other about Armand. She pounded the pallet beneath her, smoothing the lumps of crushed filling, commanding herself not to think of Cord.

"Señorita..."

She leaped, then sighed with relief at the sight of Puetas creeping into the lean-to, but her smile quickly faded when she saw how frightened he looked. "Whatever is wrong?" she said in a low voice, so as not to awaken the boy. "Where is Dolita? Has something happened to her?"

He held a finger to his lips for silence, and she saw that his hand was trembling. Kneeling beside her, he quickly whispered, "Dolita is safe. I have hidden her far away where she will not be found. Forgive me, but I had to think of her first, I love her so."

Amber was bewildered and fast becoming frightened. "Puetas, tell me what is going on. Why did you hide Dolita?"

"Because in the mountains I saw Valdis and Gerras—"

She gasped, and he quickly moved to cover her mouth with his hand. "No! Do not awaken the boy just yet. You must be quiet and listen. As I said, you must forgive me, for my first thoughts when I saw them and overheard them were for Dolita, and myself. Gerras wants her, and they both mean to kill me. They come for all of us. Tonight. I was going to stay hidden..." His voice and his eyes dropped in shame.

Amber struggled to keep disgust and anger under control. "You were going to run away with Dolita, but you decided to come back and warn me. So now what do we do?"

"We must go at once."

Amber scrambled to her feet, whispering, "Help me carry the child."

"There is no time," Puetas cried anxiously. "I do not know when they will come. It is true that I almost did not come back, but I knew I could not live with myself if I did not warn you. Call me a coward if you wish, but if you do not leave the boy and come with me now, I will go alone and leave you to face them.

"This is your doing," he added, accusing her when he saw the condemning blaze of her smoky eyes. "Señor Hayden offered to take you away, but you refused because of the boy." He tossed a scornful look at the sleeping child. "I can help you no more if you refuse to come with me alone."

"Puetas, you *are* a coward!" Amber exploded, forgetting to whisper and instantly waking Armand.

She grabbed the boy's hand and pulled him to his feet. "Do not be afraid." She forced a tight smile to her own quivering lips. "We are leaving now, Armand. We will take the blankets so we won't be cold, and we will take my horse. We will go to the mountains and hide until morning. You can show me the way." She wondered if she was really babbling to herself.

"Señorita, please!" Puetas begged. "Leave him. Come with us now. There is no *time*."

"Go!" she hissed. "We don't need you!"

There was the sound of scuffling in the darkness beyond, and the night was split by the blue-white flash of an exploding gun.

"Ah, my lovely one, surely you do not wish to leave without even saying hello?"

She froze at the sight of Valdis, his triumphantly leering face illuminated by the fire's gentle glow. He held a smoking gun at his side. "Puetas," she gasped, quickly shoving Armand behind her to shield him. "You have killed him!"

"No, no," Valdis said quickly, stepping into the lean-to. "He is not dead. Not yet. First, he will tell where he has hidden the servant girl. Gerras wants her. He shall have her. And I shall have you."

282

Amber continued to hold Armand behind her tightly, feeling his convulsive tremors. Giving her long hair an arrogant toss, she cried, "You don't give up, do you? It doesn't matter to you that I think you are ugly, repulsive, and every other filthy, rotten thing I can think of. I despise you!"

She had been waiting for the move, watching the ominous flashing of his eyes, and when he brought his arm up to strike her, she was ready. Ducking, she pushed Armand to one side and screamed, "Run! Run!" At the same time, she grabbed for Valdis' gun, catching him off-guard and jerking it from him at the same time she brought her knee up into his crotch. He screamed in pain and doubled over. Holding the weapon with both hands, she backed away, leveling the gun straight at him.

"Now, you monster," she cried, grateful to hear the hasty running sounds that told her the boy had understood and obeyed her, "this changes things, doesn't it? I have never killed a man, but I don't think it will bother me one bit to pull this trigger. I'm sure nobody will miss you."

Clutching himself between his legs, Valdis whispered, "This means nothing, bitch. If you will look behind you, you will see that Gerras has the boy. You may kill me, but when you pull the trigger, Gerras will slit his throat. Slowly."

"Drop the gun!" Gerras commanded from behind her. "Drop it or I cut him."

Amber was helpless. A movement caught her eye, and she turned her head ever so slightly to see that Puetas, drenched in his own blood, had

crawled into the halo of firelight and was holding
out a feeble hand to her. "Do as he says or they
will kill both of you."

Valdis looked around at the Indians who had
gathered at the sound of the gunshot and the rest
of the commotion. They were making no move to
interfere, but Valdis decided not to chance anything. "Let's take them and go," he snapped to
Gerras as he reached for his gun. Amber let him
have it without a struggle.

As the boy screamed and tried to run again,
Gerras clutched him tightly about his throat,
squeezing. "I will not go without Dolita," Gerras
declared. "That is why I came. You have what you
want. Now I will have what I want."

Still clutching the boy by the neck, Gerras
dragged him over to where Puetas lay facedown.
Twisting his fingers in the wounded man's hair,
he jerked his head up and glared into the eyes. "If
you do not want to die a slow death, traitor-dog,
tell me what you have done with the señorita."

Puetas' eyes were swimming with pain, and he
could feel his life ebbing from the bullet hole in
his chest. Mustering his last shred of strength, he
spat.

"Dog!" Gerras straightened and kicked him in
the face.

Armand seized the opportunity and bolted, running as fast as his legs would carry him, grateful
for the speed he had acquired during his lonely
days running in the desert, running then to while
away the miserable hours, running now to escape
the terrible men.

Valdis bellowed, "You fool! Now the boy has escaped! The Indians are angry for what you have done to a dying man. We will go now, or you can remain behind and face them by yourself."

Gerras holstered his gun, contrite. He warily observed the restless, murmuring Indians.

Tears streaming down her cheeks, and gesturing toward the villagers, Amber pleaded, "Please...please do something. In the name of God, stop them."

Valdis whacked her roughly across her buttocks and snarled, "Shut up, damn you! If I did not think it would incite them, I would give you the beating you deserve right now. And if they do intervene, be assured you will die before I do."

"Then kill me now!" she screamed, hitting him and kicking at him wildly. "Go ahead and kill me, you devil!"

The Indians began to move forward and Gerras cried nervously, "Do something to quiet her, Valdis, or they are going to jump us. I can feel it. Make her be still."

Suddenly, without warning, Valdis whirled about, drew his gun, and fired it into the air. "Stay back!" he cried. The Indians came to a startled halt. "Stay back or some of you will die!"

They did not understand his words, but they didn't need to. Immediately, they began to retreat.

"Now move fast," Valdis ordered Gerras as Amber continued screaming. "I want to get out of the glow of their campfire and into the darkness so I can make this one wish she had obeyed me."

Swiftly, they moved into the night, to their tethered horses.

The boy watched from the shadows, his teeth
chattering. Every muscle in his body twitched with
rage of a kind he had never felt before. Those men
were taking away his silver-haired goddess, the
woman who had shown him kindness and love.

How he wished the big man were here, the man
he had spied on so many hours as he hid in the
hills above the great matador's hacienda. He would
know what to do.

But the big man was not here. He was alone.

With fiery determination mingling with fury,
he threw himself onto a pony, and set out to follow
the men and his goddess.

It was raining the night the dream came to Cord.
He had found shelter in a niche in the Colorado
side of a mountain, just deep enough to draw himself into against the driving storm. Sleep was slow
in coming, for the skies were split relentlessly by
jagged, angry lightning, and the ground beneath
him rumbled continuously with thunder. When at
last sleep took him away, he dreamed he was holding Amber, their passion exploding in great waves
of ecstacy. But just as he dreamed he was releasing
himself inside her with everything he had, she was
torn from his arms. Invisible bonds held him as
he struggled to keep her from being pulled away.
He could hear triumphant laughter. There was a
great mist surrounding him, and when it finally
parted, he saw the leering face of Valdis Alezparito. Before Cord's eyes he threw Amber to the

ground and impaled her, crying victoriously that she was his for always and always.

Cord awoke with a start. He had been a fool to leave her. Valdis would never stop searching for her. Cord had left her at the madman's mercy.

✒ Chapter Twenty-seven ✒

CORD could only blink at Dolita in stunned disbelief, but then rage took over. "When?" he asked tightly.

Tears streamed down Dolita's cheeks as she twisted her hands together, eyes downcast. She could not bear to look at the anguish on Cord Hayden's face. She whispered, "I do not know exactly, señor, for I have lost all track of time. I have not left Puetas' side since he came so close to dying. He is still very weak."

"Did anyone go after them?" he cried, longing to smash something. "Didn't anyone try to stop them from taking her?"

She continued to stare at the ground as she shook her head. "I do not think so, but I was not here when it happened. The Indians almost tried to stop them, but my uncle told me that Valdis fired shots and scared them."

"The boy," Cord cried then. "What about the boy?"

"I do not know. I am told he ran away that night."

His instincts had been right! He never should have left her, Cord thought wildly, miserably. Clasping Dolita's trembling shoulders, he gently asked, "Is Puetas able to talk?"

She nodded. "I will take you to him."

He followed her past curiously staring Indians as they made their way to a crude shelter, with a roof of dried corn shucks. Puetas lay on a thick pallet. Cord knelt beside him, shocked by the pale, drawn face. His breathing was shallow, and he looked terribly weak. His eyes were closed, but when Cord touched his shoulder, Puetas slowly opened them to look up at him dizzily. "How do you feel, amigo?" Cord asked kindly.

Puetas struggled to focus his eyes. Dolita knelt on his other side, whispering, "It is Señor Hayden, Puetas. He comes in search of his lady. I cannot help him."

Puetas whispered hoarsely, "How I wish I could. The bullet was in me for a long time, until Cuelo brought a doctor from a larger village. Now it will take much time to get back my strength, which flowed from me into the sand. I am not able to ride with you, señor. Please...forgive me."

Cord patted him awkwardly. "It's all right, Puetas. But maybe there is a way you can help me. I've got to find them, and I'm sure Valdis has changed hideouts. You used to ride with him. Can you think of *any* place he might have gone besides the one we were in?"

"No," Puetas answered. "The cave where I took you was the only place I ever knew."

Cord rocked back on his heels, pressed his fingertips against his forehead, then looked once more to Puetas. "The boy. Do you know what happened to him?"

Puetas started to speak but was suddenly overcome with a spell of coughing. Dolita brought a cup of water, which he gratefully drank. Then he told Cord, "He ran away, and Dolita tells me he has not been seen since. Perhaps Valdis and Gerras caught him. Or he escaped and kept on going. But, I tell you, no one has seen the boy."

"Sometimes," Cord sighed, "I think Armand should have been told about his son. Other times I think he might have gotten killed trying to claim him, and I figure it was right to have left well enough alone. But...it was wrong to leave the child here to be miserable."

Dolita and Puetas exchanged sympathetic looks, and Dolita offered, "Perhaps he will return, señor. I will ask my uncle to look after him better. I would do so myself, but Puetas and I will be leaving when he is able to travel. We wish to marry and make new lives. Happy lives."

"Congratulations," Cord snapped, then quickly countered with a wave of his hand, "I'm sorry. Forgive me. I don't begrudge you anything."

"You should hate me," Puetas cried. "I thought first of Dolita, then myself. And I refused to take the boy, and the señorita refused to leave. Had I not been so pigheaded, perhaps we could have left in time."

Cord's eyes narrowed, but after a moment he

just looked weary. "That's something you're going to have to live with, Puetas, and sometimes living with your mistakes is the worst kind of punishment there is."

Dolita sought to break the tension. "What will you do?"

"I have to find Amber," Cord answered simply. "I wish you a good recovery, Puetas, and much happiness to you both."

After he had gone, Dolita shook her head. "He must love her very much. But then why did he leave her?"

Puetas whispered sadly, "Sometimes a man runs from that which he must deny...until he can deny it no longer. When he runs back, it may be gone. I pray for him, and for the señorita, that it is not gone."

After darkness had fallen, Cord reached the only place he could think to go—the Alezparito ranch. Moving through Alezparito land, he did not fail to notice that there were few vaqueros about. No doubt, Valdis had called in all those faithful to him.

The servant standing at the large wrought iron entrance was familiar, and he smiled in recognition as Cord dismounted. "Señor Hayden! What a surprise. I did not think you would come to the señorita's fiesta. It has been a long time."

Knowing Rodrigo was a talkative sort, Cord decided it best to let him assume he was, indeed, an invited guest. "I am glad I was able to make it," he told Rodrigo, matching his smile. "I got back only today. I must confess I'm not even aware of the purpose of the fiesta."

Rodrigo, only too glad to tell him everything, lowered his voice conspiratorially. "Do not repeat me, but Señorita Alezparito is entertaining some members of the high court, trying, no doubt, to win their favor for the time when Señor Valdis returns to claim his innocence."

"Am I the last to arrive?" Cord asked, letting the remark pass.

"*Sí*, you are late. But if you will go on up the stairs, someone will announce you."

"No," Cord quickly retorted. "I think it would be rude for me to go in now. I wish I could have arrived earlier. Would you do me a favor and send a message to Señorita Maretta that someone wishes to see her in the stable? Do not tell her who it is. I want it to be...a surprise," he added with a grin and a friendly nudge.

Rodrigo's eyes sparkled mischievously. "I will have it done."

Cord fished in his pockets for a few coins and dropped them into the Mexican's outstretched hand, then turned and went back to his horse, leading him down the rutted dirt path to the stable, set back from the road and away from the main house.

A half hour passed as Cord paced up and down on the straw-littered dirt floor. He had found a lantern, lit it, and a soft mellow glow lit the stable. As he began to think she wasn't coming, he heard soft footsteps approaching and he turned to see Maretta silhouetted against the wide doorway.

She looked shocked, then pleased, and finally angry.

The ballgown of red watered silk was cut low to display her slender bosom as provocatively as possible. Her hair was caught up in ringlets and held in place by a large silver comb, from which a scarlet mantilla flowed gracefully. She looked at him through narrowed lids, lashes brushing her painted cheeks. She paused dramatically before crying, "You have taken your time returning to one you claim to desire!"

He stepped forward and bowed slightly, kissing her hand before allowing his eyes to flicker over her appreciatively, as she expected him to do. "Time only enhances your beauty, Maretta."

She gave her head a toss and said, "Do not think you will fool me again, Cord Hayden. This time I am quite sober. I know what you want. You want me to tell you where my brother has taken the whore, and this I will not do. So, do you wish to leave now?"

Cord smiled lazily and folded his arms across his chest. "Yes, I would like to know where Valdis had taken Amber. I won't pretend with you, Maretta."

"As you did before!" she snapped.

"Was I dishonest? Did I not please you?"

Her cheeks flushed, and despite her attempt at anger, she could not help but be charmed. "Yes," she whispered in a little-girl voice. "It was wonderful. It is always wonderful with you, Cord. But you said you would come back."

He opened his arms. "Here I am."

She ran to him and threw herself against him, flinging her arms about his neck. "Oh, Cord, I knew you would not stay away. I knew you would come back to me, for what we have together is so good."

"Wait a minute, Maretta." He caught her wrists and pulled her arms away, looking piercingly into her black eyes. "I am not here because of us. Valdis has taken Amber again, and I want to find her. I tracked him down once, but he's no doubt changed his hiding place."

Her lower lip jutted out petulantly. "And why should I help you find her when I want you for myself?"

He sighed and shook his head. "Maretta, you must understand there can never be anything between us except in bed. You're a beautiful, desirable woman, and if you weren't so damned contrary, you'd have hundreds of men fawning at your feet. Why waste your time on me when I'm honest enough to tell you I'm only interested in one thing and always have been?"

She cocked her head to look up at him angrily, but then she smiled. "You are honest, Cord. I am grateful for that. Most men would not be."

He gave her an appreciative hug. She was a bitch, and probably deserved to be deceived, but he had never liked using women. "Do you know where he's hiding?"

She nodded.

"Tell me."

She merely stared at him.

"I want to take her back to America, where she

belongs. Why do you want her to continue suffering?"

Her upper lip curled back. "She is responsible for Armand's death."

"Hell, no, she isn't," he told her flatly. "You don't really believe that. You've been around bulls all your life, and you know one with faulty vision slips by now and then. Maybe Armand didn't give his total concentration that day, and if he didn't, then it's his fault, not Amber's." He shook his head grimly. "No, you don't blame her for his death. You blame her for him not wanting to marry you, and that's also a lie. We both know he didn't love you and had no intention of marrying you. Amber had nothing to do with it."

She struggled, her pride at stake, but she knew he was right. "Perhaps," she said finally, "I never wanted to marry Armand. Perhaps I used him to make you jealous."

She started to say more, but Cord had suddenly tensed, listening, the instinct that had saved his life so many times taking over. Motioning to Maretta to stay where she was, he drew his gun and, with a lightning-quick movement, leaped behind a post and pointed his weapon toward one of the stalls, crying, "Come out of there or you're dead." In a moment, his eyes widened at the sight of the frightened little boy slowly stepping from the stall. His black tousled hair hung down, partly concealing the round chocolate eyes. The child was trembling, his lips twitching.

"You!" Cord gasped, holstering his gun. "You must have been following me—and you did a damn good job of it, too." He crossed to kneel before him and place his hands on the skinny arms. "You don't have to be afraid of me, boy. Tell me why you've been following me. What do you want?"

The boy continued to stare at him in silent terror.

Cord scratched his chin thoughtfully. "They say you have never spoken a word. You don't understand my language anyway, do you? Now why would you follow me?" He shook himself, took a deep breath, and continued, wondering whether the boy knew Spanish, "Is it the lady, the one who was kind to you? Amber?"

Armand blinked in recognition, his eyes taking on a glow. He nodded. He knew the name Amber.

Cord's heart was racing. He struggled to seem calm lest he frighten the boy more. There was no knowing what he had been through since running away from his village.

"Amber," Cord repeated, pointing to himself, then to the boy. "Amber. Can you take me to Amber?"

To Cord's delight, the boy nodded, smiling. Cord slapped his thigh in jubilation and stood up. By damn, the boy knew where she was! Maybe he had followed Valdis from the village.

Cord and little Armand were almost out the stable doors when Maretta cried out, "You cannot leave me like this! This time I am not drunk. I will remember clearly the pain, the way you shame me. I will see you dead for this!"

Cord turned and looked at her. "Believe me,

297

Maretta, I am sorry," he murmured, "but it's best this way."

"You are no man!" she cried scornfully. "A real man could not walk away from me!"

Yes, he could, Cord thought resolutely as he continued on his way. A real man could walk away...if he were heading for a real woman.

✿ Chapter Twenty-eight ✿

AMBER stared about her. Another cave, but this time, it curved far down into the bowels of the earth. There was a narrow, winding stream that came from somewhere and ran directly in front of the damp hollow where Valdis had left her. He kept a torch lit, but gave her no warmth. It was not the cold that bothered her so much as the constant, eery screeching of bats hanging above.

She leaned her head back against the wall of rock behind her. Never mind the creeping insects, or the slimy worms that sometimes crawled over her. None of it mattered. Her mouth felt dry, parched, and if someone did not help her soon, she knew she was going to get sick and die. Soon, she might not even care.

Hearing footsteps approaching, she braced herself. Valdis stooped to enter through the narrow opening, and she saw that he carried a small pot and a jug.

"I brought you some food," he said pleasantly, sitting down beside her as though they were dining at home. "A delicious stew and some cool water. Eat and you will feel better."

He set the utensils aside and swiftly produced a knife to cut the ropes from her wrists. Quickly, gratefully, she began to rub them to start the circulation moving through her numb fingers, painfully aware of how weak she had become.

Valdis took her chin in his hand. "You do not look good. Almost a week now, and you are puny. The other women have told me you lose your food as soon as you eat it. What am I to do with you?"

"Let me die," she mustered enough energy to snap.

He threw back his head and laughed, the sound echoing through the cave. "No, no. You cannot die. I have many plans for us. Soon now, I will return home and declare I have found my mother's murderer. I have almost made up my mind which of my men will take the blame. I will once more rule the valley, and you will be my mistress. I will dress you in the finest gowns, and will even take you to Paris and Spain to buy them. I will build you a hacienda to make the wealthiest women in Mexico envious." He shook his head. "But what are we to do with you? You look terrible. Everyone would laugh at Valdis Alezparito for being taken with such a señorita as you have become. We must do something."

She stared. "You leave me here in this damp hole with spiders and bats. I have not had a bath or a change of clothes since I got here, and the food you bring me is slop. And you talk of fine gowns and haciendas! I think you are crazy, Valdis."

He frowned, eyes narrowing, fingers flexing. "No, I am not crazy. I am in perfect control. I have left you here to teach you a lesson. Now I am going to let you have some fresh air and a bath. The women will wash your hair. I have a lovely dress for you to wear. But first you must eat. This stew is good. I have deliberately sent slop to punish you, just as I have left you here, alone, to think of what your life will be like forever if you do not obey me."

He dipped a spoon into the pot and extended it to her lips. She swallowed. It was good. And the water he offered was fresh and cool, not stagnant and sour.

"See?" He grinned. "Things can be better for you. You have learned how bad they can be. Now you will learn how good they can be. *You* will decide how you are to live your life with me. You will either be mine, to do my bidding, or I shall hand you over to my men and let them tire of you before we feed you to the buzzards. The decision is yours."

Amber said nothing. It was not the time to provoke him. She wanted all of the stew. She wanted strength. Without it, she was totally at his mercy.

"Now," he said when she had eaten. "I will carry you up and outside. It is a lovely day, warm, with sunshine. There is a nice place nearby where you will be bathed. Then we will talk. You will find I am not so bad as you think. One day you will love me. I know this."

She did feel better after eating, but as he helped her to her feet and guided her out, she pretended weakness, leaning against him, hating to touch him but knowing she would have to feign sickness so as to put off the time when he would ravish her.

They climbed a narrow, winding trail, moving up and up, until at last they stepped into the bright sunshine. Amber squeezed her eyes shut at the sudden light and covered her face with her hands. Valdis' men, lounging about, drinking, playing guitars or cleaning their weapons, looked at her and laughed. The few women glowered at her.

Amber squinted as Valdis ordered someone to take her away and bathe her. She was thrust into the work-worn hands of a hard-looking woman. Her fleshy bosom sagged, and she was much too heavy in the hips.

To Amber, Valdis snapped, "Do as she wishes. She has little patience. Give her any trouble, and she will probably scratch your eyes out."

Doggedly, Amber followed the woman through brush and around cactus, over sand mounds and rock formations. Then they stepped into a clearing where there was a cool, clear pool in a stream beneath a small, cascading waterfall. It did look delightful, and the angry-looking woman did not have to order Amber out of her rancid clothes. The woman tossed her a bar of lye soap, which Amber quickly rubbed over her body. She scrubbed until her skin was pink, then dove down to swim beneath the water for a moment before surfacing with strong, sure strokes. Oh, it felt good to breathe fresh air, feel the warmth of golden sunshine, and to be clean!

"See the lovely dress I have for you?"

Amber treaded water and turned. Valdis was standing on the mossy bank, holding out a gown of pale green muslin. It was of a simple design, with long sleeves, one of which he held up. "We need, my lovely one, to hide the rope burns on your wrists."

He sat down upon a rock, laying the dress carefully across his lap, looking quite pleased with himself.

Amber, making sure she remained in the water deep enough to hide her nakedness, called, "Why do you wish to hide the rope burns? Are you ashamed for your men to know you keep me tied?"

"My men have nothing to do with it. It is our stubborn friend, Cord Hayden, who must not see them."

The sound of his name stunned Amber. "Cord? You have no need to fear him. He left me and the others long ago, before we returned to the Indian village."

He shook a finger at her and chanted, childlike, "Fool me once, and shame on you. Fool me twice, and shame on me!" Laughing, he gloated, "I shall not be fooled again, señorita. I have had many scouts out watching. Gerras, who never gives up wanting your little Dolita, has watched the Indian village since we left there. He saw Hayden. I was not worried, for I knew he would have a very hard time finding this camp. But then my sister came, using a secret short-cut. She tells me she thinks maybe the bastard boy is bringing Hayden here. It seems the boy has taken to you. He must have followed Gerras and me when we brought you here, for he seems to know the way. That is what Maretta thinks, anyway."

"Armand!" Amber whispered faintly. He had followed her. And he was bringing Cord! But, dear Lord, Valdis knew, and he was waiting. They would both be killed. She screamed, "No, Valdis, don't kill them. I'll do anything you ask."

She stumbled from the water and made her way over to him, embarrassed to be fully exposed, trying to ignore the sudden look of desire that leaped into his eyes.

She gasped, "I tell you I will do anything, damn you! Don't hurt them!"

He slapped her, knocking her down. "I grow weary of your fire. I may decide to kill you and be rid of your insolence once and for all."

He reached down to twist her hair. "You will put on this dress. Your hair will be brushed until it shines. You will paint your lips and your cheeks, and you will smile. When your hero arrives, you will tell him how happy you are with me. You will tell him that at long last you have found a real man to love. You will make him believe you. You will tell him to go away and leave you forever. You will even describe to him how we couple, how I make you feel." He took a deep breath, stood back and let go of her hair. Smiling, he said, "When you do this, he will go away and plague me no more." He looked at her, hard. "The boy will not be hurt. No one will be hurt if you cooperate."

"What will happen to the boy?" she asked fearfully.

Valdis looked impatient. "I do not wish to keep you tied, but I want you to be obedient. The boy will remain with us, to keep you compliant."

Armand to stay with her! She hardly dared believe it.

"Now then, we shall have no more problems, shall we?" He whacked her buttocks sharply, then squeezed. "You want the boy to be treated well, so think of that when I come to you tonight after I have gotten rid of Hayden forever. You can show me how appreciative you are of my kindness to your matador's bastard." Without warning, he crushed her in his arms, covering her mouth. When he released her, she wiped her mouth with the back of her hand and he reached out and squeezed one nipple painfully. She cried out, and he roared, "Never do that! Never shrink from my touch or look as though you do not like me. Thank me each time I favor you with my hands, my lips, or my rod of love. Soon, you will be on your knees begging me to take you, over and over.

"Remember, two lives will depend on how pleasant you learn to become—yours and the child's."

They had ridden through the morning, and already the sun was high in the sky. Cord could see the wisdom in waiting for nightfall but did not want Amber in danger a minute longer than necessary.

When a rocky knoll came into sight, straight ahead, the boy reached up from his pony to tug at Cord's sleeve.

"This is it?" Cord reined his horse in and looked down at the anxious black eyes. "All right, friend." He forced a grin. "This is where we part company for a while. To be safe, you are going over there to that clump of sagebrush and hide yourself and your pony. Wait till I come back. Understand?"

The boy stared. With a sigh, Cord led him to the dense patch of brush, and pointed to the ground. "Here." He pointed to the boy. "You stay."

Cord turned to ride away, and when the boy started to follow, he repeated his orders, harshly. This time, Armand understood.

A mountain range lay straight ahead, and to his right lay thick clumps of cottonwoods and pines. It meant going out of his way, but it was his only chance to slip up secretly on the camp. Suddenly he caught a glimpse of smoke and realized it was a campfire. He had found the hideout! He kicked his horse to a full gallop and rode straight for the cover. He picked his way through the rough terrain, using the smoke as a beacon to guide him. Finally, he figured he was close enough to go on foot. Dismounting, he took his rifle, left his horse tied, and began to walk stealthily, hunched over, pausing every so often to listen for sounds.

It took an interminably long time before he saw the fire, just on the other side of a large, jagged rock, and he crawled the rest of the way on his belly. Easing his head up ever so slightly over the rock, he stared down at Valdis' men, sprawled around the fire. Some of them had camp women in their arms. They passed bottles back and forth. Some slept. Everything was peaceful, and Cord figured no one suspected he was there.

Then, heart leaping, he saw what he was looking for—Valdis. Tremors of rage rippled through him, and it was all he could do to keep from aiming his rifle and blowing the bastard to pieces. But then he saw that Valdis was pulling a woman down beside him, drawing her to him, wrapping his arms about her possessively. He kissed her passionately. The woman was Amber. And she was not struggling.

It couldn't be. Perhaps she was drugged? Never would she go willingly to Valdis. Never. And he was not going to allow her to be violated.

He stood, a growl emanating from deep within like that of a wild animal ready to attack. All eyes below suddenly turned up to where he stood with rifle in one hand, his pistol in the other. "Let her go, Valdis!" Cord roared. "Now!"

To the others, he cried, "Don't make a move. You may kill me, but I'll get him first."

Amber rolled from Valdis' arms, and propped herself against a rock. Cord strained to see her face, refusing to believe that she was smiling.

"Amber, come up here, now," he yelled, his voice sounding hollow. Something was very wrong.

When she made no move, he cried hoarsely, "Are you able to get up, Amber?"

"Of course I am able to get up," she called out cheerfully, and the others laughed. "Come join us, Cord. We are all good friends here now."

He gripped the rifle. "Amber, you don't have to be afraid. Just get up and walk up here. Valdis, you walk slowly right behind her, because you're coming with us to make sure we aren't followed."

Amber got to her feet, and Valdis made no move

to restrain her. "You don't understand, Cord," she called out, shading her eyes from the sun. "Things have changed since you left. I have come to know Valdis for the wonderful man he really is. He has made me very happy. I don't want to go with you."

"Amber, get up here. You don't have to be afraid."

"I'm not afraid," she laughed. "If you wanted me, Cord, you shouldn't have left me. Did you think I would stay behind and rot in that horrible little Indian village? Valdis took me away, and now I'm a happy woman. We have peace here. We are happy."

Valdis spoke for the first time, shouting amiably, "Come down, Hayden. Have a drink with us. You will see how happy the señorita is. Do not be a poor loser. The best man won, isn't that so?"

Everyone laughed raucously, and Cord saw that Amber joined in, too. She allowed Valdis to draw her into his arms once more.

Slowly, Cord slid backward from the rock and turned and walked away, the ringing laughter echoing behind him. He kept on walking, not allowing himself to think or feel.

Somehow, despite the roaring in his head, Cord made his way back to the boy's hiding place. Somehow, he was not surprised to find him gone.

Gerras leaped down from a ledge high above the one on which Cord had made his stand, a triumphant grin splitting his face. "He's gone!" he cried, waving his rifle. "And not a shot was fired. He will not be back."

Valdis turned and pulled Amber into his arms and kissed her long and hard, thrusting his tongue inside her mouth. When at last he released her, he laughed, "It is over. Tonight I will reward my men with all the tequila they can drink. They performed well, watching your lover every step of the way, watching where he hid the bastard so they could bring him here. Go to him now. Let him know he will be by your side as long as you please me. Tonight, after I have celebrated with my men, I will come to you, and you can show your appreciation for my kindness."

He released her, and she stumbled away, tears blinding her as she made her way back into the cave.

Cord. Her heart cried his name over and over. *Cord. I had to say those lies. I had to.*

She struggled to breathe past the agony in her throat...dear God, she loved him so.

🕮 Chapter Twenty-nine 🕮

AMBER held little Armand's face in her hands and whispered anxiously, "Please, please, my darling, try to understand what I am going to say to you. We have to figure a way to get out of here. I don't know how we're going to do it, but we've got to try. I can't endure what awaits me, and I can't bear the thought of your having to live here."

She kissed his cheeks and fell back to sit on the ground. Armand stared up at her, not taking his eyes from her for a moment.

Lost in her misery, Amber did not at first feel the gentle poking of Armand's finger upon her shoulder. He poked harder, and she turned to him. She reached for the objects he held out to her as he smiled triumphantly. "Mushrooms? Why—?" Then she knew, and her grin matched his. Somehow, somewhere along the way, he had found mushrooms. If he knew as much about growing things as his people did, then they were poisonous. Poisonous mushrooms!

She gave him a quick hug. "Armand, you may have found a way for us to escape. They were cooking a stew. All I have to do is slip these into the pot, and the whole lot of them will be ill." It was hope, and the first she'd felt since seeing Valdis at the Indian village.

She searched for and found a smooth rock and two small, jagged stones with which to pound the mushrooms.

Armand and she worked feverishly and, in moments, had reduced the mushrooms to a residue like soft mud. Tearing a bit of material from the petticoat beneath her dress, Amber scraped the mush into it, tying it loosely to make a small pouch, which she tucked inside her bodice.

"Now," she breathed raggedly, as they both sat back, "all I have to do is get it into the pot. I suppose I will have to wait until dark, but first, I'll make everyone think I'm drunk." She giggled, reaching to clasp the boy's hand, sadness suddenly overcoming her again. "If only we could find Cord," she said wistfully. "I'd give anything if I could tell him the truth. Maybe he hasn't gotten far. Once we get out we can ride hard. But I suppose that's wishing for too much...." Her voice trailed off.

Armand tugged at her sleeve, pointing to himself, then toward the outside, nodding and grinning hopefully.

Amber stared. "Are you telling me you can take me to Cord? You can trail him?"

He nodded, eyes shining.

"You understand some of what I say, don't you?" she murmured in wonder. "I know it is probably only because you recognize familiar names, and you pay attention to gestures, but someday we'll talk easily, I just know it." Bounding to her feet, she held out her hand to him, "Come on, pardner, let's go up there and put on a good act!"

Outside, they walked into the late afternoon sunshine. Valdis, drinking with his men, jovially called, "Ahhh, you have come to join us, *querida*. Now we will truly have a fiesta."

"I brought the boy up for sunshine and fresh air," she told him evenly, careful not to sound at all eager about Armand.

He waved an arm. "Of course. Is this not his home now, too? As long as he doesn't cause trouble, we will have no problems. The boy may play as he wishes. Come and sit with me. Wine will make you relax. You look tense."

Amber motioned to Armand, and he understood what was expected. Wandering off, but not far away, as Valdis' men regarded him warily, he went about inspecting cactus flowers among the rocks, pretending to enjoy chasing a pale yellow butterfly.

Amber sat down, eyes darting quickly to the pot of stew. It was near the cave's entrance, so evening shadows would fall there earlier than on other parts of the flat space in front of the hideout. That was in her favor. The pouch tucked in the bodice of her dress was well hidden, but she would have to duck any amorous advances Valdis might make. She hoped he would wait until night before touching her.

"Come, drink," Valdis urged. "You are one of us now. Smile. You must look happy, or my people will not like you. They will think you consider yourself too good to drink with them."

"Yes, I suppose so." She made her voice tight. "If I'm to be forced to live with you animals, I might as well try to enjoy myself." She jerked the bottle from his hand and tipped it to her lips, pretending to swallow. She feigned a short coughing spell, much to the delight of Valdis' men. "Maybe if I get drunk I can stand you pigs!" A cheer went up as she drank again, and this time she swallowed some, fearing they would notice if the bottle didn't seem emptier. Then she stood up and walked around, scowling. "I hate all of you, you know that, don't you?" She grabbed another bottle from someone else, much to the delight of Valdis, who was clapping his hands gleefully. "I hate all of you, and I always will. Bandits! Murderers! I wish to see all of you dead."

"Ah, you will have your hands full this night," one of his men goaded Valdis.

Another chimed in. "This one is a wildcat. Never will you tame her."

Valdis roared, "But I will enjoy the wildcat's bites and scratches, and before the night ends, her only screams will be those of pleasure."

"Take her now!" someone called out. "Now, in front of us all. We have seen you tame others, and this one will be a real challenge."

It was all Amber could do not to protest. Much to her relief, she heard Valdis declare angrily, "No. This one is special. She is not a *puta*. She is to be my mistress when I return home. You will respect her. When I tire of her, or if she displeases me, then you may pass her around as you do these bottles. Until then, let there be no such talk."

She continued to weave through the group, pausing to sip now and then. Valdis settled into a game of cards with some of the men, and Amber felt a rush of encouragement as others wandered over to watch. She was even happier when the women all left to go down to the stream to bathe.

The sun continued to drop until, at last, the purple shadows that she had awaited so anxiously began to descend over that part of the camp where the cooking pot was. No one was looking at her anymore, and she fished into her bodice, quickly extracting the pouch and untying it. Then she began to wander toward the pot, pretending interest in the simmering contents.

A sharp voice caused her to almost drop the pouch.

"What are you doing?" growled one of the men.

She reached for the stick that was used for stirring. "What does it look like I'm doing?" She slurred her voice. "Someone must do the cooking. All you pigs do is drink."

She was rescued when Valdis snapped, "Leave her be. It will give her something to do."

Amber took a deep breath and began to stir the bubbling stew. After a few moments, she slowly looked around to make sure no one was paying any attention, then dumped in the glob of pulverized mushrooms, quickly stuffing the rag back into her bodice. Giving the stew a few more turns with the stick, she turned away, pausing to look at Armand, who was watching her in rapt attention.

She winked, and he grinned. It was done.

She wandered as far away from the pot as possible and, finding a grassy spot, lay down and pretended to sleep. One of the men snickered, "The señorita drinks too much. Now she sleeps it off."

"Let her," said Valdis with a chuckle. "She will need her rest for tonight."

They all joined in the raucous laughter.

The women returned from the stream, and Amber was thrilled to hear one of the men order that the stew be served. She heard the sounds of moving and remained perfectly still, tensing only when someone asked whether she should be awakened so she could eat.

"Let her sleep," came Valdis' voice. "Tonight, I will have some special food for her!" he added, laughing.

Soon she could hear slurping sounds as they ate, and she dared to open her eyes just wide enough to make sure all of them were eating at once.

Gerras was the first to show symptoms. "Ayo!" he cried, belching loudly. "My stomach makes noises like castanets. "I think I am going to be sick. Maybe the meat was bad."

"Maybe we drank too much," someone else said feebly.

Valdis grunted. "We also ate too much. The pot is empty. The meat was not bad. It was too *good*. Now we pay the price for being pigs."

Amber peered out from beneath half-lowered lashes and saw that Gerras was swaying on his feet. "My eyes! I can't see clearly. You are moving. All of you are moving. And now I will fly like a bird—"

Two women began writhing on the ground and several men stumbled, falling into one another blindly, mumbling to themselves. A guard who had come in from his post to eat, fell unconscious.

Sick cries blended together, making one awesome sound as everyone was struck by the mushrooms. Amber strained to see Armand but could not, and wondered frantically where he had disappeared to. Soon they would make their move, and there was no time to be wasted searching for him. Then she heard a movement behind her in the brush, and turned slowly, hesitantly, to see him crouched there, smiling at her.

She turned back to the scene once more. When she saw that Valdis was stumbling about, lost in a trance, saw that everyone in the camp was affected, she decided it was time. Rolling under the brush, she crawled on her hands and knees, Armand leading her.

When they were out of the endless stand of brush and could stand up, Armand grabbed her arm as though he knew where he was going.

Around a jutting rock, Amber was thrilled to see several horses corralled in a crude pen. Armand slipped between the railings to disappear among them, returning with a small pony. Grinning broadly, he moved back once more and returned with a horse for her. Pushing a railing aside, he led the two animals out and then mounted his pony.

Soon they were climbing up the side of a mountain. The trail was quite narrow. An animal screeched and Amber jumped, gripping the horse's mane tightly.

Hours passed, and still they plodded doggedly upward. At long last, Amber felt they were out of Valdis' reach, and she said to Armand, "We have to sleep. We've got to be on our way early."

Sleep swept over them as briskly as the cold mountain wind that blew across their huddled bodies.

Neither heard the crunching of leaves nearby, or the footsteps of the man approaching.

🕮 Chapter Thirty 🕮

CORD sat for a long time watching Amber as she slept, her face bathed in moonlight. Lying there, her long, silver hair fanned out about her, she looked, he thought, almost too beautiful to be real. He smiled. The boy was quite a scout. Cord had known that Valdis might send someone after him to kill him, so he had kept watching behind himself and had known that the two fugitives were trailing him.

How had they managed to escape? As weary as he knew she was, Cord dared not let Amber sleep any longer, because if Valdis and his men were following, then they had to keep moving.

Silently he dropped from the ledge and knelt beside her. Reaching out to touch her shoulder, he hesitated, his eyes moving to the gentle rise and fall of her breasts. Lord, she was all he had ever desired. With gentle fingertips, he touched a breast, smiling as the nipple quickly became taut. She sighed softly.

He trailed his hand down, caressing her hips, and she wriggled in her sleep. Gently, he pulled her dress upward, exposing her slim, perfectly molded legs, now shaded in a rosy hue by the first threat of dawn.

Spreading her thighs, his fingers moved nimbly between and he began to caress her. She moaned, for she was dreaming of warm brown eyes, her body on fire, and she gave way to the sweet memory of Cord Hayden's lovemaking.

After making sure that the boy was sleeping soundly, Cord undressed. He maneuvered himself on top of Amber, spreading her legs wider and cupping her buttocks. With one mighty thrust, he was inside her, and he gasped as he felt the hot velvet surround his manhood so eagerly. It was, he realized joyfully, like going to where he belonged, going home.

Amber's lips parted, but Cord quickly covered them with his own. Her fingers moved to clutch at his firm back.

Cord held her tightly, feeling the great shudders building within her as her hips rose, pushing hard against him. He knew that she had experienced her own pinnacle of joy, and he quickened his thrusts, taking himself all the way.

They clung together for long moments, and then Amber said accusingly, "This is no dream, Cord Hayden."

He rolled away from her and propped himself

on an elbow, smiling down at her beautiful, but angry, face. "Don't wake the boy," he whispered. "We've got some talking to do first."

Amber allowed her temper to cover for her embarrassment. "How dare you sneak in here and...seduce me!"

"Oh, shut up, Amber," he drawled, caressing her breasts, laughing as she tried to shove him away. "You enjoyed it, and you know it. So stop acting so damned prim. We haven't got time. I've got plenty of questions, and you'd better have some good answers. Now let's start with that scene back there at Valdis' camp. You seemed satisfied, yet you slipped away and followed me. Why?"

She lifted her head, glaring down at the possessive, restraining arm across her chest. "It was an act," she said between clenched teeth. "Valdis made me do it. He said he would kill Armand if I didn't."

"You're quite an actress, as I've told you before. Now, tell me everything," he commanded.

Stiffly, she told him all of it. When she was through, Cord made a low, whistling sound and shook his head.

They lay side by side, gazing into each other's eyes, and after a while Amber said abruptly, "I would be lying if I said I weren't suspicious of you."

He raised an eyebrow. "Suspicious? Why?"

"You told me you loved me, but I wonder if you really do."

He laughed softly, not mockingly, then he shrugged. "I guess I'm just going to have to find a way to prove to you how much you mean to me,

Amber. Right now, we've got to be on our way."

He helped her up, then awoke Armand, who blinked happily at the sight of him. Cord told him to untie the horses. When the boy was out of hearing, he turned to Amber. "Let's understand each other. I'm going to have to ride like hell to get to Wyoming by the time Major Powell begins his expedition. I probably can't make it, and if he's already gone, then I'll have to catch up with him. You and the boy are coming with me, and you will stay with me till I figure out what to do with you. There's no time to take you anyplace else, and I'm not going to let you loose. Valdis is sure to come after you. Now, we've got a long ride ahead, and it's going to be rough. Can you make it?"

"I can make it," she told him with fervor. "And I promise we won't hold you back or get in your way."

He trailed his fingertips down her face. "You won't ever be in my way. Neither will the boy. I just want to prove to you how much I care, because I know you don't trust me. Now—let's ride."

✒ Chapter Thirty-one ✒

THEY rode north for two weeks, great silences falling among them for as often as whole days. They ate whatever Cord and Armand could find. Armand was happy, but he sensed that he should stay out of the adults' way, and he rode his pony just a little ahead, appearing to ride in his own world.

Amber and Cord said little to each other, but it seemed that every exchange had a deeper import than the one preceding it. It was a probing process both needed—Amber especially. She was deeply disturbed by Cord's continual nearness. How, she asked herself, could she have fallen in love with this stubborn, wild man? And how could she have fallen in love with a man who had bedded Maretta? Who had not even claimed to love Maretta?

What kind of man was this, she wondered over and over, sometimes frantically.

But lying deepest was this: Cord meant to leave her behind while he went off with Major Powell. Just leave her, as though she were baggage he could drop off and pick up at will! This was a man who professed love? No! her heart cried. If Cord loved her, he wouldn't just leave her.

Suddenly, in Arizona, the forest ended and the world abruptly became flat and rocky. Amber looked ahead into that void, and felt a singing tension all the way to her toes. It was silent, utterly silent, as though all the quiet of time to come and time past had descended upon them.

A gray mist surrounding them turned violet, then purple. Amber trembled. It was as though that forbidding silence was crawling inside to consume her. She dared not speak, for sound would surely be blasphemous.

Suddenly, through the mist, the first sight of the canyon appeared. Armand cried out loud with delight at the spectacle, and Amber gasped, dropping the reins. It was awesome; ribbons of color ripping through the earth, all the beauty and all the splendor that the hand of God had created.

They reached a precipice, and Amber and Armand slowed their mounts, but Cord motioned to them to move along, and in a few more steps a sharp descent was visible. Gray sandstone slopes spotted with black brush bordered a narrow, rocky path, and clumps of junipers and mesquite had to be navigated. They entered a deep, narrow, twisting corridor filled with shadows. By then, only a scant glimpse of indigo sky was visible.

The cliffs enclosing them changed colors every few feet, from rich brown to vibrant scarlet, to purple, and to turquoise and pale green.

The air became cooler as they made their way on down, and Amber shivered as she marveled that it was summer. They rounded a sharp curve of rock to find an astonishing array of fresh green cottonwoods, their branches tossing in the chilly winds, and willow trees, through which could be seen the gleam of moving water.

Cord reined his horse to a stop and Amber and Armand followed suit. For long moments, they sat in silence, staring. Cord murmured, "The Indians tell me this is just a creek. At some point I think it empties into the Colorado River."

Moved by the majesty of it all, Amber's anger at being deserted was, for the first time, cast aside. "The water is so blue. How deep the color is!" she said in awe.

He nodded in agreement. "The Indians told me that when it first comes up out of the floor of the canyon, it has no color at all, but then it begins to look turquoise. I can understand the color of the ocean being like this because the sky is reflected by the water. But this creek is only about two or three feet deep. And there is no way for the sky to be reflected here, not with all the cliffs and rocks in between.

"They say there are four big waterfalls a few miles away," he went on happily, "and the water cascading down is also blue."

He looked at her beseechingly, but not apologetically. "Every time I come across something like this, my blood starts racing. I guess that's why I have the wanderlust."

Then suddenly he became serious, almost morose. "I've told you everything about my past in the last week. I feel like a new man, knowing I don't have to run from lies any longer. Being invited to join this expedition is a special gift. It has nothing to do with the way I feel about you. It's just something I have to do. Can you understand?"

Her eyes teared. "Cord, I'm trying. Believe me, I'm trying. But so much has happened to me, my life. And to complicate everything, I have to understand about your love affair—or whatever it was—with Maretta."

"I can't undo what's been done," he said sharply. "That's all in the past."

She looked away and said nothing.

He cursed softly, then said, "Come on. Let's ride."

She followed grimly, Armand close behind her.

After a while, Cord looked up, startled, and she followed his gaze, stunned to see Indians peering down at them from a ledge above.

"It's all right," Cord told her. "Stay here."

She moved her horse closer to Armand, who was grinning happily over this newest adventure, while Cord dismounted and began climbing up the side of the cliff. Amber watched as he made his way up, then disappeared behind the large rocks. Moments later, he reappeared and climbed down, four of the Indians following.

"It's all settled," he said, smiling at her. "They're going to take the two of you on down to their village now."

Amber felt a new wave of despair wash over her. There was nothing more she could say to change his mind. And how could she tell him of the despair over his leaving? Perhaps he would never return. They had discussed this on the journey, but she had hoped he wouldn't leave her here.

She stared up at him, biting her lip to keep from crying. The top of her head barely reached his chin, and she felt like a child. "How..." she gasped brokenly, "can you *do* this to me, Cord? What if you don't come back? What will become of us?"

He jerked her against him, one hand entwining fingers in her long, silver hair, pulling it gently back to see her vulnerable face. He devoured her mouth with his own. Abruptly lifting his lips, he whispered huskily, "Nothing will keep me from coming back to you, Amber. I promise. And I promise I'll find a way to prove I love you ... just as you will realize how much you love me."

He left her then, mounting his horse and riding away. He did not look back.

⚘ Chapter Thirty-two ⚘

THE ride was rough, and Cord was not surprised to find that the sight of Powell and his men made him feel exhilaration. He was vigorous again. Someday, he vowed, Amber would understand what all this meant to him.

One of the men looked up and waved with his left arm. Seeing the stump of the right arm, Cord knew it was Major Powell himself. He waved back and started down the powder-dry gully leading to the river. Powell was an unusual man, a man Cord deeply respected. He had lost his arm at the Battle of Shiloh and resigned from the army in '65 as a Major, then joining Illinois Wesleyan University as a professor of geology. Two years later, he had become a lecturer at Illinois Normal College and began a series of expeditions into the Rocky Mountains.

Cord grinned, thinking about Powell's salty personality. He was only one of thousands of soldiers who lost arms in the damned war, and he hadn't let it stop him from doing what he wanted to do—which was answering the call of the wild. He was a short man, too. Cord laughed out loud as he recalled what Powell had told him about a bet he made with his close friend, the eminent geologist, W. J. McGee. McGee was a very tall man.

"One day I was staring up at his head," Major Powell had laughingly recounted, "and I told him, 'I'll bet I have a bigger brain than you have.' Well, he just laughed at first, and then he realized I was seriously making a bet, and he accepted it. You know what we did? We both made out wills, leaving our brains to each other. When each of us dies, some doctor will take out our brains and measure them."

Cord was astounded. "But you'll never know who won!"

Powell dismissed that. "Let our families crow over who wins," and he added with a wink, "Who knows? I may go down in history for exploring that damn big canyon, and then they'll also write about my bet with McGee."

Now Powell came forward to greet him. "I thought you had changed your mind," Major Powell called. "We left Green River City a week ago. I figured maybe you'd found that little lady you mentioned in your letter and gotten yourself married."

Cord dismounted and, after shaking Powell's left hand, grinned and said, "All I said was that

I had to try and get a lady out of some trouble. What makes you think there's romance involved?"

"A man has a different look about him when he's answering the call of a woman than when he's answering the call of the wild—though sometimes the two seem the same." Powell laughed. "Welcome, Hayden. We're glad to have you with us."

Major Powell made introductions to the nine other men. Some were hunters, lusty for adventure, and others were old soldiers, but all had been carefully selected.

Powell also introduced Cord to the Chicago-built boats. "This one is 'Emma Dean,' named for my wife, and there's 'Maid of the Canyon' and 'Kitty Clyde's Sister.' Inspiration failed me, so the last one is called 'No Name.'"

Powell told him of their beginning and how everyone in Green River City had turned out to wish them good luck. Pushing the four little boats from shore, they had been immediately caught up in the swift current and carried on down.

"The first afternoon," Powell said, eyes shining with excitement, "we came to a point where the river sweeps the foot of an overhanging cliff, and we camped there for the night. There was still a few hours of daylight left, so I climbed up onto the cliffs and walked around in those strange carved rocks of the Green River badlands. I found sandstones and shales in all colors, all lying horizontal." He smiled. "Forgive me. I tend to get carried away."

"We all will before it's over," Cord said quickly. "That's why we're here, isn't it?"

331

"Of course. Now tell me about your lady."

Cord did, ending with, "I believe she's safe with the Havasupais."

"She will be fine," Powell was quick to assure him. "They're a friendly people, and she'll learn almost as much about the canyon from them as you will on this expedition. Can she take the rugged life?"

Cord laughed. "Amber can take anything, Major. She's a very special lady."

"Well, thank God you can take her home whenever you want, Hayden. I'm as relieved as you are that you don't have to run anymore."

"I never liked running," Cord said tightly. "I wanted to stay and prove my innocence."

Powell snorted. "Feelings were running so high back then you'd have wound up dangling on the end of a rope. I'm just glad you had the good sense to lay low till that fool girl told the truth. Now, let's get going."

The boats were quickly caught in the swift current. A half mile below, the river curved sharply to the left and entered another canyon carved into the mountain. The boats moved into the narrow passage, and Cord marveled at the way the walls on each side rose rapidly, stretching higher and higher.

They were swept along as the river cut abruptly around a point and to the right. Then the waters suddenly plunged swiftly down among huge rocks.

"I think this is going to be our first experience with the rapids," Major Powell cried anxiously above the thundering water. Cautiously, he stood up and cried, "I'll try to make a way among the rocks."

In seconds the boats were pulled into the swift current, each man paddling fiercely, a few strokes on one side, then a few on the other, swinging arms and oars left and right as they fought the angry water, nerves taut as bowstrings. They mounted waves taller than they were, foaming bubbling crests, washing over them in powerful slaps. Then they would plunge down into troughs, rudely splashed all over again.

Then, suddenly, the river was calm, and everyone breathed freely again. Major Powell proclaimed happily that they had met and conquered their first rapids.

Late in the day the boats reached a calm, sandy cove, and they camped there for the night. After a supper of jerky, dried beans, and coffee, Cord leaned wearily against a rock, staring at the watermelon sky. There would be a breathtaking sunset over the canyon, but they were too far down to see it.

"Marvelous, isn't it?" Major Powell said reverently as he sat down nearby.

"I'm amazed," Cord told him, "at all the greenery growing in the midst of sheer rock."

Powell nodded. "You're a true explorer, Hayden. You don't miss a thing." He pointed high above. "There's a Gambel oak, a real curiosity. When you see one up close, notice how its roots spread horizontally, shooting out at intervals to start new trees. You can spot a grove of Gambel oaks and think there are forty or fifty of them, when actually its just one big tree, holding roots, like holding hands.

"There are also ponderosas here, too," he continued, "and straggly piñon pines and junipers."

"Breathtaking," Cord breathed. "Just breathtaking, all of it."

Powell chuckled. "We've just begun, my good man. I'm afraid we've got a long way to go, and it's not all going to be sightseeing. Those rapids worry me. I wonder which will endure to the end— my boats or my men."

Cord looked at him sharply. "You're worried about the men deserting if the going gets rough?"

"I don't know. Three concern me. I sense their change of feelings since we left, especially after running our first rapids today. But," he sighed, "all I can do is talk to them and hope they get back their original enthusiasm. I made it quite clear long before we left that we were undertaking a dangerous venture, and I asked that anyone having doubts back out. No one did, so I expect everyone to see it all the way through. But, Hayden, you aren't an official member of this expedition, so you owe me nothing. Remember that, but as I told you, I'm glad to have you aboard."

One of the men approached with the last of the coffee, and they both held out their tin cups. When they were alone again, Powell said, "Campfires and coffee call for telling old tales, don't you think? One I like best is the legend of the golden rose."

Cord listened thoughtfully. He was still lost in reverie, impressed with the story, as Major Powell bid him good night and left.

* * *

A week after Cord joined the group, he stood with Major Powell and the others one rose-kissed morning and stared in wonder at the glassy-smooth water. They were about to enter the Canyon of Lodore, thought to be about twenty miles long. The sound of angry water rushing and crashing could be heard just around the next bend, and the walls above them looked at least a mile high.

Silently they crawled into the four boats, and the boats drifted slowly around the bend. In a split second they were running the rapids, and almost as quickly, they were on calm water again.

The walls were oddly shaped, standing vertically or overhanging in cliffs. Some were terraced, some receded into steep slopes broken by gulches or smaller canyons. Lichens covered the red sandstones, and there were delicate mosses and ferns festooning everything.

The next day they reached a point where they had to get out of their boats and walk among the rocks to examine the channel before attempting to run it. In midafternoon, Powell decided they were going to have to make a portage and carry their boats over the rocks until they reached a place safe enough to sail through. He landed his own boat and signaled to the others to follow, then began walking along the bank, scrutinizing the ground. The other men stayed in their boats.

Suddenly there was a shout, and the boat called No Name shot straight down the center of the falls with its three men.

"She's going over," Powell screamed. "Save yourselves!"

Cord and the others swung their oars frantically, and everyone sent up a prayer of gratitude when they turned from the grasping current and reached the shore. Scrambling out, Cord ran along the shore among the rocks to see what had happened to the No Name. The first fall was not too great, perhaps ten or twelve feet. They had survived ones like that before. But below, he realized with an icy shudder, the river tumbled down for forty feet or more, into an angry, narrow channel filled with sharp rocks that broke the waves into whirlpools, beating them into boiling white foam.

Cord and Powell maneuvered themselves around a great crag just in time to see the boat hit a rock, rebounding sharply. Helplessly they watched two of the men lose their oars as the boat swung around and struck another rock. The boat broke in half, and the three men were flung into the river.

"Grab it! Grab it!" Cord yelled above the thundering sound of the water. The larger part of the boat was still floating, and the men struggled to grab it, gasping and choking as they swallowed the water beating their faces.

"They're being carried down," Powell roared. "Let's go!"

They rounded the next bend just in time to see that the remaining part of the boat had been struck again, and this time dashed to pieces. Swiftly, the fragments—and the helplessly flailing men—were washed out of sight.

Powell and Cord scrambled along the shore, eyes searching frantically. One man had made it to the shore. They could see another man's head above the water, in a large whirlpool beneath an even larger rock.

"That's Frank Goodman," Powell cried. "He's got hold of the rock. Grab him, Howland," he called to the one on the shore.

Howland found a long stick and held it out to Goodman, clinging to the rock. Goodman lunged for it, and Howland pulled him to shore.

"Seneca, here!" Captain Howland cried, making his way toward the remaining crew member, who also happened to be his brother. Seneca was slowly making his way to shore after being caught among the rocks, and in a moment the three survivors stood on shore together.

A week later, they made camp in a small clearing on the river's shore, with cedars on one side and a dense mass of box elders and dead willows on the other. Powell went off, alone, to explore, and Cord helped the men build a campfire.

Suddenly, a whirlwind roared down from a canyon above, and before anyone understood what was happening, the campfire flames were caught in the wind, igniting the dead willows and dried wood along the shore.

Cord yelled, "Get to the boats. We're going to be burned alive. The wind is whipping a wall of fire." But even as he cried out, he felt his clothing starting to burn. The very air was on fire.

Scrambling into the boats, Cord realized that they were going to have to turn them loose. The overhanging willow limbs were burning only a few feet away. He looked down the river in the glow of the violet sunset and saw a rock-filled rapids awaiting them. Damn, he swore, where was Powell?

Captain Howland ordered, "Row out as far as you can without getting caught in the current, then stab your oar into the river as hard as you can and try to anchor and not move. The flames seem to be dying down."

They obeyed, and as quickly as the devil wind had arrived, it departed, and with it, the shooting, fanning flames died. The fire crackled slowly, and they dared to make their way back to shore just as Major Powell came running from the rocky embankment above.

A survey was taken. A few tin cups, basins, a camp kettle—that was all that was left of their cooking utensils, and there was some clothing and bedding in the boats. Everything else was gone.

A few weeks later, one of the men, physically and mentally exhausted, sought refuge at an Indian agency near the river. Powell had bid him farewell with no hard feelings, but Cord had known he was fearing that others would leave also.

❧ Chapter Thirty-three ❧

IT was August 9th when Major Powell recorded in the journal he religiously kept that the most spectacular scenery of all had been discovered. The canyon walls were of beautiful marble of many colors, perhaps twenty-five hundred feet high. Toward the bottom, washed by the waves, the marble was polished and fretted with breathtaking patterns. At one point, the sun struggled to shine through a cleft in the wall, giving an iridescent luster to the gleaming stone. No one was surprised when Powell named the site Marble Canyon.

Three days later, they reached their lowest point. Perhaps, Cord mused, the deepest descent had begun with the rattlesnakes. Powell had killed two as he walked along a stream, and one of the men had killed one in camp. It had been particularly unnerving to find the rattlesnake in camp—for it was pink. No one had ever heard of a pink rattlesnake. So far, they had stayed clear of the numerous lizards, some as long as eighteen inches, and the many scorpions, some of which were deadly.

Spirits were down. Rations were scarce and no one was getting nearly enough to eat. It had rained every day for a week.

Seneca Howland, speaking to no one in particular, said in a somber voice, "me and my brother and William Dunn have decided we don't want to go no further in the boats. We've spent the afternoon climbing around in the crags and pinnacles, and we've scanned the river. The streams have boulders washed into them, forming dams, and there are falls of maybe eighteen feet. Then there's a rapid, filled with rocks, for maybe three hundred yards. Somewhere below, there's another waterfall, and we can't tell how big it is." He looked in turn at each pair of eyes watching him, some in silent accusation. "We're going out on our own. We'll climb out of the canyon and find our way. We hope you understand."

No one spoke. The next morning, after a tense breakfast, Powell ordered that two rifles and a shotgun be given to the three who were leaving. He also asked them to help themselves to the remaining rations. They refused, saying they would hunt animals along the way.

Powell wrote a letter to his wife, which he entrusted to Captain Howland. Sumner gave Howland his watch and asked that he send it to his sister if the rest of them did not make it out of the canyon. Powell turned over some notes from his journal of the expedition.

Cord finally turned away from the leave-taking. Some of the men were unashamedly crying. Each group—the ones leaving and the ones remaining—felt the other was doomed. As for himself, he did not know which choice was the wiser. He had seen awesome beauty that would be engraved in his mind forever. But he knew the fearful dangers just as keenly.

He felt a firm hand on his shoulder and turned to Major Powell, who was looking at him with moist eyes. "Go," Powell said in a husky whisper. "Go with them, Hayden. Once you're out of the canyon, go northeast along the rim. I've spotted a few wild horses and ponies. You may be able to rope one. When you can see the two pillarlike rocks the Indians call the 'Wigeleeva,' head for that point. You'll find some Havasupais around, because the Wigeleeva have a significance for them."

"Thanks," Cord said with a curt nod, "but I'm not leaving you, Major. I joined for the duration. I won't desert."

Powell studied him hard for a moment, then said, "You did what you set out to do. You lived through wonders you will tell your grandchildren about. No need to risk your life any longer. Go with the others. One day, we'll meet again."

Powell squeezed his shoulder. "Go on. If it makes it any easier for you, I'll fire you," he added with a mischievous smile.

In that split second, Cord knew what he wanted to do. He wanted Amber, and he wanted her as fast as he could get to her. There wasn't any question about his loyalty to Powell, or his love for this expedition. But he had carried Amber in his thoughts since the beginning, and in that moment, when Major Powell released him, he knew that she had overwhelmed everything else. He would go.

Cord grinned. "I was never officially hired, Major. You just let me tag along. Godspeed."

Giving his longtime friend one piercing look, Cord turned and, hoisting his rifle, turned toward the rocky walls. He never looked back. That was his way. He had always felt it bad luck...that he would never again see that which he looked upon in departing.

After four days of blistering walking in the late summer heat, Cord was able to find a wild horse and lasso him. He spent several days breaking him, then continued in the direction Powell had suggested. He was alone, the other three men having headed in the opposite direction.

He spotted squirrels and rabbits along his way, which he shot, cleaned, and cooked on a spit. The nights were long and lonely, and it was only through sheer weariness that he was able to fall asleep at all.

At last, after many weary and anxious days, he spotted the Wigeleeva. Making his way to the rocks took a whole day, for he had to descend into the canyon, forced to leave the horse behind.

Warily, he approached the valley. The Havasupais were said to be friendly, but what if a lone warrior might be frightened of a strange, white face? But he need not have worried, for the afternoon he met three Indians on horseback, they signaled eagerly in sign language. They had heard of the expedition, for the white man's assault on the great river had not gone unnoticed among the inhabitants of the great canyon. They trusted him.

But they had sadness to relate. Making do with their sign language and Cord's hasty attempts at creating his own, they told the story of the three men who had been killed by hostile Indians. Cord gave himself time to take it all in, then asked to be taken to the village where the silver-haired white woman was living. They agreed.

For the first time in his whole life, Cord Hayden knew fear: During his time in the canyon he had searched his soul, and he knew, without any doubt, what he wanted... what he had wanted all along.

He only hoped she would still be waiting for him.

Chapter Thirty-four

AMBER looked about her at all the grandeur and wondered at such an awesome world. Never had she seen such splendor; red cliffs, lush green foliage, indigo skies, and turquoise waters.

She gazed into the distance at the two irregular red pillars, the Wigeleeva. Some of the Indians said they were a god and goddess, while others said they represented the petrified remains of two brothers, chiefs of many generations ago, who led the Havasupais into Havasu Canyon and were still standing guard over their people.

She delighted in her quiet walks along the creek, especially in the early morning light, when a lavender mist kissed the earth before rising and dispersing. She never failed to marvel at the hundreds of colorful birds that flitted about, white-throated swifts, goldfinches, little violet and green-colored swallows, tiny hummingbirds, and the gloriously blue-and-brown feathered birds which no one had a name for. Dancing in the creek could be seen grebes, kingfishers, green-winged teals and the glorious, great blue herons.

There was beauty here, and peace, and as she stared on out at the vast canyon beyond, cutting its ribbons of rocks through the earth, she could understand Cord's hunger to explore.

She walked over to where buckskins were stretched to dry in the sun, touching the glorious white color. They would, she knew, make warm and beautiful coats for her and Armand and the others, to ward off the cold winter ahead.

Winter. A knot rose in her throat. Would she spend her winter here? Was this to be her future? With each day, the fear that Cord was not coming back became stronger. Once, she had voiced her trepidation to Noahax, who had told her that the big white man had left something with their leader, saying that he was to use it if he did not return. Amber had asked the leader about it, but he had stared at her stonily and refused to answer.

She stared longingly at the creek, and lovely young Noahax, tending the turtle stew, saw her and said, "Bathing is not allowed during the ritual of death." The young woman nodded toward the bluff below where they were standing.

Amber heard a sudden howling wail of grief and knew it was the women keeping watch over the body of old Hutegu, who had died two days before. He had been taken to his hut, while a coffin was made of split logs and mud, and, his family hoped, give ample time for the dead man's son to return from the hunt he and so many of the other warriors had been on for almost a week. The hunt was for deer and antelope to dry for winter.

She admitted freely that she would miss these gentle people who had taken her under their wing and made her feel as though she truly belonged, and she knew Armand would miss them badly. He had been made to feel loved, even wanted. Perhaps, she realized with trepidation, he might not want to leave.

Amber was standing beside Noahax, when the midwife, Tuilate, called out to them.

"Go to her," Noahax said, without turning to Amber. "I must tend the stew. The other women are all mourning."

When she hesitated, Noahax snapped uncharacteristically. "You should want to learn all you can. One day, you will need to know the ways of birth," she added with a sly wink, "for when your man returns, he will sleep with you, and you will become fat with his child."

Amber sputtered indignantly, "He...he will not. I won't!" Some times she regretted the ease with which she and Noahax had learned to talk.

The young woman laughed and waved her away. "Go! You will make old Tuilate angry. Go. I will come in soon."

Amber had no choice, not really. They treated her well, and she did not dare insult them. Warily, she approached the midwife, who was waving her to hurry, a frown in the time-ravaged lines of her face.

Amber stepped inside the hut and winced at the sight of the woman thrashing painfully on the floor. Her hands were stretched up behind her head as she pulled on the rope there. Her body pushed downward in the agonized thrusts of birth.

In a minute, Tuilate grunted with satisfaction and stooped to retrieve the wet, bloody infant who slid into her hands. She motioned to Amber to kneel beside her and follow her gestures. Amber held the writhing baby while Tuilate tied the umbilical cord.

She tied the cord about an inch and a half from where it entered the infant, then cut it and dusted the stump with a powder of red ocher. The powder came from a secret place known only to the Indians. As she worked, Noahax entered silently.

Tuilate took the baby from Amber's outstretched arms and ran her fingers over its face, head, and body. This was to ensure that the boychild would be handsome and well-formed when he grew to be a warrior. Next, she wrapped a cloth around the stump of the cord. When the stump dropped off, she would wrap it once more and fasten it to his cradle.

"Why do you want to save that?" Amber asked Noahax, and was told, "When a baby boy reaches the age of one year, what is left of the stump will be ground with red ocher and deer fat. The root of his birth will then be returned to him in three lines of painted drawings, lines drawn on his body. The ritual ensures that the child will not grow up to be troublesome and absentminded."

Amber kept quiet. It was not her place to argue with their beliefs.

Together, she and Noahax tended the new mother, and when her newborn infant was asleep at her breast, they stepped outside the hut into the warm late afternoon sun.

"I wonder if Armand is still hurt because the men wouldn't take him hunting with them," Amber mused as they walked toward the simmering pot of stew. "Every morning since they left he's gotten up to wander off by himself with that bow and arrow, and he never comes back till sundown."

Noahax nodded with understanding as she dipped a wooden spoon into the stew and tasted. "He is too young in body to hunt with the men, yet too old in spirit to play with the other children. He enjoys exploring by himself. I think he would have preferred being with your man in the deeper canyon."

Amber smiled wistfully. "Yes, he would have." *And so would I,* she thought.

Some of the men came up from the mourning area and helped themselves to the bubbling turtle stew. The women would eat after they had washed Hutego's body one last time.

Amber sat off to the side, keeping out of their way, dreading the burial ceremony. She had no choice but to attend.

As the sun continued to sink, making dancing shadows of scarlet and purple, Amber became more and more gloomy. As it grew dark, Noahax held out her hand. "We go to mourn Hutego before he is taken to his final rest."

They made their way down to a flat rocky ledge deeper in the recess of the canyon. Amber mused silently that only a few hours before, she had been

349

part of a birth. Now she was going to a funeral. Life. Then death. But, somehow, only that time in between the two was mysterious.

Beside her, Noahax lovingly fingered a faded, drying flower, which she had braided with a willow frond and hung about her neck. Amber knew how much it meant to her, for the handsome young warrior Sanakaja had brought it to Noahax from the dangerous inner reaches of the canyon below. Noahax had explained that when an Indian man loved an Indian woman, he proved his love by making the dangerous descent to the special place where a delicate golden flower bloomed. The flower grew only in very deep places. Some men died in the attempt to reach it, for the way was treacherous.

Amber had been fascinated by the delicate golden blossom, so like a rose with its satin petals. A golden rose. Unlike any she had ever seen. A symbol of love. True love.

Noahax caught her staring, and Amber whispered, "I am happy for you. Maybe I'll still be here when you are married. I've seen birth here, and death, but not a wedding."

"I would like you to be here." Noahax touched her briefly in a gesture of friendship. "Perhaps one day you will have a symbol of your own to cherish. Perhaps a gift from the one who is journeying now."

Amber said nothing. Cord was not thinking about loving her. She understood why he had gone with Major Powell, wanting to be part of the expedition and to learn about the hearing held in his absence.

She recalled all she could of the nights on the trail when they had slipped into the woods after Armand fell asleep, feeling the night wind against their faces. How lovely those nights had been, the moon bathing the forest in amethyst light. They had made sweet, passionate love, and he had held her naked in his arms, kissing her body all over.

The nights had passed too swiftly. They made love so many times Amber lost count. She knew she would always remember those precious nights and she wondered if memories were all that was left to her.

❧ Chapter Thirty-five ❧

ON a plateau, overlooking the Indian village, Valdis Alezparito stood beside his horse and stared down, the blazing sun scorching him. His eyes narrowed; he removed his wide-brimmed sombrero, jerking the kerchief from his neck to rub at his sweaty face, he cursed in a low whisper.

Beside him, Gerras watched silently, as he had been doing since early dawn, knowing it was not the time to speak. Never had he seen his leader so furious, so intent upon revenge.

Tracking the woman Valdis desired so fiercely had been hard and dangerous. Too, there had been much to take care of at home. Valdis had been delighted to know of Maretta's shrewd purchase of the Mendosa land he so coveted. For a flicker of an instant, he was uncomfortable about taking her to a life within the walls of the convent. But pity quickly faded. Pity and compassion, those were what cowards were made of.

Now, after traveling countless miles over mountains and deserts, they had found Amber. Valdis' other men had settled down to await orders while Gerras stood nearby, watching Valdis grow angrier with each passing hour. Finally, he dared to say, "It is foolish to think you can take her from Indians. Leave her. Let us return to the ranch. It is a certain death for us. There are only eight of us against all of them."

But Valdis seemed not to hear.

Gerras said, "The men are getting angry. They wish to know how long you intend to remain here."

"Until darkness," Valdis replied. "Then...I take what is mine."

🍂 Chapter Thirty-six 🍂

ON the rocky ledge some of the Indians were dancing a slow rhythmic dance around the coffin. Now and then, one of the women would wail and others joined in. The eerie sounds echoed far into the canyon, to bounce back and ring round them.

When it was dark, the coffin was opened, and all filed by for a last look.

Amber did not want to see the cold, stiff body, but reminded herself once more of her duty. She tried not to stare at what was in the coffin—blankets, food, tools, and jewelry that had belonged to the dead man.

With a shudder, she stumbled away.

Noahax appeared at her side again and said, "We will remain here until dawn. Then we make the journey below, to where Hutego will be buried, near the waterfall, and—" She broke off, turning to look behind her.

Amber followed her gaze, refusing to believe what she saw. She was asleep. She had to be. "Dear God, no," she whispered, her hands clutching her throat. "It can't be!"

"Ah, but it is," chuckled Valdis, delighted, pointing his rifle at the gathering of mourners. "*Querida*, it was senseless for you to think you could ever escape me. You *belong* to me."

All around the bewildered Indians, Mexicans stepped from their hiding places. Caught in the dancing and wailing, they had not heard them slipping up to surround them, and they could only stare silently, fearfully, for the young men were away and the old people and women saw the angry, determined Mexican men were more than they could fight.

Valdis did not take his eyes away from Amber. "Well, *querida?* Have you no word of welcome?"

"What do you want?" she cried in a voice braver than she felt.

Valdis asked coldly, "Will you go peacefully, or must we kill all your friends?"

"You're a brave man, aren't you, Valdis? You have a gun and all your bandits. We have only old men and women and children here."

He hissed, "Do not provoke me. You have much punishment coming. Once I have had you all I want, then I will have you tortured until you scream for mercy. Now come. We have a long way to travel."

In that moment, all she could think of was Armand. Would he have the sense to stay out of sight, or would Valdis send a man to search for him? So distracted was she that she barely heard the swishing sound. Suddenly Valdis screamed in agony, his hands going to his face, blood spurting through his fingers. Amber watched, stunned, slowly taking in the horrible sight of the arrow protruding from an eye. Valdis fell to his knees, writhing in agony.

The Indians scattered, terrified, and Valdis' men, assuming they were being attacked, also ran.

Only Amber remained, frozen, watching as Valdis cried out as he rolled in anguish upon the ground.

A movement on a nearby ledge caught her attention, and she looked up in wonder to see Armand standing on the rock, silhouetted by the rising moon beyond him, a grim expression on his face... and a bow in his hand. Armand had shot the arrow!

"Run!" she screamed, fearing Valdis' men would return. "Run, Armand!"

He looked down at her solemnly, then turned and silently disappeared into the night.

Amber quickly found Valdis' rifle, which he had dropped when he fell. He had lost consciousness by then and lay very still. Spotting one of the old Indian women peering from the scrubs, she motioned her over. Noahax also crept forward. A few moments later, she called to Amber, "We have removed the arrow. We will pack the wound to try to stop the bleeding, but the eye is lost."

"Will he live?" Amber asked, not really caring.

"Maybe."

Amber knew that if there was one among Valdis' men who would not desert him, it would be Gerras. She called to him, again and again, her voice ringing out to echo in the canyon.

Finally, he appeared, holding his hands above his head. "Do not shoot," he said apprehensively.

"Don't make me," she warned, then nodded to Valdis. "Take him and go. Tell his men not to dare come back. The other warriors will return any moment, and they will be waiting for you if you come back here."

Amber asked Noahax to have a signal fire built at once. It would bring the hunters back. Then she left the scene and went into the forest alone.

She watched as the sun rose over the mountains to kiss the world awake, a gentle pink mist rising from the canyon depths. She stared down at Armand, who had come to her during the night to sleep, curled up with his head in her lap. Touching his tousled hair fondly, she smiled. He was going to be as brave and courageous as his father. He had saved her from Valdis, perhaps saved all of them.

Staring into the mist surrounding them, she knew the time had come to leave that peaceful place. Cord had obviously met his destiny elsewhere. It was time for her to do the same.

"Amber," a husky voice called.

Her head whipped around. She must have imagined that beloved voice, she decided, then stared in disbelief at the vision of Cord striding toward her.

"I...I don't believe it," she cried, gently laying Armand aside and struggling to her feet. "Is it you?" she gasped, "or an apparition of the mist?"

He wrapped strong arms around her and tightly held her to him. "It's me, Amber. I wish I'd gotten here sooner. Noahax told me what happened. Thank God for the boy. If I had come back and found you gone again..."

He moved back to gaze down at her, his hands framing her face gently. "I love you, Amber. I always will," he said simply.

Stepping back, he reached inside his jacket and withdrew something, placing it in her hands.

She stared down in wonder at a golden rose. "You knew...." she whispered. "You knew about the legend?"

"I knew, and I believe in it. I hope you believe in it, too."

With a cry of joy, she flung her arms fiercely around him. Their lips met in a pledge of love, a pledge that was theirs at long, long last.

There would be no more doubts, no fears, for the golden rose sealed their devotion for always and ever.